LOVELAND PUBLIC LIBRARY

D0021270

STUFF TO DIE FOR

Also by Don Bruns

Jamaica Blue

Barbados Heat

Death Dines In
(contributor)

A Merry Band of Murderers
(editor & contributor)

South Beach Shakedown

STUFF TO DIE FOR

A NOVEL

DON BRUNS

Oceanview Publishing
IPSWICH, MASSACHUSETTS

FIRST EDITION

ISBN-13: 978-1-933515-10-6
ISBN-10: 1-933515-10-4

Published in the United States by Oceanview Publishing,
Ipswich, Massachusetts
www.oceanviewpub.com

2 4 6 8 10 9 7 5 3 1

PRINTED IN THE UNITED STATES OF AMERICA

To my kids and their generation. No matter how old you are, there are still some things you never figure out.

ACKNOWLEDGMENTS

Thanks to my friend, Tom Biddle, for the use of his Miami condo, to Captain Bob Bijur and Haley Sofge with Island Queen Cruises, to Doctor James Kahn for his technical expertise, to Don Witter, Jay Waggoner, Dave Bruns, Nancy Olds, and Linda for taking the time to read the manuscript, to the folks at Bayside for their interest and help, and to Rodger McClain for steering me straight. Here's to Jason and the guys at Big Guy Media for the movie trailer, and to Fred Rea, king of movie quotes. Thanks to the wonderful crew at Oceanview Publishing, and especially to the booksellers and librarians who promote mysteries and make all of this possible.

Finally, a toast to the Miami River, the hardest working river I've ever sailed.

DB

STUFF TO DIE FOR

PROLOGUE

The brief article about Salvidor Santori's death appeared in the *Miami Herald*. When I read that they'd found his body on top of the Colony Hotel on Ocean Boulevard in South Beach, I paid a little more attention to the story than I normally would have. Santori had twenty years in the CIA with extensive training in espionage. This guy was used to the cat-and-mouse game, spy vs. spy. I read the story with interest, wondering if the death was really relevant to all the crap James and I had been through.

Maybe his murder was an isolated incident, but James, Em, and I had been *this* close to being killed, and in the process I may have lost the greatest girl I've ever known. So I thought about the story for a while, and I believe I know why Santori died. I even have a good idea who killed him. Actually, after all that happened to us, I have a *real* good idea of how Santori died.

If you ever get a chance sometime, take a walk down Ocean Boulevard, and watch the slow parade of luxury cars as twilight settles on the colorful Art Deco district in Miami. It's fun, it's entertaining, and it really makes you feel alive. I used to view the fancy clubs, the swanky restaurants, and the crazy people and think all things were possible. You just had to use your imagination.

It's just that I never, in a million years, could have ever imagined what *did* happen.

CHAPTER ONE

Believe me, when James first suggested we start a hauling business, I would have said no way in hell if I'd known we'd be hauling a human body part. And then to be accused of kidnapping and murder? But I've only got myself to blame. I've known from the start that James Lessor could get into more trouble than any ten people. I just keep forgetting that he's always dragging me in with him.

I met James in the third grade. Even then it was never Jim or Jimmy. His name was James, he'd tell everyone. "James, like in the King James Bible." And if a third grader could be arrogant, James was arrogant. And ambitious. I met him in Mrs. Waggoner's class when he bilked me out of fifty cents on the stone playground by offering to be my best friend for the school year. Fifty cents for the year seemed like a good bargain, and having someone who knew the ropes like James as my best friend seemed like a no-brainer. Then I found out that twenty-five other kids paid the same price for the same privilege.

I don't know where those twenty-five kids are today, but James and I *are* best friends. And he's still scheming, working on the next get-rich-quick idea. When we were fourteen years old, he borrowed his dad's video camera and we went to the movie theater in Miami Lakes, over by the Pep Boys auto parts store. It was a hot, sticky South Florida day and James had on this trench coat that was three sizes too big. I tagged along and we must have looked like quite a pair, James with a bulky video camera hidden under his coat, and me with a pair of shorts and a T-shirt. We bought tickets to *Barbed Wire* with Pamela Anderson, and as soon as the previews were over, James pulled out the camera.

"We're gonna sell copies to everyone in school, Skip. A hundred kids buy the movie at five bucks a crack, we make —"

"Five hundred dollars, James."

"Yeah. Five hundred bucks." He got a big grin on his face.

We crouched in our last row seats and he flicked on the camera. That's when the hand grabbed his arm and the manager of the theater yanked him from his chair.

The police officer in the lobby gave us a warning, and we were banned from the theater for life. The manager quit his job the next week and within ten days we were back watching movies — minus the trench coat and camera.

He talked me into at least ten other business ventures between the third grade and now, but none of them panned out, and half of them got us into trouble. And none of them involved terrorism, mutilation, subversive government plots, or torture. Until now.

So why is James Lessor still my best friend? Because I admire him. He's got the — what do the Jews call it? Chutzpa? He's got the balls to go out and make things happen, and for some reason that appeals to me. Probably because I'm not a self-starter. I need a James Lessor, and he needs a Skip Moore to rein him in now and then. Obviously, I should rein him in a lot more than I do.

I have to admit I got fired up about some of his ideas, and I probably wouldn't have gone to college if he hadn't decided we needed to be restaurateurs. You see, James is a marvelous cook. I don't know what sparked his interest, but about the seventh grade he was whipping up inventive omelets with apples and cheddar cheese or mushrooms and salsa, and then he graduated to seafood dishes like imperial crab and deviled oysters. He loves screwing around in the kitchen, and being his best friend and someone who enjoys the process of eating, I am a beneficiary of his sizable talent.

"We're best of friends. Have been since either of us can remember, so I know you as well as you know yourself. Am I right?" Lessor was in his sales mode. He should have been the one selling security systems. I wasn't making any headway at it, and he was always selling some dream or scheme and convincing me we should try something new. With his sculpted face, wavy hair, and crooked smile, James could convince just about anyone of anything. As I said, it was James who convinced me to go with him to Samuel and Davidson University in North Miami.

I'm constantly reminded of how it started six years ago. It was a hot, sweaty night and we were sitting in his rusted out, formerly red Chevy pick up truck behind Gas and Grocery, two thirds of the way through a six-pack of lukewarm Budweiser.

"It's like he's still with me, Skip. He's over my shoulder telling me to quit fucking around and get serious about life."

"Don't all parents tell their kids that?"

He flicked the ashes of his cigarette out the busted window that never rolled up and popped open his last can. You could always smell the pines that grew in a clustered grove beside the small concrete block building that was Gas and Grocery.

"I don't have any other father to compare him to. And now I don't have him."

My dad left our family when I was twelve. James's dad had

left this world just six months shy of our high school graduation. That'd be six years ago.

He leaned his head back and let half the liquid gurgle down his throat, belching loudly. "Christ, I wish I could talk to him. Find out where he fucked up. I never really wanted to talk to him before, you know? He was just my old man. I was embarrassed for how it ended, but now—"

He let it hang.

His old man. Oscar Lessor. Tried to start one hundred different businesses, and the last effort landed him in jail.

"All those schemes, all those businesses he started. He never amounted to shit." He stared through the windshield, focusing on something in the dark.

"The mechanic shop, the vending route, home dry cleaning, Amway—I don't even remember half of them. He was a loser, Skip."

At the end the old man had picked the wrong business. He'd partnered with a friend in selling shares in Miami property, only the *friend* never told Oscar that there were more shares than property. When shareholders came to collect, the friend was long gone and Oscar Lessor did five years in prison. Five years. When he got out, he was a broken man.

"Hey, man. Look at the businesses you've tried to start. You're not a loser. And he wasn't a loser. He just never got where he wanted to be."

"You know what he told me a couple of weeks before he died? The doctor had told him that the cancer was going to get him before the end of the year, and he'd pretty much accepted it. I brought him a cup of coffee, and he reached out and took my hand. Didn't have much strength, his hand was shaking, but he squeezed mine and he said 'I never drove a Cadillac.' "

"A Cadillac?"

"Yeah. I never told anyone that. Sounds really stupid. But

that's what he wanted. I think my old man thought if he drove a Cadillac, it was his way of saying that he'd made it. He'd finally arrived."

"And your point is?"

"I'm not going to fuck up my life. I'm going to make it long before it's my time to go. My old man is still hanging around, telling me to get my act together, and he's right. I'm not going to be the loser he was."

"So what are you going to do?"

"I'm not going to die before I drive that Cadillac. What we've talked about. We'll get the student loans and go to school. You take the business courses, I'll do the culinary thing, and when we get out we'll start our own restaurant, right on South Beach. We'll be the hottest spot in town."

Seventeen and eighteen, right out of high school, I suppose that sounded like a chance to hit the big time. My mom was just happy that I'd decided to go to college. Sam and Dave U. — 2300 kids — smaller than our high school. It was nicknamed Sam and Dave U in honor of the two sixties singers who had the hit "Soul Man," but there wasn't a lot of soul at Sam and Dave U. And no one seemed to know who the real Samuel and Davidson might have been. They'd used Miami's standard for building complexes: rows of pale stucco buildings with orange tile roofs and palm trees that sprouted more dead brown branches than live green ones. The faculty lacked soul and the students lacked soul. The institution was structured like a trade school, with a minimum of fine arts or anything else for that matter. Talk about a minimum campus. We should have figured it out from the brochure the university sent out.

CAMPUS ACTIVITIES.

MANY GROUPS PLAN OFF-CAMPUS TRIPS TO CULTURAL AND ENTERTAINMENT VENUES.

That was it. Off campus.

And four years later, after almost being tossed out two or three times for minor and major infractions of campus rules (organizing a wet T-shirt contest in front of the Student Union for one), we found that the placement office was not up to the task of finding high-paying, steady jobs for two students who barely squeaked by with a 1.9 and 2.1 grade point average. With student loans in the tens of thousands, the dream of owning our own restaurant was a distant memory.

"Skip, think about it." James was selling harder than usual. "Working as a line cook at Cap'n Crab isn't what I envisioned after four years of Sam and Dave. And you?" He waved his hands in the air, the look of total exasperation on his face. "Dude, you've got a head for business and you're selling some goddamned security system to home owners who don't have anything to secure. Our dreams, man. What happened? We were supposed to own our own business!"

"I remember. It's just going to take a little longer than we planned."

I knew it wasn't what he wanted to hear.

"Look at this crappy apartment, Skip. Jesus, our dorm room was bigger than this."

I took a deep breath. When the breeze was just right you could smell the thick, cloying, greasy smell of fried food from the Denny's about a block away.

"Shit. I don't have the time, bro. You know what I think?"

I shook my head. Long ago, maybe in fourth grade, I'd given up trying to tell what James was thinking.

"I think someone should take this city and just flush it down the fucking toilet."

I smiled. "De Niro, *Taxi Driver*."

"Hey, very good."

James had spent far too many nights watching classic movies, but he always had some great quotes. I'd watched most of them with him but his unbelievable memory captured the best lines. I had trouble remembering the plots. James was a riot at parties.

"So, as I was saying, security systems. How many have you sold in the past six months? Three? Four?"

"Two."

"And you're coming off salary, right? Now it's commission?"

"I've got some stuff in the works."

"Bullshit. And me? I come home every night smelling like fucking fish. I can't get the stink out of my clothes, my hair—" He paused. "This isn't what I had in mind, Skip."

"It's temporary, James. We'll get some of the loans paid off, move down to Miami and—"

"Yeah. And one or two years stretches into five and six years. It's going to start happening now, bro. It's time to break out. Skip Moore and James Lessor, entrepreneurs. Moore and Lessor, or Lessor and Moore. Have truck, will haul."

I put down the magazine, the one with Jamie-Lynn DiScala on the cover. Tony Soprano's little girl was all grown up in a miniscule bikini and a come hither look on her face."What the hell are you talking about?"

"Come to the door, my man. I want you to see our future."

I should have avoided the door. I should have turned my back, bolted out the rear of the apartment, and never talked to my best friend again. But, of course, that didn't happen.

If it had, there would be no reason for this book, and Jackie Fuentes would probably be sleeping with the fishes. Literally. But I went to the door to see what the future held. You always want the future to look bright—rosy and beckoning. You just never expect the future to be a Chevy one-ton box truck.

CHAPTER TWO

EMILY GOT US THE FIRST JOB. James had business cards printed with my cell phone number. I guess he thought we'd just pass them out and everyone would call.

HAVE TRUCK WILL HAUL.
555-4628

It was supposed to be that simple. It almost was.

"Furniture, clothes, machinery, junk, whatever somebody wants hauled, we can do it. You're the salesman, Skip. When they call, close the deal."

I'll be honest. The first thing I thought about was hauling illegal merchandise. When you grow up in South Florida you don't read about waving palm trees and white sandy beaches. The people up north read about that. *You* read about drugs, contraband, stolen goods, and hijacked commodities. You hear about shady characters, organized crime, and boats, planes, and trucks that make unannounced rendezvous at strange hours in the morning. Bales of marijuana floating on a black ocean and

Colombian drug lords who import their form of terror into the United States through Florida. And you think about Cuban refugees who are escaping a life that must be hell. But, what the *hell,* it was another James Lessor scheme and since I'd bought into all of them before, there wasn't much to lose. Or so I thought.

James had bought the used truck for $12,000, an inheritance from an aunt who lived in California.

"I met her once." He sucked on his cigarette, letting the ash grow an inch before he flicked it off. "I must have left some impression, or else she just doled out $12,000 to everyone in the family."

"James, you should have paid off some of your student loans. They're going to hang over our heads for half of our lives."

We were sprawled on cheap plastic lawn chairs on what passed as our apartment patio. It was a slab of cracked and pitted concrete, stained with a lot of beer, wine, and black smudge marks from ground-out cigarette butts. Some of those stains had actually been there when we moved in.

James took a slow swallow of beer from the brown bottle and gazed over the top of his sunglasses at the two girls three apartments down. Dressed in shorts and halter tops, they worked over a charcoal grill, trying to fan the briquettes into hot coals. "Skip, it's that old adage about giving someone fish, or giving them a fishing pole. Give 'em a fish, they eat one meal. Give 'em a pole, they can catch fish the rest of their lives. If I put the money toward the loan, I wouldn't have any money left. But," he held up his index finger for dramatic effect, "but if I buy a truck, then I can use the profits from our little business venture to pay off the entire loan and at the same time build a business empire."

"Empire?"

"I'm not thinking one truck here. Think Ryder. Think U-Haul, Penske. Think big, Skip. People are more mobile than ever, and they have more stuff than ever. Stuff, buddy. Stuff. They need trucks to haul that stuff." He stood up, stretched his six-foot, lanky frame, pulled his baggy green shorts up around his bare waist, and walked barefoot down to the girls' patio. I could see him showing them how to get maximum heat without stinking up the meat with charcoal lighter. Four years of culinary college had paid off. He could pick up girls by dispensing barbecue advice.The phone chirped. I checked the number. Emily.

"Em. How goes it?"

"Whatcha doin' for dinner? Want to grab a pizza?"

I looked down toward the girls' patio. James was laughing, drinking one of their green labels, and they seemed to be amused at something he'd said. "Sure. I think my roommate has plans."

"Oh, so I'm runner up?"

"No. Just an observation. Sure, let's get a pizza. I want to run a business idea by you."

"Me?"

Her, indeed. Emily's dad owns a construction business in Carol City. Carol City Construction. He's built some of the most palatial homes in the Miami area, and runs a very successful company. When Em graduated from the University of Miami with a computer engineering degree, she was offered about a zillion jobs, with salaries approaching $150,000. But she went to work for Dad and figured out how to make the main guy in her life another gazillion dollars. If anyone knew good business, she did."You."

"What about Jaystone?"

"I'm not quitting. Jaystone Security is still paying the bills."

"Barely. You know you could always work construction, Skip. Dad could put you on at about a dozen sites right now."*Dad* didn't realize I couldn't drive a nail even if I had a sledgehammer. And furthermore, he didn't like me a whole lot. It wasn't necessarily that I was dating his daughter or that I had a crummy job.

It was more about not dating his daughter seriously. And I'm not sure he knew that was by her choosing. Em liked different guys. She liked to flirt, to party, to have her little affairs. She'd been that way since she went away to some hot-shit private school as a junior in high school and we'd broken up. But she still liked to get together with me and just get comfortable. And sometimes it was very, very comfortable.

"James has an idea—"

"Oh, Jesus." I could picture her shaking that pretty little head, her short hair bouncing around that kissable face. "He's always got ideas. You're not buying into something with him are you?"

"Em, let's go get a pizza. We can talk when my minutes aren't on the line, okay?" Cell phone minutes, just like money, meant nothing to her. It's the problem with rich people. They don't think about how tough it can be on the others, trying to keep up. Every now and then I've got to bring her up short.

"I'll be by in half an hour."

"Dutch treat, Em. There haven't been a lot of sales this month."

"Then I hope to hell this business venture pans out, Skip. If it doesn't, you might just starve to death."

Did I mention that besides being rich, she has this sarcastic streak a mile long? Still, when she's comfortable, she's very comfortable.

Half an hour later to the minute she picked me up in the T-Bird convertible, the tan top already down and the red paint job waxed to a blinding shine. If I have to rely on a woman for my ride, I'm glad it's a classy ride.

CHAPTER THREE

PAULIE'S HAS THIS GREAT CRUST that's crisp and thin and has enough flavor to make you wish they'd just forget about the toppings. Seriously. Sometimes we just get a twelve-inch without anything and eat the crust.

Em ordered a fourteen-inch mushroom and Italian sausage with a pitcher of beer to wash it down, and we sat out on the faded wooden deck under a cheap umbrella, the sun cooking everything that wasn't covered.

"So what is this big venture?"

"Promise me you won't laugh?"

"No."

"No, you won't laugh?"

"No, I won't promise you. Skip, that's one reason I keep seeing you. You make me laugh."

She laughed.

I read one time that if you can get a girl to laugh, you can get her into bed. I'm always afraid that they'll laugh *while* we're in bed.

"I'll tell you anyway. James wants to go into the hauling business."

"The what?"

"Hauling business."

She was silent for a moment while she rolled that idea around in her head. "Well, he's had to haul his ass out of a lot jams and he's always been pretty successful."

"He bought this box truck, and—"

"A box truck?"

"A box truck."

"Like a U-Haul?"

"Yeah. Sort of. It's this fourteen-foot aluminum box on the back of a cab. And you can haul just about anything."

A smile played on her face.

"You're gonna laugh."

"No. Actually, it's not a bad idea. For a sideline. And you could use the extra income."

"That's what I'm thinking. But James is thinking more than a sideline. He wants to have an entire fleet. He says people have too much stuff and they always want to move it."

"Or store it."

"Huh?"

"Skip, there's this lady, Jackie Fuentes, and she's got a ton of stuff she needs to store. You could haul it for her."

There it was. We hadn't handed out the first business card, and we already had a customer. This was going to be easier than I thought.

She sipped her beer and crossed those awesome tanned legs of hers. Her shorts rode up another couple of inches. I started to wonder if we were going to get comfortable tonight.

"She lives near the causeway off Indian Creek Village. Dad built her house about five years ago. God, Skip, it's this huge mansion."

Em's dad lives in a 10,000-square-foot home in a gated community called Silver Bay, so when Em's impressed with the size of a house, it must be awesome. And Daddy's little princess lives in a condo that looks out over Biscayne Bay and South Beach from twenty stories up, so she's not doing so bad herself.

"Her husband is involved in financing. I think he's like a venture capitalist. He arranges high-interest loans to fund new businesses. And apparently he arranges extramarital affairs, because Jackie caught him with a little blond and threw him out of the house."

In my relatively short life, I have always found it hard to fathom people who live that kind of life. And even with Emily, my own little rich bitch, I have to bite everything off in very small chunks. Christ, the apartment James and I live in isn't 600 square feet, and our combined income is about $30,000 a year. Ten thousand square foot homes on fancy islands and high-finance engineers just don't register.

"Eugene?"

She caught my mind wandering. Whenever she was serious she'd call me by my given name. I wish my mother had *given* it to someone else. And Skip? When I was younger, people would ask my name and when I said Eugene they'd invariably say "What?" I got to a point where I'd just say, "Skip it." Over the years the name Skip took hold and I am so thankful for that. Of course, people I've known for years sometimes revert to Eugene. Sometimes when they're serious and sometimes when they just want to piss me off.

"Yeah. Go on."

"As I was saying, Jackie Fuentes threw her husband out."

"And?"

"And she's throwing all of his stuff out."

"Stuff. That's what James was talking about. People needing to move stuff."

"She's been going through his closets, the storage rooms,

and she's got a huge pile of stuff that she wants to move out. You could call and offer your services."

Em gave me a big smile. I love that mouth. "Em, how do you know all this?"

"She confides in me. I see her at the club, and—"

The club. Em's friends belong to the club, and how can someone like me identify with the "club"?

"She told me."

The waitress brought the pizza, the steam still rising from the hot, melted cheese. I took a whiff. I believe that God created pizza for the regular people. Em can be regular when she wants to. It's cheap, it's filling, and there isn't a bad pizza out there. There are great pizzas. There are pizzas that aren't as great as the great, but there are no bad pizzas. That's what I believe.

"She said that Rick—"

"Rick?"

"Ricardo, her husband. She said Rick had moved the little blond into a condo and she wanted his stuff out. And then she told me something that I probably shouldn't say to you. Hell, I shouldn't say it to anyone."

I loved this about Em. She fought with herself. Usually she was conflicted about her financial and social status. She wanted to be a pizza person, but she was this little rich bitch who could afford filet mignon. She had a lot of battles over that. But this time, it was something totally different. And again, I should have heard it and walked away. Away from her, away from the truck idea, and away from James. But no, I actually encouraged my cute little Emily. Partly because it was fun to torment her a little, and partially because I really was trying to understand how the other half lives.

"Come on, Em. Tell me. Please?"

She picked up a corner piece of pizza and took a tentative bite. Not too hot.

"I shouldn't."

"Em, you're asking me to do a job for this lady. Tell me."

"All right, but you can't go to James with this."

"Maybe. After all, he is my partner."

"Eugene!"

"No James."

"She thinks that Rick might be working for some subversive group."

"Subversive?"

"I think she's paranoid."

"Subversive?"

"Things that he's said. Spanish-speaking guys who call at all hours of the night."

"So what's he doing for these foreign guys?"

"I told you. He raises money for risky business ventures and charges a hefty percentage."

I scraped the cheese off a square piece with my teeth, chewed and swallowed it, then took a bite of crust. I've asked some of the people at Paulie's what was in the crust, and they act like it's a secret. Actually, most of them are Puerto Rican and they don't speak much English. They might have told me the ingredients, but I wouldn't have understood.

"So he's raising money for a Spanish business."

"It's probably just that. But she says they call or show up at all hours of the night. I think she just got freaked out. She thinks they are" — she paused dramatically — "terrorists — part of a subversive plot."

I bit off another piece of pizza and this time savored the sauce.

"Anyway," she asked, "should I call her?"

"Yeah. I think so. I mean, what's to think about. The terrorist thing sounds like a lady who's paranoid."

"She thought about going to the FBI or CIA, Skip. She was that scared."

"She was really going to turn her husband into the CIA? Maybe this isn't such a good idea."

"I shouldn't have said anything."

Terrorists? God, it seems that everything that happens any more is terrorist related. "Well, hell, we could use the money, we've got the truck, we can load it. Where does she want it hauled?"

"Probably a storage unit. Maybe to the condo where the Mr. is keeping the mistress."

"How much do we charge?"

Em shook her head and drained her glass of beer. "Skip, Skip. You're a business major. Did you learn anything at all at Sam and Dave?"

"To be honest?"

"Call a couple of companies and ask what they would charge."

And there it was. Our first hauling job. Hauling away the remains of some philandering guy's marriage. Hauling away the possessions of some rich bastard, Rick Fuentes, who might be an international terrorist. And I wondered if U-Haul and Ryder started out like that. I bet they didn't.

CHAPTER FOUR

You can see the Marlins' stadium from in front of our apartment. It's this space-age looking building, and when the Marlins play at home you can literally smell the noxious exhaust fumes from the thousands of cars leaving the game. It's South Florida at its finest. Acres and acres of concrete surrounded by palm trees. From our spacious five-by-ten cement slab out back, we look directly at the back of the next row of apartments. Seven apartments to the right, the border of our property is defined by a narrow stream with shallow, dirty, brown water flowing slowly by. On the patios are broken tricycles, cheap rusting barbecue sets, and tenants' freshly washed underwear thrown over old picnic tables and plastic chairs to dry in the hot South Florida sun.

Our neighbors behind us have a playpen all set up on their slab, with a plastic duck and some foam building blocks, and the only people we've ever seen coming in and out of the place are a black couple in their late sixties. We've never seen a baby.

"I told you. Listen to me, pally. In three months, we'll have a second truck and we'll be hiring employees." James was figuring longhand on a brown paper bag. "Jeez, Skip. If we charge a couple of hundred a load, and we could get three gigs a day—"

"That would be six hundred a day."

"See? That business degree is paying off." He sat straight up in the cheap lawn chair. "And six hundred a day is like $3,000 a week. And $3,000 a week is—" He scribbled with his pen.

"$12,000 a month and $144,000 a year. The problem is, James, that I don't think we can do three loads a day five days a week."

He paused, squinting into the bright Sunday afternoon sun. "Yeah, I guess it would be pushing it. So, we up our price."

"You've got to stay competitive." I sipped on a Coke and watched water flow through the muddy dirt ditch that ran by on the edge of our complex. A big sign was posted.

NO FISHING, SWIMMING,
SOAKING, OR WASHING

Like there was the slightest desire.

James tossed back the last of his beer—the last of our beer. He hadn't contributed to the communal beer fund and I was damned if I was going to buy another six-pack. He drank four out of the six anyway.

"When is she calling?" James asked.

"Any time. She was meeting Jackie at the club."

"Oh." His finest English accent. "The club. The veddy important club. The fucking rich asshole's club."

"That's the one."

"Tell me, Skip. If you *could* belong, would you? Huh?"

I let it slide by. When I was very young, my father used to say to me, "I wish I had enough money to buy a herd of elephants." I'd always counter with "What would you do with a herd of elephants, Daddy?"

"Well, son," he'd say, "I don't want the elephants. I just want enough money to buy them."

Would I join the club? Hell, I wish I had enough money to make that decision.

"Anyway, we've got a job. An honest to God job. It's just a matter of time, Skip. Hey, you can do a business plan, right?"

"Yeah, Basic Business 101."

"Well, we need a business plan."

"You need to have some goals. Some idea of where you're going. Right now you cook crab and I suck at selling security systems. Where do you see this new venture going?"

James looked out over our dark brown stream. He tugged a Marlins' cap over his perpetually sun-burned forehead. "I see us being successful. I see us light years ahead of my old man. This isn't a hair-brained scheme, Skip, it's real. It's finding a need and coming up with the solution."

"It's a part-time job that lets us pick up a few bucks."

He squinted his eyes and looked at me. "I see us making a million dollars in two years."

"Jesus! You're out of your fucking mind."

"Two guys started Google at our age. What about them? And Ben Affleck and Matt Damon. By our age they had already written that movie *Good Will Hunting* that made them millionaires. Why can't it happen to us?"

"Because you're talking about hauling somebody else's shit. That isn't the same as Google or a hit movie."

James slowly stood up. I almost told him that the client's wife thought her husband might be an international terrorist. I almost broke my promise to Em, just to jab him a little bit. But hell, he would have loved the intrigue. James looked down at me from his perceived lofty position. "I'm going down to Gas and Grocery and picking up a six-pack. Hell, you don't bother to get the beer around here and after listening to your negative attitude, I could use a drink."

CHAPTER FIVE

THE THREE OF US MET AT CHILI'S. If you want a drink and a decent meal in Carol City, Chili's is about it. And the sad part of that story is that Chili's isn't really in Carol City; it's across the border in Miami Lakes. There's no place in Carol City to get a decent meal *and* a drink.

"James." Em nodded at him, an icy tone from her usually warm mouth.

"Em. Looking sexy as usual." In her skintight jeans, she did.

She grimaced.

"Of course, it's all for show. I happen to know you're frigid as hell." He smiled, shrugging his shoulders as if it was all a joke we should share.

"And you're an asshole, James. Now that we've got the pleasantries out of the way shall we discuss your business?"

I jumped in. "How much did you tell her we charged?"

"I told her $1,500."

"How much?" I thought James's eyes were going to pop out of his head. To be honest, I thought mine would too.

"Well, she didn't balk at it. I called a moving company and asked them what they'd charge. I think it's worth it to her to have the stuff moved. She just wanted someone to take responsibility."

The bartender brought us three short drafts, and we sat silently for a minute, sipping the dark bitter beer and watching the happy-hour crowd walk through the doors.

"Jackie is expecting you guys this weekend. Can you do it Saturday?"

"For that kind of money I'll move it at three in the morning. Oh, by the way, Skip, did you say something to Angel about the job?"

"Angel?"

"Angel. The Bahamian guy who hangs out at Gas and Grocery."

I stared blankly at him.

"He asked if we needed any help moving the stuff from Jackie Fuentes's house. Said he could use some extra cash."

I thought for a moment. Angel is almost always there. He's hanging out in the parking lot, looking at the magazines inside, or just appearing out of nowhere. He's always a little wacked, but I like him. He's someone who seems very real. "No. I don't remember talking to him."

James shrugged his shoulders. "Well, he seemed to know about it, but I told him the first job we were doing alone. Couldn't afford a third split."

I shook my head. No third splits! Maybe down the road. And I was certain I'd never said a word to Angel.

"Anyway, he asked, and seemed disappointed when I said no. By the way, where are we taking this stuff?" James raised his frosted glass and took a long swallow.

"She's rented a small storage facility." Em had all the information. "Once it's in there, she can quit paying on it, and the owners of the facility will eventually haul it away or sell it. Apparently people do it all the time."

"Pretty sneaky." James seemed pleased with the scam. Make it a little shady and he was there.

A pretty blond waitress walked by and smiled. "Hi, James. Busy this weekend? I'm off." She stopped and brushed the hair off his forehead.

"It's tempting. Let me get back to you. I may have to work."

"Saturday night? After Cap'n Crab closes?"

"I've got a second job."

She frowned.

"Got to make a little more money so I can take you down to Miami and have a proper date."

She smiled. "Proper. I'll hold you to that." She moved on, looking back over her shoulder, giving him a wink.

Em had that disgusted look on her face. She couldn't see the charm. Given the time and the desire, James could win her over. I would bet he could get her into bed. He just has this winning way about him. However, I wasn't about to give him the time or encourage his desire.

"Can I see the truck?"

"Out in the parking lot." James kept his eyes on the blond's cute rear end as she disappeared into the kitchen.

I took a final swallow of my Amber Bock and we got up from the bar. Em left half a glass. She always does. I was paying, and Amber Bock isn't the cheapest beer that they serve.

The sun was cooking the parking lot, the heat radiating from the black asphalt. Our truck sat at the back of the lot, shining in the bright sunlight. James had insisted on a truck wash. I told him that the cleanliness of our truck didn't mean anything to the lady off of Indian Creek Village, but he insisted that a clean truck showed a serious attitude about the business. I agreed with him, until I found I had to pay half the cost of the wash. Eight bucks. From now on, it was half-and-half on the expenses, and only a third of the profits until he'd made the $12,000 back.

"I got a glimpse of it at your apartment the other day," Emily said. "What's inside?" She started to open the cab.

"No. Let me show you where the money is made first." James pulled on the rear heavy metal latch and slowly pushed up the sliding back door.

"Well," she let her eyes wander over the interior, "it's the back end of a truck."

James scowled. The future was not something to make light of.

Plywood panels lined the walls and the floor. Hooks had been screwed into the left wall and a shelf was mounted on the right. It was an amateur job all the way around, but it seemed to fit us perfectly. We were two of the biggest amateurs in the business.

"Now the cab." James walked around to the front and opened the driver's door. Two cloth seats, an automatic transmission, and an add-on CD player. Nothing fancy. James beamed. "Then there's this little storage area." He pulled down the passenger seat and there was a concealed door behind the seat. James hoisted himself into the cab, opened the door, and stepped into the storage area. "See? There's a false wall in the truck, and we can put our personal stuff back here." He stuck his head out. "Room for three people."

"So, if you get thrown out of your apartment you've got a place to stay?"

He stared at Emily and stepped down from the truck.

"Have you ever tried to back it up?" she asked.

I studied her for a moment. "I don't think so. Why?"

"No rearview mirror. You've got to use side mirrors."

James looked into the driver's side mirror and ran his hand through his sandy brown hair. "How hard can that be?"

"It takes some getting used to."

"And how do you know?" She came off like an expert, this girl who drove a drop-top Thunderbird.

"Skip, I worked for Daddy a lot of summers. I've driven about every kind of truck imaginable. Trucks with eight forward and four reverse gears. Trucks that hauled lumber and all types of building materials. And I've driven plenty of trucks with side mirrors. It's not as easy as it looks."

I'm sure my eyes widened a little. I saw a look of awe on James's face. I had a new admiration for Em. She was full of little surprises.

"Maybe we should make her a partner?" I couldn't believe James said it. He'd only had one beer.

"James, I would never partner with you on anything. Never. Not if you were the last job in the world."

He shrugged his shoulders. "Pretty girl like you might attract a lot of customers. Of course your attitude would turn 'em off."

She gave him the finger.

"I'll call you and let you know when," I said.

Em got into her 'Bird and drove off, a slight squeal to the tires when she hit the open road.

"Let's go up to Pep Boys and get a quart of oil. It seems to drink a little of that. Fifteen hundred dollars, pardner. So if we could do fifteen a day—"

"James, the girl in there—"

"Nancy. Part-time. Once in a while."

"I never met her before."

"You and me, Skip. We're not cut out to be in long-term romances. At least not right now. Hell, we've got tomorrow to think about." He reached up and raked his hair down, giving me a wide-eyed stare. "Dude, we are sucky boyfriends."

"Ashton Kutcher, *Dude, Where's My Car?*"

"Wow. One try. You got it."

"Man, you are scraping the bottom of the barrel."

CHAPTER SIX

If you haven't seen the homes in the North Bay Road area, get on the Internet and find the Coldwell Banker Web site. They usually have some pictures of these $25,000,000 mansions. I don't think I've ever seen anything like Jackie Fuentes's house.

Emily led the way in her T-Bird past the North Bay Road mansions, past their heavy stone walls covered in ivy and bougainvillea, where we could catch glimpses through wrought iron gates of palatial estates of pink, yellow, and aqua stucco. Parked in circular driveways we could see gray Hummers and mint green Astin Martins, race yellow Porches and silver Volvos, like modern sculptures adding to the landscape of these waterfront properties. We stopped at the gate on La Gorce Circle and each of us had to show a photo ID. The uniformed guy came out and made us open the back of the truck. I don't know what he thought he'd find, but he spent a good thirty seconds gazing at the empty bed. Then we drove down the pine-lined winding road, finally pulling in the service entrance at the rear of the sprawling home. Sprawling means probably 20,000 square feet. The house featured an eight-car garage and a pair of tennis courts immediately to its right.

"Come on around to the front. You won't believe this." Em grabbed my hand and James followed close behind.

We got to the far corner and she said, "Close your eyes." I did, and she tugged me out front.

When I opened them, there was a long, deep blue, glistening pool of water that seemed to stretch out forever. The pool was lined with palm trees stretched out perfectly down the length of each side. A marble-tiled patio led up to the house where the porch was supported by eight massive pillars that appeared to be made from the same marble as the patio. Streaks of purple, green, and earth tones meandered in a swirling pattern through the elegantly shaped structure.

Four glass-topped tables sat on the porch, each with a pitcher and glasses as if a lemonade party were about to begin.

"Jesus." I looked up and up at the towering home. Two and three stories high and about ten miles wide. I exaggerate, but at least ten different roof levels looked over the pool. There were angles upon more angles and orange-tiled rooflines that went every which way. I remembered our home, with the one angle where the garage met the house. Flashing was laid under the tiles so the water would run down into the gutter, but it leaked every time it rained, no matter how much caulking Dad put on it. If the angles on Jackie Fuentes's house leaked the mansion would flood.

The white stucco gleamed, and through wide-open windows gauze curtains fluttered in a mild breeze.

"Come on, you've got to see this waterfront." Emily took my hand again and pulled me down to the pool and beyond. I glanced over my shoulder and James was following along behind, looking in every direction, obviously as impressed as I was.

Fifty yards farther we were at the water's edge. A sand beach that seemed to run forever stretched out on either side. Blue-green water lapped at the shore, and the soft sand felt so fluid under my feet I was tempted to take off my canvas Sebago shoes and run barefoot as far as I could.The three of us stood there, two of us simply awestruck by the view. No one said a word for sixty seconds. Finally, James opened his mouth.

"Dude."

I know, on the surface it's not the most expressive term, but it summed it up for the moment. Its deeper meaning was, "Have you ever seen anything this impressive in your life — other than that unbelievable house up there?"

That's what's nice about "Dude." It's just one word, but it conveys a whole lot more than just one word

"Hey, you guys."

We turned around and there was this gorgeous little brunette, maybe five feet tall, in a black bikini bathing suit. She had a grin that almost stopped my looking any farther, but that would have been a shame because the rest was awesome.

Jackie Fuentes was put together like a *Playboy* model. Ample-sized breasts, the halter top barely covering her nipples, and a narrow waist with a diamond stud in the belly button. The thong that hugged her crotch let every feature show through. I'd never seen a woman who was completely shaved. There was no doubt about this one.

"Dude," I said. I looked at James. He didn't say anything this time.

"James, Skip, this is Jackie. Put your tongues back in your mouths." Em gave us a stare.

Jackie Fuentes laughed. "Thank you so much for coming. I will be so glad when his things are out of the house." She motioned to the mansion. "Follow me and I'll show you where everything is."

We would have followed her anywhere. So this was what trophy wives looked like. I couldn't begin to imagine how beautiful and sexy the blond he'd left her for was. Em is one good-looking woman, but Jackie Fuentes was unbelievable. Maybe a little Latin and Italian and just plain gorgeous thrown in together.

Her cute, almost-naked butt led the way back to the house. She picked up a short robe from a chair by the pool and threw it around her shoulders. An attempt at decency, but the indecent part was already burned into my mind.

She opened the door and walked into the foyer. Marble tile continued from the porch and a huge living area spread out in all directions. I glanced up and saw the largest chandelier I'd ever seen in my life, even in a picture. Shining brass and hundreds of bulbs in a free-form fixture cast shadows below.

She escorted us down a wide hallway, carpeted like an expensive hotel. All right, the only expensive hotel I'd ever stayed in was when our high school swim team went up to Gainsville and I beat Fred Rea in the 100-meter breaststroke. But that was a pretty fancy hotel and this carpet reminded me of it.

"That's the theater there." We passed a room with five rows of seats and a large screen mounted on the wall. "And over there *was*," she said the word in a chilly tone of voice, "his weight room. I hope you guys are up to moving his weights."

James finally got his voice. I'd never seen him so awed. By the house, by the ocean view, and by Mrs. Jackie Fuentes. "Mrs. Fuentes, we'll move whatever you have."

She stopped and looked back at him, smiling a delicious smile. "It's James?"

"It is."

"And I'm Jackie. Not Mrs. Fuentes. I never want to be called Mrs. Fuentes again."

"I never meant to offend you."

"You're cute, you know that?"

Em rolled her eyes.

At the end of the hall we entered a large room with boxes

piled eight feet high. Clothing hung on wheeled aluminum racks, and in the far corner someone had set out his weights, a bench, and several barbells. I hadn't lifted weights in six years. I'd like to think that I'm still in shape, but I don't condition anymore, my diet isn't exactly the best, and the number of beers consumed each week seems to increase at an alarming rate. What the hell, there were two of us. We could lift them.

I had a brief flirtation with the idea of buying them from her. We'd set them up on our patio and work out every afternoon after work. I weighed the two options. Lift weights, drink beer. As I said, it was a brief flirtation.

James, on the other hand, seemed to have more than a brief flirtation with Jackie Fuentes. She laughed at something he'd said and I could see the old James Lessor confidence oozing from him.

"Jackie?" Em broke in. She didn't seem to like where this was going. "Why don't you tell the guys what goes and if you have any specific packing instructions."

"Sure." She shook that pretty head and pulled the robe around her. "There's a back entrance just at the end of the next hall. You can back your truck up there and just load it all in. I've got the address you'll be taking it to."

James touched her hand. "Leave it to us, Jackie. We'll take care of everything."

James was being a total idiot. For a minute I thought he might offer to do it for free, or for the chance to see her without that swimsuit. No, this was our future. You can't screw up your first job because of a good-looking lady. I mean, it's conceivable you'd find a good-looking lady at a number of your jobs. But, as I said, if I'd known what was in store, I would have stopped the whole project then and there.

I looked at Jackie Fuentes, and *imagined* her without the robe or bikini. It was cheaper that way.

CHAPTER SEVEN

JAMES MANEUVERED THE TRUCK up to the door. Em had been right. Backing up was a bitch. He swerved this way and that trying to get a feel for what he was seeing in the side mirrors. I stood by the door, yelling when he was in danger of hitting some of the landscaping, the small porch, or the house itself. There were several moments when I thought he might.

Finally, he had the rear of our Chevy somewhat lined up with the back door. He jumped out and surveyed the angle of the truck much like a painter or brick mason might step back to admire his work.

"Not too bad."

"It took you fifteen minutes."

"I'll get better, Skip. You want to try?"

I didn't.

"How should we do this? One of us could stand in the back of the truck and take the stuff to the rear after the other brings it down the hall — how does that sound?"

"Doable. We'll take turns. You do truck duty for the first

half and I'll do it the second half." I wanted it to be fair for all concerned.

We went at it for two hours, taking turns bringing boxes down the hall, lifting them into the back of the truck, and repeating the process dozens and dozens of times.

"The first thing we're investing in when we get paid is a dolly." I mopped my brow with the sopping wet T-shirt that I'd removed over an hour ago. If this became a steady gig, I wouldn't need the weights. Thank God Jackie remembered she had a dolly about halfway through the job.

Light, heavy, the boxes kept coming. Some of them were open and we could peer into corners of Rick Fuentes's life. There were desk items like pen sets and a crystal globe. Another open box had dozens of videotapes with titles like *Tax Audits Involving Business Travel* or *Setting Up Your Own Off-shore Bank.*

"It's shit like this that is the difference between the haves and the have-nots," James said.

Em walked in and pointed to the last pile of envelopes and boxes by the door. "Jackie says that's all the mail he's received in the last four weeks."

"She hasn't even opened his mail?" If I went four weeks without opening my mail the power and water would be shut off.

"Apparently he called her and asked her to open it. He said if there was anything important he needed her to call him, but she didn't. I don't think she wanted to know what he was involved in. I told you, she was scared."

We each grabbed a load and carried it out, shoving everything into the truck.

"Long Island Ice Tea, boys?" Jackie came out of the house in a loose-flowing, long peach-colored summer dress. I could see through it, and she didn't wear a bra. She carried a tray with these very fancy glasses, napkins, and glass stirrers topped with miniature pink flamingos.

I grabbed one as she offered the tray. It appeared we weren't going to drink on the front porch by the pool, but at this point it made no difference. An iced alcoholic beverage was a beverage from heaven no matter where we drank it.

Em came out the door sipping hers. She'd kept Jackie company while we did our dirty work. James and I sat down on the small concrete porch and the girls joined us. I closed my eyes and tilted the glass, draining a quarter of it in one gulp. Sweet syrup with a bite. I could immediately feel the relaxing warmth in my veins. I would have settled for just this drink. James seemed interested in more than the drink or the money.

"I don't want to sound like I'm coming on to you, but—"

Jackie smiled. "But you are?"

"Skip and I can keep this in the truck overnight and unload it tomorrow."

Which was new to me. I'd thought we were going to unload it tonight at the storage unit and be done with it.

"So," he continued, "would you like to grab a bite to eat after I get cleaned up?"

"You're cute."

"You said that already."

"Yeah. It hasn't changed. However, I really don't think going out with you works."

James was in his selling game. "Jackie. Is it a class thing? You're rich, I'm poor? Or is it an age thing? Because you can't be more than a year older than I am and—"

She leaned over and kissed his cheek. "You're a charmer. However, I really don't want to be seen with someone new at this point. My attorney cautioned against it. It's that simple."

And that was it. We finished our drinks with some mild banter and hopped in the truck.

James had the address for the storage building and we drove away.

"So that's the line. 'Want to grab a bite to eat?' "

"She has some class, and some money, bro. I couldn't use my standard line, 'Wanna fuck?' "

The storage unit was in a small industrial park about seven miles from Indian Creek by the map and about ten million miles from Indian Creek by the status of the community. What the hell, it reminded me of Carol City. We drove through the narrow drives dividing the single story units until we saw number 352.

"Are you going to back it in?"

"We could just park it alongside."

"It's going to be a lot easier if you back it in."

"All right. Get out and guide me."

I didn't envy him. The space between the two buildings was narrow and I would guess even an experienced driver would have a tough time. He stuck his head out and surveyed the concrete area in front of the unit.

"How close am I?"

"Cut the wheel, more."

"It only cuts so far, pardner."

Now he was wedged. The truck was cockeyed in the space.

"Straighten it out and start over."

He hit the gas, still in reverse. If I hadn't jumped about four feet sideways I would have been smashed. Instead, I landed hard on my ass as I heard him yell, "Shit."

The truck rammed the building and I heard a thud and a crunch as the side of the building and the back of the truck buckled.

"Skip, are you all right?" He jumped from the driver's seat and jogged to the rear as I picked myself up. I patted myself down, checking to see if anything was broken.

"Oh, shit." James covered his eyes with his hand.

I walked over to the truck and surveyed the building. "Man, you caved in the side of the unit."

"I don't give a damn about that. Look at the truck."

"We'll get it fixed, James. What about the building?"

He gave it a quick glance. "We'll unload and take off. Nobody can prove we did the damage."

Of course, he was right. The aluminum siding was damaged, but it could be repaired as well.

James reached into his pocket and took out the key. He turned it and gave a tug as the garage door opened into the cavernous storage space.

I fought with the heavy metal latch on the truck, finally forcing it open. The sliding back door eased up as dozens of boxes and envelopes spilled out onto the concrete apron.

"Shit." James stared at the four weeks' worth of mail strewn across the front of the unit.

"Help me pick this up." I gathered an armful of envelopes and put them back into an open box.

"What the—" James picked up a manila envelope.

"We're not going to make much progress one envelope at a time," I said.

"Something is wet and sticky here."

"Did you break something?" I didn't see how that could matter. Someone was probably going to haul this stuff away in a couple of months and sell it or take it to a dump.

James examined the envelope, then tore it open. He peered into the opening and froze.

"What?"

He didn't speak, just kept staring.

"What is it?"

"Oh, shit. Oh, shit." He dropped the envelope and shuttered.

"James."

I picked up the envelope and glanced inside.

"Take it out."

"Oh, God. You take it out."

"No, man. It's gross. It can't be—"

I shook it out of the red-stained envelope and it fell to the concrete. Coagulated blood covered the stub of the severed finger. A blue-stoned class ring circled the knuckle. I shook the brown envelope again and a smaller gray envelope fell out. I stared at the finger, wanting to believe it was something else. Wanting to believe it was a magicians trick or a joke that James was playing. But deep in my stomach I knew it was real. Someone in Miami was missing a finger and we were the lucky guys who had found it.

I lost my Long Island Ice Tea on the cement.

CHAPTER EIGHT

There's a line in the movie *The Mexican* that says, "Guns don't kill people, postal workers do." Despite James' affinity for that quote, he had a belief that bank tellers would be the next group of employees to go ballistic.

"Seriously, Skip," he had said one afternoon on the patio. "Tellers stand there for six or eight hours and watch people come up to their windows. Some of these people have nothing, and the teller feels sorry for them. They're taking out every last cent they've got and the teller knows they have nothing left. After a while they start to feel really bad." He sucked on his green bottle and puffed on a cigarette. With Psychology 101 behind me, I've always felt he has an obsessive personality.

"Then, they get all these rich assholes who come in and deposit hundreds of thousands of dollars. Or take that much out. They tell the teller that they're making a down payment on a yacht or a cottage in the South of France, or whatever. After a while, these bank employees *should* go nuts. They're making what? Ten bucks an hour. More than the poor people and a whole lot less than the rich."

"What's your point?" I asked.

"Bank tellers are going to start to kill people out of frustration."

"Who? Which class?"

"The rich people. They're going to start shooting the wealthy."

I got to thinking about that. In a way, Rick Fuentes was a banker. He arranged financing for business people. He'd raise the money, make the loan, and collect the interest. Maybe the people who gave him the cash weren't happy with the way he was lending it. Or maybe a client who had borrowed money from Fuentes wasn't happy with the terms. Seriously, maybe this was a banker thing.

We'd found a neighborhood bar about a mile from the unit. In a back corner booth we nursed our drafts. I hoped that this drink would stay down.

"Read it again." I waved at the bartender and he pulled two more Buds from the tap.

James pulled the letter from the small gray envelope.

"*We ask you to reconsider your decision. If you agree with us, we will give you the rest in relatively good shape.* Jesus, Skip, what the hell does it mean?"

"It means we should go to the cops."

He shook his head. "No way, compadre. It's a federal offense to open someone else's mail."

"James, my God. It's someone's finger." I left the rest of our discovery hang in the air.

"Not just *someone's* finger." James wasn't going to leave it alone. "Someone who graduated from St. James High with us."

"Yeah, there's that." We were both silent for a moment. The St. James ring with our graduation date engraved on it was firmly planted on the severed digit.

"And, Skipper, now that our fingerprints are all over the

fucking envelopes and the letter, we're going to get our asses kicked. The cops will fuck us, man. I have experience — or at least my old man had experience! I think we take it back to Jackie Fuentes and explain what happened."

"What? That you don't know the difference between forward and reverse with a fucking automatic transmission?"

He looked at me through half-slit eyes.

"I'm sorry. Now isn't the time to start on each other. You're probably right. We need to go back to the Fuentes house and give her the finger."

James smiled, the first time since he'd wrecked the truck.

The bartender brought the two beers, picked up the money and silently walked back to his bar. Alan Jackson and Jimmy Buffet sang *It's Five O'clock Somewhere* on the juke box, and two good-old-boys in cowboy hats at a table up front sang along. Other than that, there was no one in the room.

"Well, I want it out of my truck. I sincerely do."

"Let's go back to Jackie's right now." It was way past five o'clock.

"I'm ready." James slammed the full glass down on the table and stood up. I've known James Lessor since third grade and I have never, ever seen him leave a full beer on the table or anywhere else for that matter. This time he did, as he headed for the door. I remember taking a fast swallow and following him out. After all, I'd paid for the beer.

CHAPTER NINE

THE GUARD ASKED FOR OUR IDs and James opened the rear of the truck.

He gazed up and down at all the boxes. "Someone moving in?"

"We're moving some stuff back to the Fuentes house." James kept nodding his head.

"Nothing on the sheet here. I'll have to call the house." He picked up the phone and closed the door to the booth. We waited, not saying anything to each other. We'd been in trouble before. That was nothing new to us; however, it had never been this serious. The guard opened the door.

"Mrs. Fuentes said she is not available for dinner tonight. She said that would be clear to you."

James opened his mouth, but nothing came out.

"Can I speak with her?" I asked.

"I'm sorry, she said she can't be bothered any more this evening. Perhaps you could call her tomorrow.

James had fire in his eyes. "Look, bud, I've got something of hers that she needs and I need to get back there and give it to her."

"You look, *bud.*" The guard frowned. "We have our own police force here, and with one touch I can summon a patrol car that will be here in sixty seconds. Would you like me to do that?"

"Cops?"

"Cops."

"No. I'll call Mrs. Fuentes later." James spun on his heel and I followed him. I checked on the rear door latch to make sure it wouldn't spring open and we got back in the truck.

"Want me to call Em?"

"Why?"

"She can call Jackie."

James was hot. I could almost see steam rising from the top of his head. "Honest to God, Eugene, no one else can know anything about this. Do you understand the severity of what we've got here?" That's about as serious as I've ever heard him.

"I don't have to tell her anything. I can just ask her for Jackie's number. Tell her you left your cell phone behind or we're missing something."

He thought about it for a moment. "No. It's not Jackie Fuentes's mail, is it?"

"Technically, no."

"Whose mail is it?" James was pissed.

"It was addressed to Rick Fuentes."

"Exactly. Fuck Jackie Fuentes. She won't see us, we'll go to the end user. Remember Em telling us he'd moved into a condo over in Bal Harbor?"

I did.

"We're taking it back to Mr. Fuentes."

"Jesus, James. That complicates things. We've got a load of his stuff in the back of the truck, and our client is his estranged wife. Now you want to go to the old man and admit that we not only have his stuff, but we've been opening his mail?"

"Whose mail is it?"

"Come on, man. This is so fucked up. You can't be—"

"Whose mail is it?"

"He's going to be so pissed. And Jackie is going to be in trouble, and Em is never going to let me forget this."

"Whose mail is it?"

"Rick Fuentes's."

He swerved, avoiding an almost invisible pothole in the road. "I think it's time we deliver Mr. Fuentes's mail. Come on, Skip, it's the only thing that makes any sense."

"We put it in the storage unit."

"Can't. Fingerprints are all over it. Jackie knows we were carrying the mail."

"We go to the cops, James. Now."

"Like hell! My whole life was fucked by the cops. Because my old man's business partner split with the money, the *cops* arrested my dad. The cops threw him in jail when he didn't know a goddamned thing. They convicted him and put him in prison for five years, Skip. Five ball-breaking, rip-your-guts-out years. That's the way it was. You think I want to go to the cops with my fingerprints all over this thing? You think I want to put this finger and envelope in that storage unit so somebody can come back and claim we were involved in some sort of mutilation or murder? You think I want one damned thing to do with the law? You've got another thought coming. Mr. Fuentes is going to get his mail. Tonight. You on board?" He kept his eyes straight ahead, driving, as far as I could tell, without a destination. Steam was just about rolling out of his ears.

For some reason I thought about our young Bahamian friend, Angel. Angel seemed to be high on drugs most of the time or totally blown away on alcohol, but we both considered him a friend. He's learned to function in society in spite of his addictions, or as he calls them, *his afflictions*. Regardless of what they are, or in spite of what they are, Angel has a pretty good head on his shoulders. Angel can be very philosophical at times and I lay it on his intelligence and intuitive nature. He also reads a lot and memorizes these passages. They often have relevance — unlike James's movie quotes. James says it's the drugs he takes, but I think Angel is brilliant.

I've heard Angel spout off philosophical sayings, and most of those times I'd have to agree with James. It was the drugs. However, one of Angel's aphorisms immediately came to mind when James asked if I was on board.

"No task is a long one but the task on which one dare not start. That task becomes a nightmare."

I know, it's a stretch to believe a person high on chemical substances can think like that or remember it from verse, but he does. That's Angel. But I was still confused how he knew about the hauling job. James must have mentioned it and then forgotten. There were many nights when that was more than possible.

"All right. I'm on board. How do you propose to find this Rick Fuentes? I mean, we could call Jackie and —"

"No. Can't call Jackie. Let's keep her out of this."

"All right. We know he lives in the Bal Harbor area. We could —" I was out of ideas.

"Call information."

I stared at James as he concentrated on the road. We were headed down to the Bal Harbor area. I recognized the well-lit streets with high-end shops, perfectly groomed palms planted at regular intervals, and elegant high-rises that looked out over the harbor.

"Dial it."

411.

"City and state please."

"Miami, Florida. Bal Harbor — a listing for Rick Fuentes."

It was a recording. The operator picked up. "Miami?"

"Yeah."

"Name?"

"Rick Fuentes."

"Please hold while we dial that number for you."

Son of a bitch. That charge would show up on my bill. Minutes and information charges, these things kept adding up.

The phone rang. "Shit, James. He's actually listed. What the hell do I say to him?"

"The truth."

"What?" I was near panic at this moment. Rick Fuentes could pick up the phone at any second and I'd be left going, "Ah, uh, ah, uh . . . ."

"Can you just tell him that we have some of his mail and we'd like to deliver it? Would that be so hard?"

"No. I can do that." Well thought out. I had to hand it to my man.

James pulled over to the side of the street. We were in the area. Neither of us had a clue how to navigate in this well-to-do neighborhood. I'd been here once with Em. We shopped at Saks Fifth Avenue. *She* shopped at Saks Fifth Avenue. I didn't spend a penny except for the six bucks for parking and the forty-dollar lunch. Two sandwiches and a shared salad. This was one expensive neighborhood.

"Hello. We can't come to the phone right now. Please, leave a message and we'll call you as soon as possible."

Was there an original message anywhere in the world? One that said. "Hey, taking a crap, but once I'm done, I'd love to talk to you." Or one I'd almost done at our apartment in Carol City. "We have caller ID. We know who you are. If we wanted to talk to you, we would have picked up, but obviously we didn't. If you have anything at all that's important to say, you'll have to say it on the machine."

"This is Skip Moore. I have some mail for Mr. Fuentes. If you'd like us to deliver it to you please call me back." I left the cell number.

"We could sit here till next summer."

"He'll call back."

"Next summer?"

"These rich guys. They need to stay in touch, but they screen their calls."

"James, you are always sooooo wise."

The phone rang.

"Hello."

"This is Rick Fuentes."

"We have some mail for you."

"Bring it by. Here's the address."

Shit.

No task is a long one but the task on which one dare not start. That task becomes a nightmare.

CHAPTER TEN

CARL ICAHN IS A FINANCIER who lives in the Indian Creek Village area. According to what I've found on the Internet, this man supposedly has had more financial encounters than most rich people. He proposed a hostile takeover of TWA and tried to take over Marvel Comics. I mean, Spiderman's home turf? Come on. He owned the Sands in Vegas and a billion other companies. When we were driving by the mansions on the private island, James pointed out a palatial estate that he thought was Icahn's. I'm not sure how he knew, but I think he'd seen pictures.

I was thinking about Icahn as we drove back into Bal Harbor following Rick Fuentes' directions. I asked James what these people did for a living. Here were condos. Hundreds, maybe thousands of condos that started at maybe $800,000 and went up to four or five million. What the hell did all these people do?

I knew what Icahn did. He played with other people's money.

"You want to know what these people do?"

"I asked, didn't I?"

"I can tell you, but you won't like the answer."

"Humor me, James."

"They make a lot of money."

Shit. As usual, James was semiuseless.

"It's eBay mentality, Skip."

"What's that, *James*?" When he's being an asshole you have to call him on it. This time it didn't faze him.

"It's the mentality of *stuff*, Skip. It's the reason we have a Chevy truck."

"I have no fucking idea what you're talking about."

"It's the reason we're going to be able to afford one of these two-million-dollar condos in a couple of years. Listen, bro, people are into stuff. I told you this before. They buy tons and tons of crap on eBay. They collect junk. Books, cars, antiques, memorabilia, stuff they'll never use. Stuff that has no earthly value to them. Stuff, Skip. Stuff, and more stuff."

"What does that have to do with the price of a condo?"

"If you have stuff they want to buy, you can get rich. Norman Branon lives in Indian Creek Village. He owns four car dealerships in Florida and three in Colorado. Acura, Audi, Bentley, BMW, Porsche, and," he drew a deep breath, "Cadillac. People buy his stuff, pardner. Lots and lots and lots of his stuff."

"And that's why Norman is living in Indian Creek."

"And why we live in a one-bedroom piece of crap in Carol City. This guy gets rich off of stuff. Hell, Skip, he used to own the Philadelphia Eagles."

"And we don't have this stuff."

"Never will. Don't even want it." He paused. "Well, I still think I'm going to buy a Cadillac. But we can haul all this stuff. We'll get a bigger truck next time and haul Mr. Branon's Cadillac wherever he wants."

"So if you don't have stuff, you learn how to leverage everyone else's stuff?"

"I should have the business degree." He watched the street signs carefully and finally jerked the truck to the right, following a winding road. "Skip, you lack vision. With you it's all nuts and bolts. I like that, don't get me wrong. Someone has to sound the alarm once in a while, right or wrong. Someone has to ask about the fiscal responsibility of a certain project. But—" he braked for what looked like a low-riding, racing-yellow Maserati that came popping out of a side street, "but someone has to have the ideas. If we can't afford stuff that people will buy, we'll haul and store people's stuff. The guy who started Waste Management started with one truck, Skip. He hauled people's stuff. He's now worth about a gazillion dollars."

"Body parts, James. Who would have thought that body parts would be part of people's stuff?"

He didn't say anything. We'd been avoiding the subject for a while. It was weird enough to have the finger riding in the rear of the truck, but the class ring made it even stranger. And I was feeling a lot of guilt about not calling Em. She had arranged the job and probably should be aware of what had happened.

"It's through those gates." James pointed at a guardhouse to the right. There was another side business. The security companies that guard people's stuff. The problem with my company was that in my assigned territory, Carol City, no one had stuff worth guarding. I needed to be selling security systems in Bal Harbor or Indian Creek Village. Someone was making a fortune right here.

The guard called ahead and got approval. He handed James a small map and pointed out the condo about an eighth of a mile back. "Mr. Fuentes informed me you were delivering some mail to this address. We'll expect to see you back at the gate within, let's say, half an hour?"

James bristled. "That depends on Mr. Fuentes."

The elderly, uniformed guard stared at him under the shiny

bill of his blue cap. "Half an hour, sir. If it's longer, please ask Mr. Fuentes to call the guardhouse."

We pulled away. "Mr. Fuentes—half an hour. Fucker practically threatened us."

"Just protecting people's stuff, James."

He was silent and sullen. We pulled up in front of a pale stucco and brick building and parked in a guest-only spot.

"Well, pardner, who's going to carry the mail?"

It was a moonless night, bright lights bouncing off the water on the shore side of the towering structure. I could only imagine what it looked like from thirty stories up.

James opened the sliding truck door and I picked up the box with most of the mail, the opened manila envelope with the severed digit lying on top. I shuddered.

"Neither snow nor rain nor heat nor gloom of night . . ."

"Yeah, yeah. Let's just get this over with." I never would have done this by myself. There's courage in a crowd, even if the crowd is only two.

CHAPTER ELEVEN

THE DOORMAN POINTED US TO AN ELEVATOR on the far side of the spacious lobby. A gigantic vase of multicolored fresh flowers sat on an onyx table in the center of the vestibule, and luxurious couches and rich mahogany-colored leather chairs surrounded the table. On the wall was a painting that had to measure fifteen by ten feet. Thick textures of muted greens, yellows, and blues formed an underwater collage, with plants and tropical fish etched on canvas for eternity. I'm not a big fan of art, but I stopped to admire the sheer expanse of the piece.

"Come on, man. Half an hour, remember?" James was at the elevator, pointing at his watch.

"We're just going to hand him the envelope?"

"I think we owe him a quick explanation."

"What? We're hauling your stuff to be stored and in the process we opened some of your mail?"

The door slid silently open, and we stepped inside. Plush carpeted walls hushed the sound of doors closing and cables shooting us to the top. In less time than I hoped for, the doors opened and we looked out on a birch-paneled hallway.

"This is going to be very strange, James."

"Very."

We walked down the thick, heavy carpeting, looking for his door. There were four units per floor and Fuentes's was the last. James pushed the buzzer on the door and we waited. An interminable amount of time passed. Finally the door swung open and we were face to face with Rick Fuentes.

"You have mail for me?"

I was immediately taken with his angular face, his deep green eyes, and his steel gray hair. The man looked like a matinee idol a couple of years past his prime. His Latin features and deep tan added to the look as he studied us, a puzzled expression on his face.

I looked at James, and he had his mouth half open, nothing coming out.

"Apparently your mail isn't being forwarded." I shrugged my shoulders, the envelope heavy in my hand. "We were asked—hired to take it to a storage unit, and—"

"You decided to bring it my attention instead?" There was no denying a Cuban accent. "And this is all the mail you were hired to pick up?" He motioned to the envelope.

James was staring at me, waiting for my next move.

"No. There's a lot more in our truck. This package, this envelope seemed to be leaking something and we thought maybe something had broken. So we opened it."

"My mail? You opened it?"

"Yes."

"And was something broken?" He made no move to invite us inside. I was glad. There was still a chance to race down the hall, jump on the elevator, and make a clean get away.

"Mr. Fuentes, we found a finger. Here." I thrust the envelope into his hands. I desperately wanted to walk away from it all. I motioned to James who still appeared to be frozen.

"A finger?" He peered into the envelope, then reached in, pulling out the severed digit. His eyes grew wide. Dropping it on the marble entranceway, he backed into his condo. "What do you want? How could you do something this hideous?"

"Mr. Fuentes, we didn't do anything. We thought it was something you should see. There's a letter —"

"What do you want?" His voice was higher, louder than before. James shifted his gaze between Fuentes and me.

"Nothing. What I want to do is leave."

I turned and grabbed James by the arm.

"Young man?"

I turned back. He had a revolver in his hand and it was leveled about crotch high.

"Please come in. Now."

I should have kept on walking, but I didn't. We followed Rick Fuentes into his condo.

CHAPTER TWELVE

WE SAT AT A CARVED MAHOGANY TABLE in ornate chairs. He'd deposited the finger somewhere else, but the letter and the class ring sat in front of us, a reminder of how our first job had become a lot more complicated than we anticipated. The girlfriend had served coffee — deep, rich, stay-awake coffee that you could almost chew. There was no chance I was going to sleep tonight, coffee or not.

"So you see," James had finally found his voice, "we're on our first hauling job. That's it. And we seriously know nothing about your mail. If we did, we'd tell you." The handgun lay on the table in front of Fuentes, another reminder that we certainly weren't out of the woods yet.

"And Jackie knows nothing of this? She was to open all my mail."

"We can only speculate. She didn't seem to."

He frowned and picked up the blue-stoned class ring, rubbing the jewel with his thumb. "Do you know whose ring this is?"

"No. I only know that Skip and I graduated that same year from the same school."

He took a deep breath, squinting at us. He didn't know whether to trust us or not, but I could sense he needed to trust someone.

"It's my son's ring." There was a tremor in his voice.

"Your son?"

"Victor."

Victor. There was no Victor Fuentes in our class. I didn't know everyone personally, but the name certainly rang no bell. I looked at James and he shook his head.

"Vic Maitlin."

As in captain of the football team Vic Maitlin. As in senior class president Vic Maitlin. As in get the girls Vic Maitlin.

As in saved my life Vic Maitlin?

"When I divorced my first wife, she took back her maiden name and she registered him as Maitlin. His true name is still Fuentes." Rick Fuentes stared at us with his piercing, emerald eyes. "Where is my son?"

"Honest to Christ, we don't know." I looked at James and shrugged my shoulders, doing my absolute best to remain calm. "Mr. Fuentes, we could have gone to the police. Instead, we came straight to you, sir. We have the rest of your mail in the truck outside. There is absolutely nothing we want from you. Please, believe me. If we had an agenda, we would have told you by now." I shuddered. There was only one Vic Maitlin. This was no mistake. The young boy who'd saved my life. And I swear to you I have never, ever mentioned this to anyone. Not to my mother, James, or Em. I had a hard time catching my breath.

He buried his head in his hands, a tremor shaking his body. When he raised his face again, he appeared at ease. His blond mistress walked into the room and put her hands on his shoulders, gently massaging them. She looked all of nineteen years old, a petite little girl dressed in gray sweats.

"You know Vic?"

James tore his eyes from the blond. "Of course. We weren't really close, but sure, we knew him. Everyone knew Vic."

Fuentes smiled softly. "You haven't kidnapped him? You have no idea where he is?"

"None."

"I want him back home." He looked over his shoulder at the girl, probably four or five years younger than his son. "*We* want him back."

She nodded.

Vic Maitlin. I couldn't get past the name. Jesus, my worst memory. My best memory. I wouldn't be standing in front of the father if it weren't for the son.

"Help me find him."

"What?" I didn't think I'd heard what I heard.

"Help me find him. I have an idea where he is. I need corroboration. That's all."

"Mr. Fuentes, we're not in the missing person business." I shook my head emphatically, realizing that I had the chance to finally pay Vic back. But it made no sense. I wasn't the hero. Vic was.

"There will be no danger."

"You've got a finger that tells me otherwise."

He frowned. "All I need is for you to verify his location. It should take a couple of days. How much would that be worth to you?"

"Five thousand dollars." James leaned forward, his eyes on fire.

"No. Mr. Fuentes, we have jobs. We're not available." I pushed my chair back and stood up. Everything told me to say no. But I owed this Vic Maitlin. Still, I held back.

"Five thousand dollars!" James stood too, and glared at me. "Mr. Fuentes, we'll give you your corroboration. For five grand."

"Half now, and half when you find him."

It was like a movie. It was happening on the big screen, and even though I was involved I was powerless to stop it.

"Why us? You don't even know us. Two minutes ago you thought we were responsible for your son's abduction. Now you're willing to pay us to find him?"

Fuentes grabbed the hand of his girlfriend and squeezed it. "I have no one I can trust."

"Well, you can't trust us. You know nothing about us." I prayed he'd take back the offer. I wasn't the person his son was. I didn't put myself out on a limb.

"If I've made a mistake, I'll know it in a very short time. I want my son back, at any cost. Find him, and I'll pay you more than the five thousand dollars."

Sinking back into my chair, I felt weak.

"Tell us where you think he is, Mr. Fuentes. We'll start immediately." James was on fire.

"He's with an international group of businessmen."

"Spanish?" I couldn't help but ask.

He paused. "Cuban."

James looked at me, a puzzled expression on his face.

"Em told me."

"You knew about this?"

I took a deep breath. I knew nothing, and I knew everything. I knew that we'd gone way too far already. I knew that the damned box truck just might be the death of us.

"I know this is a mistake."

Fuentes picked up the revolver, never pointing it, but balancing it in his right hand. "Mr. Moore, I'm willing to pay you for this service." His Cuban accent had a regal, formal air to it. "The two of you and Cynthia and I are the only ones who know about this. I have no one else to turn to. I'm afraid I must insist that you do me this favor. If you don't, a missing finger may be a minor inconvenience."

James seemed hypnotized by the pistol. Rick Fuentes kept his eyes on mine. I was the one he had to convince. He was doing a very good job of it.

"I'm going to tell you where I think he is. Confirm that for me. I would like an answer in twenty-four hours. After that, I'll send someone to look for you. Understood?"

I nodded. James nodded.

He pulled a pen from his shirt pocket and scribbled an address on a napkin, pushing it over to James. Cautiously, James picked it up and held it gingerly.

"Cynthia." It was the first time he'd addressed her. She left the table and returned with a checkbook. Fuentes tore out a pale blue check and penned in the amount, signing with a flourish. He pushed that over to James as well.

We walked out of the condo, Fuentes still sitting at the table, the blond rubbing his shoulders. The last thing I saw was Rick Fuentes, tapping the barrel of the gun on the table. His eyes were like a cat's, calculating and cunning. We had his money and we had his address. I had a debt to repay. We had no choice.

CHAPTER THIRTEEN

We were thirteen. James and I, Em and Vic. Twelve or thirteen, and it was a school field trip. You remember field trips. Sometimes they were to the zoo or maybe an aquarium or one time to the Miami River. And we were always paired up with a buddy. I was paired up with Vic, and even though we weren't close, I was excited about the pairing. Vic was playing junior high basketball and was already the star athlete of the seventh grade. His dark features, athletic prowess, and quick smile made him a candidate for most popular kid in the entire school.

Teachers loved his wit and intellect. Girls loved his looks, personality, and gentle nature and they weren't even sure why. Guys found him to be easy to be around, with a self-effacing nature and a natural humor. There was nothing not to like about Vic Maitlin, except for two guys he palled around with. Justin Cramer and Mike Stowe. Mean, nasty, and full of themselves, these two guys made the school bullies look like choirboys. Vic distanced himself from their antics but hung with them just the same.

This field trip, Vic Maitlin was *my* buddy. He accepted the role with ease and grace and we acted like we'd been best friends since first grade.

And after the incident at the sinkhole, with Cramer and Stowe, Vic told me to keep everything to myself. He swore me to secrecy, for my entire life, and even though it was a childhood promise, it stuck with me. I never had any intention of going back on my word, and if his life hadn't been in danger, I would have taken the secret to my grave. But Vic was in trouble, serious trouble, and it was time to repay my debt.

CHAPTER FOURTEEN

"ALL THE REST OF HIS STUFF is in the truck. Should we go back and—" James pointed back at the high-rise.

"Jesus." I stared at the back end of the truck. We'd gotten so wrapped up in the finger that we'd forgotten the rest of the mail. I gazed back at the condo. We'd be back to report, and frankly I'd had enough of Rick Fuentes and his gun for one night. "Nah. It's late and we've pretty much used up our half hour. We'll bring it back when we give him our report."

"You didn't sound too sure about this job."

"I'm not." It was hard not to tell my story. "Man, we could get our asses shot off. Or fingers hacked off. This could be dangerous."

We stood in the parking lot, gazing out at the harbor. A long, lean ship moved slowly, lights strung from towers fore and aft. Finally, James spoke up.

"Listen, amigo. We've made $1,500 for hauling Fuentes's stuff. We'll make $5,000 plus a bonus for finding his son. Hell, Skip, that's more than half of what the van cost. Not bad for our first day in business."

"James, you know if we don't find Vic, Rick Fuentes is going to jump our asses. It was more of a threat than a request. Do you understand that?"

He was quiet. I slid into the truck, and he stayed outside, lighting a cigarette and taking a drag. The crickets chirped in the foliage and a couple of night birds called out. From somewhere in the bay I could hear a motor boat bouncing on the water and the yapping of a young puppy.

"We're in some deep shit, bubba." James blew a smoke ring into the night, the lights from the condo casting shadows all around us.

"Duh! We could have given it back to Jackie or gone to the cops, but—"

"Let's not lay blame. What's done is done. Vic Maitlin is with a group of Cuban businessmen. Why do you think they're cutting off his fingers?"

"Fingers? Are there multiples?"

"No. Just a thought. If we don't find him, there may be more."

"Let's think about it. All we have to do is stake out the address and see if Vic is being kept there. We get a yes or no, and we're done with it."

"Stake out?" He chuckled, finding humor in a very tense situation. "You've been watching too many cop shows, Skip."

"Give me a better solution."

"No, you're right. We'll go over there tomorrow and see if there's any activity." He pulled the address from his pocket and scooted into the cab. Holding it to the light, he silently read. "Little Havana. I don't know where exactly, but I recognize the street."

"James, we've got twenty-four hours. I think tomorrow is a little late."

He studied me, flicking the ashes from his cigarette out the window.

"Half an hour."

"What?"

"The guard. He gave us half an hour. Fuentes gave us twenty-four hours. I'm not used to having people hold a stop watch to my activities," he said.

"I'm not used to finding body parts and being threatened with a gun."

James started the truck and pulled out. We stopped at the guardhouse, the old man nodded to us, and we continued on our way. He reached over and turned on the radio. We hadn't taken the time to punch-set the station settings since we played CDs most of the time. A Spanish station played some brassy salsa music and he left it there, just trying to put some noise over the stone-cold silence in the cab.

Finally he spoke. "Regrets are a bitch, Skip."

"Huh?"

"What do you regret?"

"What the hell are you talking about?"

"You very seldom regret the things you do. You regret the things you don't do."

A fair statement.

"I don't want to have regrets. I want to go out doing everything. I want to own my own business. I want to be worth a million dollars in two years. I want to make love to a hundred beautiful women and settle down with the best one. So what if it means taking chances? My old man took chances—"

"Your dad probably regretted what he did more than what he wished he'd done." As soon as I said it I wished I hadn't. I regret the fact that I didn't get to know my old man a lot better. But I'm not sure it's *my* regret. It should be his.

"But not regrets about never having tried. He tried, Skip. He got blind sided by a partner. But, God how that man tried. He regretted never having ridden in a Cadillac. That was his regret.

But my God he tried!"

"Your point is?"

"I'm trying, just like he did. But *I'm* going to succeed. We're getting a nice windfall here, and if we play our cards right, this business could be a huge success. I don't want to regret that I didn't give it a chance."

I gazed at him, my best friend. He motivated me. I never would have gone to college if he hadn't pushed the restaurant idea. He was right, of course. A man should do everything during his life to avoid having regrets. I believe that, maybe because James believes it, but it seems like a mantra to live by. Live your life so that when you die there are no regrets. But then, I'm twenty-four years old and when I'm thirty-five or forty, I may laugh at what I thought when I was twenty-four. When I was sixteen, I thought I'd know a lot more at twenty-four than I do now.

"I've got one regret already."

"What?"

"I didn't call Em." I pulled my cell phone from its plastic holster and hit speed dial.

"Jesus. You don't want to tell her that—"

"Hello?"

"Em."

"Are you guys done unloading? I've got your check. Want me to stop over?"

I looked at James and he was shaking his head, watching the oncoming headlights as they whizzed by. He had a big frown on his face.

I put my hand over the receiver for a second. "You were ready to make her a partner when you found out she could drive without a rearview mirror. In retrospect—"

"What do you want to do? Have a conference with her?"

"Not here on the phone."

"Good." He spoke in a loud whisper.

"I want to stop by and see her. I want to tell her what's going on."

"Oh, that's brilliant. Put her in danger too?"

"Skip? Skip? Are you there?"

"Yeah. Hold on just a sec."

"She's out of danger. *We're* in danger, Jackie Fuentes may be in danger. Vic Maitlin is definitely in danger, but Emily is on the outside. We could use some advice from someone on the outside."

"I guess we don't have to take it." He frowned. "All right. Do what you need to do."

"Em, we're going to stop by. We need to talk to you about something that's come up."

"Skip, that doesn't sound good."

"It's not, Emily." I almost quoted Angel's line about starting a task that becomes a nightmare, but she wouldn't have understood and it probably would have scared the hell out of her.

CHAPTER FIFTEEN

Em lives twenty stories up in a high-rise overlooking Biscayne Bay. Everyone we know seems to have a water view; James and I are the only ones that have a brown water ditch to look at. Em looks out at South Beach and the cruise ships that dock across from the causeway. It took us about twenty minutes to get to her condo.

"Come on out on the balcony."

She brought out three Heinekens and we stared out at the lights from the Saturday night party that South Beach was putting on a mile away. You can see some of the Miami skyline and you can see Indian Creek Village from her place. The drawbridge was opening on the causeway to South Beach to let a large-masted sailboat through and a dozen or so cars, trucks, panel vans, and buses were backed up on either side of the bridge. One rich boater, holding up the progress of twenty-four working-class slobs. Florida is all about water and boats and the rich and famous who can afford to live on the water and own those boats. Maybe James was right in his pursuit of the golden goose. Someday he'd be that rich asshole with the boat, holding up the little people on the bridge.

"So, what's so important?" She handed me the check for $1,500. I had to agree with James, we'd lined up more money in one day than either of us made in three months.

James looked at me. "We had an accident."

Em frowned and glanced at the check, still in my hand.

"What kind of accident?"

I believed in fast and factual. "We hit the storage building, the mail spilled out of the back of the truck, and we found an envelope with a severed finger."

I've never seen Emily get such an incredulous expression on her face before. The three of us sat there as she absorbed the short story. Finally, she found her voice.

"A severed finger. Somebody's actual finger."

"Yes. We tried to take it back to Jackie, but she wouldn't give us permission to come back to her home and—"

"She knows about the finger?"

"No. I don't think so. So we—"

"Came here instead?"

James squinted. "Not exactly."

"Where did you go? To the police. You went to the police. My God, a human finger."

"Uh, Em," I cleared my throat. "We didn't go to the police."

"Tell me."

"We went to Rick Fuentes."

"Oh, Jesus."

"Well, James pointed out that it *was* his mail."

"This is a joke. You guys made up this story just to mess with me."

"No."

"Tell me it's a joke."

"We'd be lying."

She stood up and started pacing, taking short swallows of beer as she walked. "Jesus, what am I going to tell Jackie? Why this finger?"

"Well, it's not her business is it? And we're not sure why the finger. It came in the form of a threat to Fuentes."

"Of course it's Jackie's business. And what kind of threat?"

I shook my head. "Em, it's Rick Fuentes's business. The threat seems to be from some Cuban guys who have an ax to grind with Fuentes. And we haven't got to the bad part yet."

"Give me a break. Tell me that it doesn't go any further."

"It's his son. Vic Maitlin."

She dropped the green bottle and it shattered into a dozen splintered pieces, watery brown beer running into the grout between the white ceramic tiles on the balcony.

"Vic? Oh, my God."

"You remember him?"

"I went out with him. We dated. His dad wasn't—I don't remember. Maybe he'd left his first wife by then. I don't remember anything about his father, but Vic Maitlin was the first—oh, my God."

She let it hang. I knew they'd gone out before Em and I had started our off-and-on dating.

"It gets worse."

"How? How could it possibly get worse? How?"

"Trust me. Since there are a limited number of people who know that this finger was sent to Fuentes—"

She held up her right hand. "One, Vic Maitlin. Two, the person who cut it off." She held up her third finger. "Three, you. Four James. And five, Rick Fuentes."

"Seven." I was the business major, math was my strong suit.

"Seven?"

"Seven that we know of. You. And Fuentes's girlfriend, this little nineteen-year-old blond."

"Un-fucking believable." I'd never heard her use that word in my life. "And it gets worse?"

"Fuentes asked us to find Vic."

"You said no."

"Actually," I gave James a nod.

"Actually, I said yes."

"Are you crazy? Have you completely lost your minds?"

"He's paying us $5,000. And he claims to know where Vic is. He just wants confirmation.

"You are crazy. You're both idiots. I simply gave you a lead for a little job and you've got yourself involved in a what? An international incident? Dismemberment? You're nuts. I don't even know you." She glared at me, bending down, and picking up shards of green bottle.

I leaned over and helped.

"Here." She held up her finger, a thin line of blood running down her hand. "Now I've cut my—" She stared at the blood then walked into the condo leaving James and me in the warm Miami night.

We finished picking up the pieces.

"Are you happy with all the advice she's given you so far?"

"Fuck you. How would you expect her to react? I'd rather have her know than not. I don't think Emily is someone I want on my bad side." A ship horn sounded and echoed over the bay.

"I've always been on her bad side."

She walked back onto the balcony, a Band-Aid on her finger. Stepping to the railing, she looked out at the water. Lights glimmered as far as you could see.

"You know where Vic is?"

"We know where his father thinks he is. All we're supposed to do is sit outside and see if there is any sign of him. In twenty-four hours we report back to Fuentes."

"It doesn't sound difficult, not even particularly dangerous."

James smiled at me. "And I didn't think that sounded like bad work for five grand."

"But we are talking about people who cut off fingers and threaten lives. I am still amazed that you guys could get in so much trouble in such a short amount of time."

We both stared at the tile floor, watching the beer settle into the discolored grout.

"Tomorrow is Sunday." She never looked at us but kept staring out at the water. "I don't work, Skip doesn't work, what about you, James?"

"No Cap'n Crab tomorrow."

"All right. What if the three of us keep an eye on this place tonight and tomorrow. We can use my car and your truck and alternate. We've got our cell phones if one of us sees anything, and we'll call Fuentes either way."

James let out a deep breath. "I'm surprised. I actually think that's a good idea. We can go over there now, and a couple of us sleep while one watches the property. I knew this was going to work."

Em turned around and gave James a hard look. "I didn't take a cut on your hauling job. You guys worked hard for that."

"Thanks. We appreciate that." James smiled at her.

She didn't return the smile. "I'm taking a third of this."

CHAPTER SIXTEEN

The area known as Little Havana isn't too far from Em's condo. The address Fuentes had given us was just a couple of blocks from American Airlines Arena, the sprawling building where the Miami Heat play. It's almost forty concrete steps up to the entrance of the arena, and once you get inside you can climb twice that many steps and stand at the top for ten bucks. With a pair of binoculars you can almost make out the game.

Next door, in the shadow of the old stone Trinity Episcopal Cathedral, is Bicentennial Park, an overgrown brick terrace that leads down to what once had been a fountain. A handful of anemic palm trees surround the pitted, broken bricks that line the once proud structure, and flattened cardboard boxes litter the ground where a homeless community spends its nights. It's not a safe area.

Passing the park, Em took a right and two lefts. I was surprised when she pulled up to the structure. It looked like an office building. All Fuentes had given us was an address, and we'd figured it was a house. You'd keep a hostage in a house. This was no house. Two stories, stucco and brick with a gray steel door and two lower story windows that appeared to be painted black. The upper windows had curtains or drapes drawn across them and there was no sign of any light. A small, paved parking lot ran alongside the building connecting it to a closed restaurant. Castero and Sons. I suddenly realized how hungry I was. James used to make a pork sandwich, with tomato and his own anchovy mayonnaise between two pieces of thick, buttered, and grilled Cuban bread. I could have eaten one of those right now.

Two late-model Chevys were parked in the back. As we coasted by I saw the small sign above the front door.

CUBAN SOCIAL CLUB

I was in the T-Bird with Em.

"We can park half a block away and see just about anything from the front." Em parked the 'Bird. James had pulled ahead a block and called me on his cell phone.

"Hey, pard. Where do you want me?"

"There appears to be an alley that runs behind the place. If there's a rear entrance someone should probably watch that."

I saw him drive the truck down one street then pull into the alley.

"There's a door at the rear."

I told Em.

"Well, have him watch that and we'll rotate. One person sleeps, while the other two watch the front and back."

I told him it was my idea. He'd never go for it if he knew it was hers.

James took first watch of the alley, Em from the front. I was supposed to sleep for the first three hours. It's eleven o'clock at night and we've all had one of the craziest days in our lives. We're on an honest to God stakeout, and I'm supposed to sleep? Oh, I'm sure that around three in the morning, when it's my shift, I'll be ready to crash, but not now.

"There's something I was going to talk to you about—" Em shifted in her seat and didn't say anything else.

"What?"

"Tomorrow, when this thing is over, we need to discuss a couple of things."

"Don't do this, Em. You know my imagination will make up all kinds of stories and it's better if you tell me now." She pressed the same buttons with me that I pressed with her.

"No. I shouldn't have said anything. Tomorrow, I promise. Get some sleep."

Parked on the street, we watched the occasional car drive by, but traffic was almost nonexistent on this side of town. No restaurants, bars, or any sign of social life. James called about twelve-thirty just to make sure we were still there.

"Are you going to tell Jackie?" I asked her.

"Do you think I should?"

"Somebody should. She's involved even though she doesn't know."

"Yeah. I wish I had some coffee."

"You'd just have to pee in half an hour."

"How do cops do it? Stakeouts and thermoses of coffee?"

"I don't know. Maybe they piss in the thermos when it's empty."

She was quiet for a moment. "Pretty small target for a female cop, don't you think?"

I hadn't thought about it. How would I know?

The sharp knock on the window scared the hell out of both of us.

"Jesus!"

A bright white light shot into the car, blinding me. "Who the hell are you?"

"Roll down your window, please." A heavy Spanish accent.

"Em, start the car."

She turned the key and the engine roared to life.

"Ma'am, I'm a police officer. Please turn off the vehicle and roll down the window."

"Let me see some ID."

He shone the light on an official looking silver badge. Em looked at me for approval, and I shrugged my shoulders. She cautiously rolled the window down about a third of the way.

"Is there a reason the two of you are parked here on the street at this time in the morning?"

We turned and looked at each other. Em glanced back at the shadow outside her car window.

"We were making out."

"Ma'am?"

"Making out. He was trying to talk me into something beyond just kissing."

"Move on. I don't want to see the two of you here again. Understand?"

She shifted into drive and slowly pulled away.

"Was that a cop?"

She inched ahead, not making a lot of progress.

"Well, was it?"

"Shut up. I'm watching the rearview mirror. I want to see what he does."

I shut up as she inched ahead, turning at the next street and coasting down the avenue until she came to the alley. She pulled in, driving behind the parking lot with the two Chevys, and she stopped just before she reached the two-story building.

We could see beyond the front of the building, where the cop had been. There was no sign of any police car and no sign of the man.

"Shit. I was hoping we'd see where he went."

My cell phone played "Born in the USA" and I grabbed it. Let it ring for twelve seconds and I swear I pay for another two or three minutes. I've got to get another cell plan.

"Hello."

"Somebody just went into the rear entrance." James was parked up about fifty feet.

"Into?"

"Into."

"James, where did they come out of?"

"I have no idea. They went into the rear entrance. My guess is they pulled up in front."

Emily gave me a look, questioning my half of the conversation.

"James says someone walked into the rear of the building, but he didn't see them come out of that entrance."

"What did he look like?"

"What did he look like?"

James hesitated. "Well, he was pulling off a cap, but he was too far away to really get a good look."

Em watched, eager for information.

"James says he was pulling off a cap. Could be the cop."

"Or not."

"Not?"

"I don't think he was a cop. It could be someone who is guarding the building. A security guard."

"He said he was a cop. I'm pretty sure he was. He showed us his badge."

"Badges are a dime a dozen. I don't think it was a real cop."

I digested the idea. Security guards wore uniforms and displayed bright shiny badges. If Vic Maitlin was being kept hostage here, someone had to be watching him.

"We had a cop come up to the car and tell us to keep moving."

"No shit? A cop?" After all that had happened this day, James still sounded surprised. Hell, we shouldn't have been surprised at anything.

"Em doesn't think it's a cop. She thinks it's some guy in a uniform with a fake badge."

He was quiet.

"James?"

"So someone is already onto us?"

"God, I hope not."

"Skip, I've got ten digits and I'd like to hang on to every one of them."

"James, it was your idea to get involved."

Em frowned. "I think it's a little late for the blame game, Eugene. Tell your friend we're going to drive around the block and find another place to park. Maybe he should watch the alley from a little farther up."

I passed on the information and we pulled out of the alley, went up two streets, cut back, and ended up on a side street where we could still see the front of the building. I could make out a row of concrete tables lining the sidewalk where old men played dominoes from early morning till the sun went down.

"Em, what do we have to talk about tomorrow?"

"There are times I wish I smoked." She gazed out the window.

"What?"

"It gives you something to do. Purpose. Taking a drag on a cigarette, playing with the smoke, letting it stream out of your mouth. Blowing rings and tapping the ashes, it's more the ritual than the actual smoking, isn't it?"

"You wish you smoked so you could do all that and not talk about whatever it is you want to discuss."

"Yeah."

"Serious?"

"Could be."

"Are you thinking about us not seeing each other any more?" I thought about it a lot. She was too good for me, and I'm sure it crossed her mind from time to time.

In the dim light I could see her smile as she leaned over and gave me a kiss on the lips. "No. We'll talk tomorrow."

I leaned back and drifted off. I had just hit sleep mode and was lazily watching a fishing stream with trout and bass that became our muddy ditch, and James was casting this huge garbage can lure into the brackish water when the world exploded.

CHAPTER SEVENTEEN

I HEARD IT, I FELT IT, and I saw it as my eyes flew open. The upstairs windows exploded in a blast of shattered glass as a ball of fire roared out of the building. In less than a second the street in front was blazing with orange chunks of flame thrown from the stucco and brick building, and we watched spellbound as a brilliant blaze shot into the black Miami sky, the inferno engulfing the structure.

Em started the car and peeled out.

"Where the hell are we going?" Talk about feeling the heat. I was sweating from fear and the intense fire from half a block away.

"Anywhere. We've got to get out of this."

James. "Jesus, James was back in the alley." I frantically dialed his cell phone. No answer.

It rang and rang. Finally voice mail.

"The person you have called is unavailable at the moment. Please leave a message and—" I hung up. I dialed again. Same thing.

"Em, we've got to check out the alley."

"Skip, are you crazy? That fire is roaring back there."

She was three blocks down, moving at a good clip, and had run one stop sign already.

"Em—"

"Shit!" She spun the wheel, making a sharp U-turn in the middle of the deserted street. "Call 911."

"Yeah." I did.

She raced back the way we came, squealing to a stop as we saw the parking lot. The two Chevys were swallowed in flames. One had exploded and flaming pieces littered the melting blacktop. I jumped from the car and ran toward the alley, tasting the thick smoke and holding my arm across my face, trying to keep from filling my lungs with the fumes from that noxious cloud. The fierce heat cooked my skin and I thought for a moment I might pass out. I hit the back alley on the run and stopped short, peering into the haze. White-hot flame spewed from the vehicle, more black smoke pouring into the alley. There was nothing I could do.

I jogged to the T-Bird, coughing, gagging, and choking.

"What?"

"Jesus Christ, Em, it must be the truck. It's a roaring inferno." We could hear the sirens in the distance, whining with the occasional barking of the horns as they sped toward the blaze.

"James?"

All I could do was shake my head.

"Skip, is there anything we can do?"

There was nothing.

She stepped on the gas and we went speeding down the street, as far away from the burning building, the incinerated truck, the uniformed man, and the fire engines as we could. I was leaving my best friend behind, and I had never felt so helpless.

CHAPTER EIGHTEEN

I WAS TWELVE YEARS OLD when my father left home. My sister was eight and Mom was thirty-two. I remember things about him, like he smoked Camels. He worked in a machine shop and Mom would sweep up metal shavings that he tracked into the house on a daily basis. I'm not sure why he walked out. I don't think it was another woman because he didn't remarry. For a while anyway. I remember he smelled like tobacco and he'd bring home red-hot candies and we'd eat them until our mouths burned.

James was six months older than I, and I leaned on him as much as a twelve-year-old can lean on another twelve-year-old. I didn't go home from school because the pain was too much to bear. I'd go to James's house and Mom would end up calling, wondering where I was. I think she was glad I had a home away from home because it made life easier for her. One less problem in her life.

James was the brother I didn't have, the best friend that everyone should have, and an inspiration that encouraged me to reach farther than I probably would have. James was always there. Always.

"Skip, I'm sorry. So sorry." Em slowed down and pulled into a deserted parking lot a mile from the fire.

"How the hell could a day turn into such a catastrophe? A little side venture, some extra money."

We could still hear the sirens in the distance as more engines came to the rescue. An orange hue lit up the sky and plumes of smoke climbed into the night, drifting over the neighborhood. I could smell the acrid odor in my clothes and hair. The 'Bird would smell like smoke for some time to come. I tried to push James from my mind, but it didn't work.

"We've got to go to the cops."

I nodded.

"If Vic was in that building—" She trailed off.

"If James was in that truck—"

"And that's why we've got to go to the police. Skip, this is my fault. I should have talked you guys out of this."

I gave her an icy stare. "Get over yourself. You couldn't have talked him out of it if you'd tried, and I'd pretty much bought into it myself. You had nothing to do with it."

"James." She rested her arms on the steering wheel, gazing out the windshield at the darkness. "God, I could have tried harder. I could have had a little more understanding, compassion."

"Born in the USA" chirped in my pocket. I grabbed the phone and flipped it open.

"Skip?"

"Oh, my God. James!"

Em grabbed the phone from my hand and yelled into the mouthpiece. "You son of a bitch. Goddamn you to hell! Where the hell have you been?"

So much for understanding and compassion. James was alive and things were back the way they had been.

CHAPTER NINETEEN

Esther's sits on Twenty-seventh in Carol City and doesn't serve alcohol. So if you want a good meal and a *drink*, you've got to go to Chili's. However, if you want some of the best home made grits, biscuits and gravy, sausage, baked chicken, or peach cobbler *without* a drink, Esther's is your place.

We sat in the vinyl and wood booth and looked out at the Kentucky Fried Chicken next door. It does strike me that most of the time we're the only white people in the restaurant. Living in Carol City, an "urban" community as my friend Carl, the manager of Walgreens, calls it, I'm a minority. You get a good sense of how minorities feel in an all-white community when you live in Carol City.

"So do we go to the cops or not?" I watched their faces, looking for signs of surrender. We were all set to tell everything we knew until James called. Now we weren't sure.

"You guys have a cop ask you to leave the area. I think I see who could be your cop go into the building. Five minutes later a cop car pulls up behind me with his light flashing—"

"And why didn't you call us about that?" Em frowned.

"He gets out of the car, tells me to either leave or follow him to the station, and I was just pulling away when all hell broke loose. I was busy putting the pedal to the metal."

I sipped on my third cup of coffee. A heavy-set black lady in the next booth shoveled a heaping spoonful of red beans and rice into her mouth. "Are you sure it was a police car?"

He thought for a moment. "No. But he had a bubble light on top."

"Could have been a security vehicle, or just a car with the light. You can buy those. Scott Morrissey had one, remember? Used to put it on his car and scare the hell out of the people making out at night down at Boynton Beach."

"Yeah." James stared out the window.

"So, James, do you think that car was the vehicle I saw that was on fire?"

"I didn't stick around to find out. If there was a vehicle burning in that alley, it might have been the same car."

I still smelled like smoke. I'd showered, put on clean clothes and still could detect the sharp pungent odor.

Em frowned again. "Quit sniffing yourself. You're fine."

"Do we go to the cops or not?"

"Not." James was adamant. Since his father's arrest, he's avoided cops at all costs.

"Why not?"

"Have we done anything wrong?"

I pondered that. "Good question."

Em chewed on a piece of toast. "I'm sure we've broken the law somewhere."

"Where? I doubt there is a law that says you have to call the authorities when you find a finger. And I know that sitting outside the Cuban Social Club was not against the law. Moving belongings isn't illegal. So where have we broken the law?"

"All right, maybe we haven't. But they're going to want people to come forward who saw what happened."

James held his hand up. "Hold on, miss do-gooder. What exactly did you see? A fire. That's all. We didn't see how it started."

"How about the cop—or the phony cop. We could tell someone about that."

"I don't think we're obligated to do that. And I don't want to cross Fuentes."

"Would the second installment on the five thousand dollars have anything to do with that?" Emily smirked. Somewhere between a smile and a frown.

"I believe you cut yourself in on that, so we've all got something to lose."

She was quiet.

"There's one upside to this mess." I'd been thinking about the positives. There weren't many.

"We don't have a building to watch today."

They both shook their heads. James dragged a sausage through gravy and stuffed it in his mouth. He chewed it carefully. "So the question is, do we call Fuentes? We did our part, kept up our end of the bargain. Now we need to know where he stands."

We agreed. Fuentes needed a phone call, and *they* agreed I should make the call.

James left to drive down the road to our humble abode. Em offered me a ride in the smoky T-Bird.

"James is gone." I looked into her eyes. "What was it that you wanted to tell me?"

She hesitated. "Nothing. Not right now. It's something that can wait, okay?"

"Em?"

"Later." She paid at the register and we drove back to the apartment in silence.

CHAPTER TWENTY

We sat in cheap plastic chairs on the cement slab. Em had a Sprite and even though it wasn't quite 8 a.m. James and I had beers. The older couple behind us were nowhere to be seen, but the playpen was set up like always, with a faded blue blanket draped over one side.

"I think it's too early to call."

James tapped the phone on my lap. "We need to tell him before it makes the news."

I punched in the numbers and the little blond answered.

"Hi, this is Skip Moore. Can I speak to Mr. Fuentes?" Moments later he came on the line.

"Mr. Moore. Do you have news?"

"Uh, yeah. Sort of." I never did well in speech class. "We watched the building last night—"

"And?"

"And it caught on fire. It was a huge fire and—"

The thick Cuban accent sounded like that guy from the old TV show, *Fantasy Island.* "Caught on fire? What do you mean caught on fire?"

"It was more like an explosion."

"And the occupants?"

"We seriously don't know. We were approached by a policeman just before the building exploded, and he told us to leave the area."

Fuentes was quiet for a moment. Then, as if he were talking to himself he said, "So the fire was preplanned. They knew that I knew."

"Knew what, Mr. Fuentes? That Vic was staying there?"

"Have you told anyone? That you were watching?"

"No." I glanced at the co-conspirators. "We haven't said a word to anyone."

"Don't. Do you understand? This entire incident—you looking for Vic—this must remain in strictest confidence."

"No problem."

"Mr. Moore, I can't stress this enough. You could be in a lot of danger if you mention this to anyone. I'll be in touch with you in the near future." He hung up the phone and I sat there looking at the receiver, more confused than ever.

"What?" James took a swallow of beer.

"I think I was threatened."

Em looked up from her coffee. "Threatened?"

"He said the fire must have been preplanned and they knew that he knew too much. Then he said to keep it to ourselves or we could be in a lot of trouble and he'll be in touch."

"Make any sense to you?"

"None."

"Anything about the $2,500?" James, the guy watching the bottom line.

"Maybe he's a little more concerned that his son was in that inferno. Maybe that's a little more important that our $2,500 right now."

Em sipped on the Sprite. "The local news should be on at eight. Let's go in and see what they're saying."

We got up and walked in the rear sliding-glass door. It didn't exactly slide anymore but if you jiggled it enough it opened and closed.

"Skip, the playpen out there — still just the old couple and no baby?" Em had noticed it before.

James turned on the television and we sat on the ratty, faded cloth couch that passed as the best seat in the house. "I saw the old guy a couple of days ago and asked him," he said.

"You just asked him what the playpen was for?"

"Well, he volunteered. He was out, I was out. He nodded, I nodded, and he motioned to the playpen. He said 'For our grandson.' I asked him how old and he says, 'Six months. We've never seen him.' So, I said, 'He must live far away,' and he says, 'No, in Coral Gables. We never approved of the baby's father, and when he was born my daughter decided to shut us out of her life.' "

"How sad." Em had tears in the corners of her eyes. "So the playpen sits there and they wait for their grandson to visit?"

"I don't know. The old guy shrugged his shoulders and walked back inside."

The local Sunday morning anchor led with the story.

"A huge explosion in Little Havana rocked the community last night as a building called the Cuban Social Club caught fire about 2 a.m. Firefighters spent three hours battling the blaze." Footage of the fire flashed on the screen and a fireman in full gear spoke into a reporter's microphone.

"We don't know the cause of the fire yet. It could be days before we are sure what happened. There appear to be three vehicles that caught fire as well."

"Were there any casualties?"

"We haven't been able to get inside the building, so we don't know. The heat is just too intense."

"Would you say, due to the intensity of the fire, that there may have been some accelerants involved?"

"All I can tell you at this time is, we are still fighting the fire. When it's safe to go in, we'll do a thorough investigation."

The scene faded and the anchor came back on. "A source close to the location tells us the Cuban Social Club is the headquarters for a group of Cuban refugees called the Old Militia. The Old Militia is apparently comprised of Cubans who are known as *Los Historicos*. We'll have more information as it becomes available."

"What was that all about?" Em stared at the screen as the weather map came on.

James punched the remote and the screen went black. "*Los Historicos*—families that left Cuba when Castro took control. I think a lot of them had property that was seized by the Castro regime."

"That was almost fifty years ago."

"Yeah. And they still want their property back."

"How old would those people be?" Em asked.

"It's not just them. It's their sons, daughters, and grandkids too. They've never even been there, but they want what was their inheritance."

I remembered junior high history. "These are the ones who launched the Bay of Pigs invasion. They were trying to take the country back in the sixties."

James nodded. "Yeah. And the story is that the United States was going to support them, and President Kennedy and the CIA backed out at the last minute. A lot of people got killed."

We were all quiet for a couple of minutes. Finally Em spoke up.

"I wonder what the hell we've gotten ourselves into?"

All three of us jumped when we heard the sharp knock on the front door.

CHAPTER TWENTY-ONE

No one ever came to our apartment. If there was a social event, we went there. Em and a handful of girls that James saw were the only ones who ever visited and only when they were invited. Our pink stucco hovel was not a place to invite polite company.

The staccato knock came again, and we looked at each other. A lot of the units around us had iron grates covering the windows and front door. I'm not sure why, because no one had much to protect. I knew that from selling — or attempting to sell — my security systems. Still, this was one time I wished we had the iron bars. Maybe to protect our lives.

I looked through the peephole and saw two guys, mid-thirties, in polo shirts and slacks. One guy had a huge mouth and he was licking his lips. They had dark skin, probably of Latin descent. The second guy shifted back and forth on his feet, anxious, maybe nervous.

"Two guys, dark skin, casual dress. Anyone want to see what they want?"

There was no response from my colleagues. If this involved

the fire and last night, James was the one who got us into this mess, but it was obvious he wasn't going to answer the door.

I opened it just enough to slip through the opening and stepped out on the front porch.

"Can I help you?" I was scared to death.

They were muscular, both carrying maybe twenty or thirty pounds too much in the mid-section. The nervous guy spoke first.

"You own the truck there?"

"No." I wanted to be truthful.

"How about the Thunderbird?" He squinted, maybe trying to look intimidating. I was amazed I was out here with these two intimidators, but I was, and I wasn't going to make this easy for them.

"Nope. Neither one is mine." I kept thinking one of them would pull out a pistol or a knife.

They looked at each other, obviously not sure what step to take next.

"You James Lessor?"

"No, I'm not."

"Well, can you tell us where he is?"

James could have been in the apartment or maybe he was on the back patio. He could have gone to the bathroom or the little kitchenette. I really didn't know.

"I have no idea where he is." They were going to figure me out in a second.

"How about—" The guy with the mouth pulled out a piece of paper, "— how about Emily Williams?" That heavy accent. Could have been the guy who flashed his flashlight and badge at us last night.

"Seriously. I don't know."

The first guy, with a rough complexion and slicked-back black hair, took a step toward me.

"Look, we ran the plates on these two vehicles in front of this apartment. Now maybe you don't know where these two people are, but it's important we talk to them."

I was sweating bullets. "If I see them, why don't I tell them to call you."

"The car and truck are both here. *They've* got to be here. Why don't you invite us inside just to see for ourselves."

"Can I ask you why you want to see them?"

The greasy one looked for approval from the mouth. The big guy shrugged his shoulders.

"Both these vehicles were spotted in Little Havana last night, just before a building exploded. We'd like to talk to the owners about what they might have seen."

"Are you with the police?"

"Yeah." They said it almost simultaneously.

"Miami Police?" I didn't believe it.

"Sure."

"Do you have identification?"

The mouthy guy drew a deep breath. "If we find that either of these people had anything to do with the fire or if they say anything about what they might have seen, the cops will be the least of their worries. You need to tell them that. You need to tell them that whatever they saw or thought they saw last night needs to stay with them. Do you understand the message?"

I could feel drops of sweat running down my chest. "I think so. I'll be happy to pass the message on."

I saw him round the row of buildings in front of me. He just cleared the structure, paused, and stood there, like a silent sentry. I watched him for a second too long, and my two visitors both turned their heads and saw him too. He continued to stare at us, arms folded, an imposing black statue. Our own Angel.

They turned back to me, the look on their faces a little less certain. The greaser spoke. "You can't begin to imagine what will happen if they tell anyone about last night. Please tell me you understand this." He looked back over his shoulder.

"I understand."

The mouthy guy with the accent put his hand up, and for a moment I thought he might strike me. "One more thing. If you ever watch a property again, don't use the old 'we were just making out' routine. It's very dated."

They spun around and walked off the porch, getting into a big blue Buick.

I stood on the porch for thirty seconds, waiting for my heart to stop racing. Angel was nowhere to be seen.

CHAPTER TWENTY-TWO

Like I said, everyone liked Vic Maitlin. Even if you were envious of his swarthy good looks, his talent, his scholastic aptitude, and his sexual prowess, you still couldn't help but like him. You could overlook the fact that he hung around with those two hoods, Cramer and Stowe. He was a guy's guy. He'd hang with the regular guys and make everyone feel his aura. I know it sounds almost supernatural, but he had an aura. You wanted some of it to rub off on you.

"I wanted some of whatever he had. It just seemed that you should be able to bottle him and pour it over yourself whenever you needed a dose of cool." James sat on the arm of the couch, watching the news babe, the sound a low babble.

"With a missing finger and threats from beefy guys like those two, I don't think I'd want to be Vic right now." I pulled a beer from the refrigerator. "Em?"

"No. I'm fine. These two guys actually mentioned what I said about making out?"

"Why would I make that up? Yes. The one guy seemed to

know exactly what happened last night." I twisted the top off and took a deep swallow. I needed something to calm me down.

"The phony cop."

"That would be my guess." I drained half the bottle.

"And they said to keep it quiet? Hell, we didn't see anything."

"Between the three of us we saw two guys in uniforms. Or maybe we saw the same guy. We saw the windows blow out of the building."

James kept his eyes on the TV. "You said you saw three vehicles burning. Two in the parking lot, one in the alley after I'd left."

"So what could we have seen?"

"Either we're not aware of it or they think we saw something we didn't." Em stared at my beer.

"You sure you don't want one?"

"No. A glass of water? Never mind. I've seen the glasses you've got in the cupboard. Chipped, stained, and I believe I saw mold growing on a couple of them. Get me another Sprite."

"Wasn't mold," James said. "There was a sale on fuzzy glasses down at Gas and Grocery."

Em feigned a smile as I handed her the cold green can.

James finally turned his head. "I think we drive back to Bal Harbor and confront Fuentes. He obviously has an idea of what the hell is going on."

"I get the idea he may be responsible for what's going on. I agree. Now that you're a target —"

"I'm a target?" James looked at me questioningly.

"You and Em. They know your names and your vehicles."

"Yeah. And they know you and Emily lied about making out in the car."

"I don't think they know who I am."

"Nobody ran the plates on your '96 Prism?" James asked.

"It wasn't there, James."

Orange flames licked the television screen and James increased the volume.

"More news on the horrendous fire in Little Havana early this morning. Police and fire investigators say that two bodies have been pulled from the rubble. At this point, Captain Ed Stabil said the remains were too badly burned to be identified."

"Jesus, I hope one of them wasn't Vic." Emily looked up at me and for the second time that morning had tears in her eyes. She usually wasn't the weepy type. "God, Skip. This just keeps getting worse and worse."

CHAPTER TWENTY-THREE

"All right, I'll call her." Em struggled with the idea. We'd brainstormed for an hour and decided that Jackie needed to know. She was the one who told Em that she thought there were terrorists involved. We thought maybe we could get a little more information before we confronted Rick Fuentes.

She dialed the number, and we sat drinking the last two beers and contemplating what the conversation might lead to. I looked at her, my eyes going up and down her body. I glanced at James and he was doing the same thing. So obvious. She wore tight pedal pushers and a top that exposed her stomach. It hit me that we hadn't made love in a week. To be honest, I thought about it every day. Every hour. Every couple of minutes. Em's got a great body, very fine skin, and fine golden hair that she wraps around every part of a guy's anatomy. I wish I could say 'wraps around every part of *my* anatomy only,' but I'm sure there are others.

"Jackie!"

She paused, smiling.

"Hey, me too. I thought the same thing."

One phone. No extensions. What the hell, it was fun to imagine what was going on on the other end of the line.

She broke out laughing. "No. Well, if you say so. I think they had other things on their mind."

I saw James perk up. He thought the same thing I did. *They* referred to *us*.

"No, seriously. They had something to deliver to you."

Silence while Jackie apparently talked.

"Uh-huh. Jackie, please listen to me. I'm going to explain what happened and it's sort of complicated. Just listen, and when I'm done with this story we can talk, okay?

Silence for a half-minute.

"Okay. Now please, no interruptions."

She proceeded to tell the story. There were no interruptions that we were aware of, no pauses. Em told her about the finger and Rick's reaction. She told her about the stakeout and the fire and the two Cuban guys who visited us just an hour or so ago. When her litany was delivered, Em drew a deep breath and sat back on the sofa. She listened for a moment, then nodded, as if Jackie could see her.

"Well, we thought you should know."

Em was silent for another minute and I wished to hell we had an extension. Every damned outlet cost a ton of money. We both had cell phones, and my guess is that in ten years a landline will be a thing of the past, but right now I just wanted an extension. Finally, Em hung up.

"Jackie isn't surprised."

"Well, I figured she'd be stunned."

"She said it doesn't surprise her because she knew something was going on. She thought Rick was involved with terrorists. What surprised her was that we've gotten into this so deep. She also said that she hoped and prayed that Vic wasn't in any more serious trouble. She's only his stepmother, but she really liked him and she really took the finger thing hard. That's the part that just confused her. She didn't realize this was a life and death situation."

"So did she mention anything about a Cuban connection?" James was chomping at the bit. I wondered why he hadn't been this anxious when the two bozos who visited us had been camped in front of our apartment.

"She told me again about the Spanish-speaking men that hung around her husband. They apparently stopped by the house frequently. That was it. You heard my half of the conversation. It didn't last that long." She paused. "Oh, and James, it pains me to tell you this, but she said to tell you she still thinks you're cute."

He grinned.

"No ideas?" I was looking for a solution.

"I think she's going to sleep on it. I agreed to talk to her in the morning."

"Morning. Shit!" James stood up. "I've got to be at work at 10 a.m. tomorrow."

"I can do you one better. I'm supposed to be at the office at nine and on the road by nine-thirty."

"Skip," she looked at me with disdain. "Why don't you ask Daddy for a job. You'd work out fine, and this job you have—" She trailed off.

"What? This job I have what?" My dander was up—whatever the hell dander is.

"This job you have is not going to last! You've got to actually sell a security system now and then, and you've got the worst territory anywhere!"

CHAPTER TWENTY-FOUR

I COULDN'T FOCUS. There were hazy dreams that had me up every twenty minutes, cold sweats that had me up every ten minutes, and a sense of dread that had me up almost every five minutes. I don't remember ever having a night with as much turmoil. When the alarm went off, I was just drifting off into a really good sleep.

I slammed the off button with my fist, not really worried about damaging the clock. After two minutes of twisting and turning and feeling the Florida humidity clogging my pours, I got out of bed and walked into the bathroom. I pissed, brushed my teeth, and stepped on the scales. 168. I'd graduated at 155. This was not a good sign. I stepped into the shower, wondering if a covering of moisture would increase the weight factor by half a pound.

I drove my '96 Geo Prism five miles to the office, past several lots with deserted block houses, their roofs caved in, past empty lots covered in weeds and trash, and past rows of bleached-out stucco homes that were far from the Florida lifestyle so many people dreamed of. I parked in the reserved-for-employees spot. There wasn't a mall, restaurant, drugstore, or anything else within half a mile of Jaystone Security so I can't imagine who else would have parked in one of our spots.

Sammy was in his office and motioned me in.

"Skipper," he smiled a toothy smile, "you've had a couple of really good sales these last six months."

He nodded his head up and down as he always did.

"And, Skipper, we admire your work ethic. You're here almost every morning"— there were a couple of Tuesdays that I'd missed and last Thursday — "but as you know, we have to put you on commission first of the month. Based on your sales to date, you'll make —" he paused and figured on a paper — "maybe a couple of hundred dollars a month."

He looked at me and gave me that ugly, nasty, phony toothy smile. "Hard to live on that, eh, Skipper?"

I wanted to shove those teeth down his throat. I'd been threatened, thought I'd lost my best friend, almost caught in the fire, and offered a sizeable sum of money all in the last thirty-six hours. For this little asshole to tell me my job was on the line, well, I was almost ready to —

"I don't want to sound negative, Skipper. No, not negative. However, if we don't see some improvement here —"

"What?"

It took him aback.

"What the fuck are you going to do? Fire me? Jesus, Sammy. Do you really believe this is the best job in the world? Maybe you can't get beyond this, but as far as I'm concerned, Carol City and this security business can go to hell."

"Wait a minute, Skip. I'm not suggesting you quit."

Sammy glared at me. He was ten years older than I was, dressed beyond my means, and as far as I was concerned, he was stuck in his job and his ego.

"Why? Because you'd have to hire someone else, string them on for six months, and have them quit too?"

"You've got till the end of the month. Do me a favor and make something happen, okay?"

I hoped the company hadn't spent a lot of money to teach Sammy how to motivate. I had five appointments lined up for the day. People signed up for appointments at convenience marts, gas stations, and Esther's. They didn't really sign up for an appointment or because they wanted a security system. They signed up because we told them they'd be entered in a drawing. This month I think it was a hot tub. Sammy would get a cheap plastic hot tub and put a drawing of it on a pad of slips.

When people signed up, they got a phone call. A lot of the poor suckers figured they'd better let a salesman call on them if they wanted to up the chance of winning, so we got appointments. When they realized what we were selling, they'd go into the kitchen to discuss it with their spouse and sometimes never come back. Seriously. I had one couple who went to the kitchen, snuck outside, started up the family car, and left. I was alone in the house with a schnauzer and a glass of ice water they'd poured for me. If they weren't concerned about me being in the house alone, they certainly didn't need a security system.

My first call was on Mrs. Mosely, a white-haired lady in her late sixties who lived by herself in a rundown row house, and while I was there she had three neighbors stop in to make sure she was all right. Talk about security. Before I left she asked if she was going to win the hot tub. I told her no.

My cell phone rang while I was driving to the second appointment.

"Skip, I had visitors."

"The two Cubans?"

"Yeah."

"You're sure?"

"The guy with the mouth? The last time I saw a mouth like that it had a hook in it."

I paused. "*Caddy Shack*, Rodney Dangerfield." I saw most of those movies with him. "Did these guys threaten you?"

"They ordered food. No conversation. I know it was them, and I can't figure out if they came in to intimidate me or they really don't know who I am."

I thought about it. It could have been a coincidence. "James, Sammy's got a computer in his office. When you get off work, let's get online and see if we can scare up some information on Rick Fuentes. I'd like to get a whole lot more information on exactly what it is he does."

"Good thought, Amigo. I've got a better one. We still have a truckload of merchandise."

He was right. His truck was loaded with the belongings and mail of Rick Fuentes.

"I say we unload it, *then* see if we want to check things out on the Net. Maybe we'll find out what this guy is up to."

If you're knee deep in something, I guess the best thing to do is see what it is you're knee deep in.

CHAPTER TWENTY-FIVE

Gas and Grocery was about three minutes from our pink stucco apartment. I had no idea where Angel lived, but there were very few times I stopped by for a six-pack or cold cuts that Angel wasn't there. This time I was not disappointed. For all I knew he might have slept in the back room. Actually, that would have been impossible. The squat cement block building wasn't big enough to have a back room.

"Angel!" He was speaking with a customer in the gravel six-car parking lot in front. He turned and nodded, his shaved head glistening in the afternoon sun. The man he was talking to ducked his head and quickly walked away, headed up the street.

"Hey, man." Angel gave me a vacant stare.

Angel was black. Coal black. His sleeveless pullover showed off his bicep tattoos, a marijuana plant on his massive left arm and what probably was the Ethiopian flag on his right arm. I assumed it was the flag because I'd seen pictures of Bob Marley posing with the national flag. Angel's colors were faded, but the same colors nonetheless.

"Sup?"

"James and I are unloading a truckload of stuff into a storage unit in about an hour. If you're free—" Angel seemed to be free his entire life, "we'd like you to give us a hand. It's worth fifty bucks."

"I thought you didn't want any money comin' out of the kitty."

"There was a little more money than we anticipated."

"I'm there."

"I'll pick you up in about fifteen minutes.

Angel nodded. "Should I bring something for the journey?"

I didn't know what he had in mind, but the last thing we needed was an illegal substance. Somebody was already running our plates and checking out James and Em. We didn't need to encourage them.

"No. Thanks anyway. We'll be by with the truck. Pick you up here?"

He nodded again.

Fifty bucks would save us maybe an hour. I guess the thought of $1,500 for the load and the $5,000 we hoped to be paid by Fuentes was making me feel like I could spare a little of that to shorten the job time.

I drove the green Prism back to the apartment and waited for James. He rolled in ten minutes later, and ten minutes later Angel, James, and I were squeezed into the cab of our one-ton moneymaker, rolling down I-95 to the storage units.

Billboards whizzed by, advertising everything from retirement communities to radio stations.

PALM ESTATES STARTING AT $189,000
Z92! CLASSIC HITS FROM THE '70S, '80S AND '90S

Then there would be a couple of miles of gleaming white shopping malls, factories, and clustered housing developments with small pale houses and orange-tile roofs.

We passed my favorite billboard.

MR. BIDET
FOR A CLEAN, HEALTHY TUSHY

Em has one. I mean, she has a bidet. But I assume her tushy is healthy and clean too.

CHAPTER TWENTY-SIX

JAMES WHEELED INTO THE LOT, stopping at the locked gate. I took out the private key that only about 150 other people had, jumped out, and opened the padlock. We pulled in and drove down the dusty gravel drive.

"Which one was it?"

"The one with the crunched side, remember? You ran into it."

He found it and parked in front.

"Man, would be much easier to unload if you backed it into the opening." Angel studied the position from inside the truck.

James and I both gave him a frown and he backed down.

We got out and opened the back.

"Let's keep the mail separate." I took a box of letters to the side and James and Angel followed.

We started hauling boxes and items to the back of the unit and two hours later we'd reached the front.

James surveyed the rear of the truck, empty now except for Rick Fuentes's mail. "If we'd get rid of that false wall and the storage space, we could haul a lot more."

"Let's get this finished and we'll consider it." I pulled the unit door shut.

"Guy had a lot of stuff." Angel wiped his brow.

"Stuff." James smiled.

"We've still got his mail." I leaned against the building, catching my breath. Too many beers and fast-food joints.

James drew a deep breath. "Hey, bro, we had reason to open the man's mail the last time."

"You think? We had a package that was leaking blood."

"Then I say we have more reason than ever to open it now."

"Okay. But only if it looks like it's pertinent to the situation."

"What's the situation?" Angel was in the dark.

"Long story, Angel. Why don't you take a breather in the cab and Skip and I will sort this stuff out. Okay?"

He gave us a frown, studying the situation for a moment. Then he nodded. "No problem." I think he relished the idea. Maybe catch a little nap before his night of whatever. Angel got into the truck and rolled the window down and watched us.

We divided the packages and mail and started wading through the envelopes and boxes while we sat cross-legged on the ground. A good ten minutes went by and James finally looked at me and said, "I don't know how we'd know what to look for. There's nothing here that looks like it would give us any information."

"Hell, we're fishing, James."

"Have no idea what we're going to catch."

I pulled out the manila envelope at that exact moment. It looked just like the envelope with the finger. The return address was Cubana Coffee Inc., Jacksonville, Florida.

"James. Here's some mail from a company that has Cuba in its name." I handed him the envelope. He stared at it for a second, then handed it back.

"Another guy's mail, I don't know—"

"The guy who planted condoms in the dean of students's desk drawer? The guy who stole Professor Owen's Boston Whaler and took a joy ride down South Beach? When did you get religion?"

"All right. Open it."

"Me?"

"You."

"This could screw up our $5,000. You know that."

"Yeah."

"At the same time it could save our lives."

"Skip, it's probably nothing. Now quit talking and open it up!"

"The problem is getting him to shut up."

He smiled. "Mike Myers, *Shreck*."

I carefully tore open the envelope. I kept thinking I could repair the damage later on and no one would know. Obviously that wasn't going to happen. Once you've crossed a line — and we'd definitely crossed it when we opened the bloody envelope — then it's a whole lot easier to keep, excuse the pun, pushing the envelope.

"Open the damned thing, will you?"

I pulled out a sheaf of papers and scanned the opening letter.

> *To whom it may concern:*
>
> *We represent a group of investors who are funding a company called Café Cubana Inc. Said company will consist of a series of franchised and company-owned coffeehouses initially located throughout the state of Florida. The operation will have a central warehouse where a special blend of Cuban coffee will*

be packaged and shipped to the individual locations. The operations will profit from retail sales of in-store sales of food and beverage, in-store sales of pre-packaged product, and mail order and Internet sales of product. Café Cubana Inc. will eventually move into the eastern corridor of the United States, targeting New England and the New York State market.

I read it back to James.

"Shit. There's a brilliant idea. I wish we'd come up with it."

"I think your hauling idea is about as involved as I care to be right now."

He wrinkled his forehead. "Okay, wiseass, what are the rest of the papers?"

"Lists of investors." I shuffled through about fifty sheets. "Man, there must be hundreds of thousands of dollars committed here."

"What level?"

I flipped through the first five. "Twenty-five thousand, here's one for one hundred thousand, another twenty-five—" I handed him half the stack.

"And this is what Ricardo Fuentes does for a living, right? Finds investors for companies and takes his cut off the top. Christ, Skip. If there's a million dollars here and he gets just 10 percent he's pocketed one hundred thou."

Five minutes later we compared notes.

"Almost four million dollars pledged. And I get the impression there's a lot more where this came from."

"Holy shit. Rick Fuentes takes home four hundred thousand dollars in commission? Un-fucking believable." James looked at the stack of papers. "Can you imagine fifty people investing four million in our hauling venture?"

"We could buy a lot of trucks."

"Trucks and a warehouse and a staff and some advertising." He was lost in his own little fantasy world.

"James, look at the names."

He concentrated on the page I waved in front of him. "That can't be the former governor."

"Same name."

"And this guy?" He pointed to a name on the list. "Christ, is this the same guy who heads up the amusement park and movie company?"

"At that level of money, I would guess it is."

"Holy shit." He ran his finger down the list. "And this is the big car dealer?"

I nodded. "This is a huge project, James."

"Amigo, this is the mother lode of projects." He continued to scan the list.

The blue Buick had glided silently in, unannounced. I heard the door slam shut and glanced up. Big mouth and his friend stood there with their arms folded, both dressed in black T-shirts that defined their big chests, biceps, and the bulges at their waistlines.

"Mr. Lessor?"

James seemed to shrink back toward the wall of the building. Never quite the bravado I think he has.

"Mr. Moore." The other guy gave me a sickening smile. "We took the time to find out about you two. It's too bad your female friend isn't here."

"What?"

"What? We want the stack of papers you've been sorting through, the mail that belongs to Ricardo Fuentes, and then you're coming with us."

"I don't think so." *What the hell was I going to do about it?*

Big mouth reached into his waistband and pulled out a pistol. This was the second time I'd looked down the barrel of a gun, and I can tell you it is truly a frightening experience. Honest to God, it looks like you're looking into a dark tunnel and there's no end in sight. That's the first thing I thought of. I decided then and there that I was getting out of the hauling business as soon as possible.

CHAPTER TWENTY-SEVEN

James finally spoke. "We don't know anything. We can't possibly be any problem for you."

The jittery man with the greasy hair grabbed my half of the papers and leafed through them.

"Café Cubana." He glanced at his partner then back to us. "What do you know about Café Cubana?"

"Nothing. Nothing but what we've read. A coffee shop with Cuban coffee."

"Jesus Christ. What do you have?" He shuffled the papers in front of his gun-toting sidekick. "These are the donors." He looked back at me. "How the hell did you get these papers?"

I shrugged my shoulders. "It was part of the mail that Mr. Fuentes left at his other house. Honestly, we were told to store them in this storage unit." I watched the gunman the entire time I answered. If he so much as twitched, I was prepared to throw myself on the ground.

"This," he shook the stack of papers, "this was not supposed to be for your viewing. This was to be mailed somewhere else."

The guy was getting red in the face with beads of sweat dotting his cheeks.

James was frozen. His complexion was almost gray, and I could see fear in his eyes. For good reason.

"The official prospectus calls for Cuban baked goods, Cuban sandwiches, and, of course, the coffee." The mouth held his gun in front of him with his right hand, pointing the barrel at me. "Maybe the two of you would like to invest in our little venture?"

James's dad would have invested in Café Cubana if he'd had fifty bucks to his name, because it was right up his alley. A new business venture, a new chance to reinvent himself. But he never had the fifty bucks and he wasn't around any more.

I tried not to concentrate on the barrel of the gun, which started looking more like a cavern than a tunnel.

"I think we've invested in one too many businesses already." I watched James, who was now sitting on the ground and shaking his head.

The greaser, with papers in hand, leaned close and I could smell his foul cigar breath. "You were never to have seen these. This changes everything. Both of you, get up. Pick up all those papers, envelopes, and boxes and put them in the trunk of the Buick over there." I hesitated, still not believing this scenario. Apparently I was moving too slowly.

"Now!" The gunman shouted. "I'll shoot you, and your friend will have to clean that mess up too. Do you understand?"

James struggled to his feet, and I tried to fathom a way to knock the gun out of the man's hand. It was only a dream. This was no time to be brave.

"You won't shoot anybody. Because if you don't lay down the gun, I'm going to blow the back of your head off. Do *you* understand?"

Angel, big, black, and menacing, had a gun in his hand and

it was pointed at the back of the mouth's rather large head.

The big-mouthed man spun around, his right arm stiff and the pistol aimed at Angel's midsection. It was a split second and it seemed to last forever. Angel squeezed the trigger, and I swear I could see it in slow motion. The explosion thundered in my ears and I thought I saw fire belch from the barrel of his pistol. The Cuban jumped into the air and swatted with his left hand like he was fending off a wasp. He came down on his hip and crumpled there on the asphalt pad outside Jackie Fuentes's storage unit. Blood ran freely, a stream of the sticky, red fluid heading toward a drain.

"Jesus." The greasy guy's head swiveled from Angel to James, back to Angel and then to me.

James didn't move, but tried to speak. "A . . ." He said it again. "A . . ." Finally he got it out. "Angel. You killed him."

Angel looked down, squeezing his eyes shut for just a moment. Then he leveled the pistol at the other Cuban. "Would you like to try something?"

The man was wide-eyed, frozen in his spot.

Angel shook his head. "I prefer rogues to imbeciles, because *they* sometimes take a rest."

I let out a breath I didn't know I'd been holding. "James!" He seemed to snap out of his trance. "Pick up the mail. Get it into the back of the truck."

We threw the mail into the truck in less than sixty seconds, and I pulled down the sliding door. Angel stood still, his gun aimed at the Cuban's head. The man never moved an inch. He just kept breathing heavily—like he'd run two miles.

James and I jumped into the cab, and Angel backed away from the man, finally climbing into the passenger side.

"What the fuck do we do? Just drive away?" James seemed frozen, his hand clutching the truck key.

I shoved him. "Hey, it was self-defense. And there's still one of them alive. I'll like our chances a lot better far away from here, James. Come on."

He turned the key and stepped on the gas and the truck threw gravel thirty feet from where he spun the tires. I was happy we'd left the gate open. We hit the road forty seconds later and never looked back.

CHAPTER TWENTY-EIGHT

"CAN'T CALL THE COPS." James was hunched over the wheel, staring at the road. I had no idea where we were going.

"We've considered that how many times in the last three days?" There was always a reason not to call the cops.

Angel rode shotgun, silent since we took off.

"Angel, where did you get the gun?"

"The Colt 380? Part of the package."

I must have looked surprised.

"When you hire Angel, you get the complete package."

I wasn't sure I wanted to know any more.

"He may be dead." James looked like he was in a trance as the truck raced down the road.

"I can't imagine what kind of trouble we're in."

"Hey!" I couldn't let that stand. "Angel probably saved our lives. Jesus, the man was shot in self-defense and you're worried about the trouble we're in. James, think about not knowing the trouble we're in. Think about us not being here to worry about it."

He was quiet for a moment. "Yeah. There's that."

"Angel, what was the thing about rogues and imbeciles?"

He smiled. "Alexander Dumas."

James and his movie quotes. Angel's quotes from great literature. And I had nothing.

When we pulled into the apartment complex, it was almost dark. No one had said another word.

"Do you think this is a good idea? Here, where we live?"

James shrugged his shoulders. "Where would you go? These guys have tracked us through the DMV, so they obviously know where Emily lives. They know where we live. I would guess they know where Jackie and Fuentes live. Maybe you have a better suggestion." Bitter and cold, and he was right. We'd run out of options.

Angel stepped out and I scooted over the seat and saw Em's T-Bird right in front of our apartment. Not a good time.

She was dozing in the driver's seat and I tapped on the window. She blinked and opened her door.

"Hi, babe."

"Em, what are you doing here?"

The three of us stood there, looking into the car.

"Em, this is Angel. Angel, Em."

They nodded at each other.

I figured she had to know what had transpired. I didn't want to go from beginning to end, so I started at the end. "Angel saved our lives tonight."

CHAPTER TWENTY-NINE

My father never called me. When he left, it was as if he'd disappeared, maybe died in a foreign war, and what memories I had would have to suffice for my lifetime. Oh, I heard about him from time to time. He sent my mother regular checks, although they were a fraction of what the courts ordered him to pay. Someone sent my mother a notice from a Phoenix, Arizona newspaper that he'd been picked up for DWI. A friend sent my grandfather a picture of my dad winning a father and son Halloween contest somewhere in Arizona, so I knew that he'd started another family.

In my fantasy life I wondered if I had been rich and famous —a movie actor or recording artist—I wondered if my father would have come out publicly and announced that I was his son. And I always wondered if I'd done something wrong. Had I been less than a diligent offspring? Had I somehow been a bone of contention in my mother and father's relationship? Something had caused him to leave our family. Maybe he didn't want children. I worry that question to this day. And when it's feasible, I'll find him. I'll hunt him down and make him answer the only question that seems to have any merit. "Why did you leave?"

I often considered that when I was stressed. What would cause me to leave? I really had nothing to leave. Em? She wasn't mine to leave. James? He was my best friend, but eventually we'd split and go our own ways. My mother? We hardly ever saw each other. My life was fluid, and leaving something as important as a family or a spouse wasn't something I could fathom.

"Maybe we should leave." Em sat on the sofa and James straddled a vinyl dinette chair. "They know who we are, they know where we are, and now you've shot one of them."

Angel stood by the window, looking out at the parking lot, like a dark sentry.

"The guy totally tripped when he saw we'd opened the Café Cubana envelope." James kept clasping and unclasping his hands. "What was it that he said?"

I tried to remember the exact wording. "Something about '*this* wasn't for your viewing.' As if some of the mail *was* for our viewing."

"Some high-powered names on that list, pard. Maybe they don't want anyone knowing who they are."

Em's cell phone chirped and she reached into her bag. "Hello." She stood up and walked back into our small kitchen.

James looked at me with his hands held up in surrender. "Where the hell would we go? Man, we are so screwed." He glanced at Angel. "Angel, man, you probably did save our lives, but where the hell do we go from here? They can't let us kill some guy and just walk away. Can they?"

"James." I was afraid he might lose it and God I needed someone with some strength tonight. "We don't even know who *they* are." I knew where the answers were. "We see Fuentes. We see him tonight."

"Oh, hell, he's part of it. He's the reason we're in this mess."

James rocked back and forth on the chair until I thought it might tip over.

"Fuentes can give us the answers and then we can decide whether to go to the police."

Em walked back in from the kitchen. "Want to know how they found you at the storage place?"

James kept rocking. "Oh, Jesus, more bad news?"

"Jackie. They stopped by her house."

I pictured the two bruisers trying to get past the guard. Apparently we weren't pushy enough. "Jackie told them?"

"They told her they worked with her husband and needed some of the things you had hauled. She remembered them hanging around when Rick worked out of her home. Remember?" She nodded at me. "She thought Rick was mixed up with terrorists. Well, these were two of the guys she was worried about. And, she thought you guys had unloaded everything by now so obviously she didn't see any harm in telling them where it was. She just wanted to get them out of there."

"Couldn't she have called Fuentes? To see if it was all right?"

"Skip, she really didn't care. Fuentes was screwing around on her and all she wanted was to get rid of him. These two guys had been in her home before, so she saw no harm. And she felt a little intimidated. She says that Fuentes told her he was having all the mail transferred to his new home, and then he insisted that she look through whatever else came to see if anything important showed up. Like she told us, she never bothered. Of course, now she feels like crap."

James stared through her. "Yeah. I'd feel that way too if I almost got someone killed. Jesus, she only missed a person's finger, a class ring, and papers on the Café Cubana multimillion-dollar deal. Maybe she should have looked through some of that, you think?"

"And maybe," Em stared daggers at him, "maybe Ricardo

Fuentes should have made sure all that mail went directly to him. Or maybe he should have kept his dick in his pants and stayed with Jackie so this never would have happened."

"In a perfect world, Emily. You're the only one who lives there." James stared back.

She ignored him. "I say we visit Rick Fuentes. Ask him what the story is on Café Cubana and let him tell us how much trouble we're in. Because that's the real question here, boys. How much trouble are we in? With these Cuban people and with the law."

"You can't go." I couldn't see it. We had to quit dragging everyone into the pit. First it was just James and me. Then we involved Em. We took Angel along. Now Jackie was knee-deep in the muck.

"I can't?"

"No. We need somebody to stay behind and put out fires."

"No pun intended?"

"And we can't tell Fuentes how we know about Café Cubana. Only that these two guys brought it up. Why don't you go back home. James and I will drive over to Rick Fuentes's place and talk to him."

James shook his head. "You're right. He can't know we opened more of his mail. It's like a disease with us. We just feel compelled to open envelopes addressed to Ricardo Fuentes."

"He doesn't have to know. Just tell him that these guys thought we knew something about Café Cubana. We don't have to tell him everything."

"None of this sounds good."

Em nodded. "But we're involved. You've opened two pieces of Rick Fuentes's mail and every time you do you just get deeper."

James threw his hands up. "Okay. Let's get rid of his fucking mail. Take it back to him, dump it, tell him it blew out of the truck—"

"James, settle down." I wanted time to think. This wasn't a

time to make irrational decisions. "Those two bruisers would have shown up regardless. Angel would have had to shoot one of them, even if we hadn't opened the mail."

"Yeah. But, Skip, we take his mail back tonight. That stuff is bad luck."

Angel kept his steady gaze out the window. "Do you need Angel anymore tonight?" he asked.

I thought about it. Obviously the man made one hell of a bodyguard. "No. We've probably got you in enough trouble for one night." I went to my bedroom, pulled down *Where the Sidewalk Ends* by Shel Silverstein. One of my favorite childhood poems is in that book. It's about a magical eraser. When a young girl makes fun of the poet for thinking he has a magical eraser, he erases her. I needed that eraser right now. I pulled fifty bucks from the inside of the dust jacket, checked to make sure I still had two hundred dollars left, and went back into the living room, handing the bill to Angel.

He tucked it in his pocket and nodded to us, walking out the door and never looking back.

I shouted after him. "Do you want a ride?"

He just shook his head and kept on walking.

"Strange dude," James said.

"Thank God for the strange dude," Em said.

"Amen." I said it softly, but with feeling.

CHAPTER THIRTY

We didn't call ahead. We both decided it was better to surprise him, and given the fact that we had some very pertinent information, I assumed he'd see us. We got to the guardhouse and he wasn't home.

"I believe they are out for the evening." The stone-faced guard dismissed us and we pulled out of the drive.

"Now what?"

"Maybe they went to dinner. Maybe they're shopping."

"A late dinner maybe."

The only bar close by served cracked crab and at first James refused to go in. "Isn't it bad enough I have to live with that stench eight hours a day?" Finally he relented and we went in and ordered two drafts. A handful of patrons around us used small forks and crab crackers to extract the meat from the crustaceans. James shuddered.

"We need a plan." I put a dash of salt in my beer. I've found it gives cheap beer more flavor.

"Things are not good, my friend. I'm usually the one with the plan. When you have to come up with the plan, things aren't good."

"I don't care who comes up with it. We need one. Listen to me, James. We've involved Em and Angel. It's up to us to get them — and ourselves — uninvolved."

"Dude. We were there when someone was killed. It was our guy who did the shooting if you remember. You don't get *uninvolved* from a killing."

"We don't know anything. The shooting was to save our asses. We can make that case."

"What if no one believes us?"

"We try, James."

"But after tonight, if we meet with Rick Fuentes, what then? What if he tells us something? You see? We're headed into the belly of the beast. We're constantly involving ourselves further and further. It's like we want to know what we're involved in. And after you find out what kind of a mess this is, you can't pretend you don't know anything."

He was right. I was afraid for Em, for James, for myself, and even for Angel. And I was afraid for Vic Maitlin. I didn't want to make too strong a case to James or Em, but I had an opportunity to return a favor, and I prayed Vic was still alive so I could at least have the chance. I really wanted to keep going. This was like a really good Hardy Boys mystery, except it involved people I knew. And it involved me.

"What do you want to do?"

He stared at the beer, then took the short glass and downed it in one single gulp. "I want the rest of our money. And I guess we're just going to have to see Rick Fuentes to get it. This is a business, Skip. I lost sight of that. Somebody is trying to screw with my business before it's even off the ground. It's time to show a little backbone. Let's see what the Cuban financier has to say." He smiled at me and ordered two more beers.

CHAPTER THIRTY-ONE

He was home when we called.

"You've got more information?"

I hesitated. "We do, but we'd like to see you personally."

"No problem, I'll alert the front gate."

"Mr. Fuentes?"

"Yes?"

"No gun this time." I said it firmly, but felt like it was more of a plea. I couldn't deal with another gun tonight.

He was silent.

"This visit involves our business. We're business people. There's no point in waving a gun around."

"Okay. No guns." The man sounded exactly like the *Fantasy Island* guy, Ricardo Montalban.

"Oh, and one more thing."

"Yes?"

"We'd like to collect the rest of our money."

"Your money."

James was right. It was our business. "The $2,500 you owe us. We did watch the building."

"The gate will let you through." He hung up the phone.

"He didn't sound happy about the money situation, James."

"Skip, there are going to be a lot of things he's not happy about tonight."

We pulled through the gate and parked the truck.

"Do you think the big guy with the greasy hair is up there with him? What if he's up there just waiting to kill us?"

I'd considered it. "James, if Fuentes wanted the rest of that mail, he could have asked us for it. We told him we had it. Instead, these two goons went to Jackie and asked about it. If they're in with Fuentes, he would have told them *we* had all the mail. I think they were by themselves."

He thought for a moment. "Skip, they obviously are part of this Café Cubana thing. The guy was really upset, finding out we had the donor list. Fuentes and these two guys are involved, and just going up there tonight could put us in a world of shit."

"Yeah." I knew we were possibly walking into the lion's den, but there was no other choice. We were being hunted and we had to find out why. "Jackie Fuentes said that the two overweight Cubans had visited her house a number of times when her husband lived there. Somehow they *were* connected with Fuentes."

We got out of the truck and James and I retrieved two boxes of mail from the back. I started to pull the back door down as James yelled.

"Hold on. We can't give him the Café Cubana envelope." He held it up like it was slimy and untouchable. "Come on, amigo. It's torn open. Christ, we cannot, cannot go to this guy with another piece of opened mail."

"We didn't see a problem with this when we opened it. Ah, fuck it." I took the offending manila envelope from his fingers and tossed it in the back of the truck. "Hell, he doesn't know what mail came to Jackie's house. Now, pick up the box and let's get rid of this other stuff." I pulled down the back door of the truck, leaving the brown envelope lying by itself in the middle of the floor.

We entered the magnificent lobby where an entirely new arrangement of hundreds of flowers blossomed from the vase in the center of the vast room. I glanced at the vivid painting on the wall and marveled at the details. Seahorses and clams, neon fish with flashing eyes, and wispy strands of plant life all worked together in a potpourri of colors. We rode the elevator in silence, neither of us wanting to concentrate on what or who might be behind Rick Fuentes's door.

He answered the door looking as if he'd stepped off the cover of *GQ*. Gray linen slacks broke over highly polished black alligator shoes. He wore a black silk shirt, open at the collar, and a narrow silver necklace with a simple mother of pearl cross. In my jeans, *Dive Bahama* T-shirt, and sandals, I felt woefully underdressed.

"Gentlemen." He let us in. "You've brought something?"

James nodded. "The rest of your mail."

He motioned to a narrow entrance table and we put the boxes down.

"Come. Sit." This time he escorted us into the living room and we sat in overstuffed chairs, surrounded by furniture that was made to look at, not use. My mother would have had fits if we were even *in* a room like this. Plush carpeting, soft fabrics, muted tones in the textured walls—it was a room to view, not to sit in.

I struck first. "Mr. Fuentes, have you heard anything about Vic?"

"No." He pounced on it. "I was hoping that was why you were here. Have you heard anything? Anything at all?"

"Let me ask you something else. What is Café Cubana?"

You could see the surprise on his face. "I'm sorry. What is the question?"

"Very simply, what is Café Cubana?"

Fuentes cleared his throat. "Café Cubana is a business venture put together by several investors. It happens to be a private concern and I'm not at liberty to discuss it with you at this time."

"Could this business venture have something to do with the Cuban Social Club blowing up two nights ago? Or is it possible Café Cubana could have something to do with your son's apparent kidnapping?"

"This is why you came to see me?"

James finally spoke. "This, and the $2,500."

Fuentes stood up and walked to a polished mahogany desk. He reached into the top drawer and I froze. If he turned around with a gun — it was a check. I seriously about had a heart attack.

"I promised you I would pay you. This is a check for $3,000. I appreciate what you did and how you may have put yourself on the line." He handed the check to James and stayed on his feet, obviously waiting for us to get up and leave.

"Mr. Fuentes, we were threatened by two Hispanic men tonight. One of them had a gun." I hesitated to go much further. It was one thing to say we were threatened. It was probably very dangerous to tell him that one of our team had killed one of theirs. "It had to do with your mail that Jackie asked us to store."

"I don't think I understand. Two men threatened you over my mail?"

"Apparently they thought we had some of your mail that dealt with a business deal on Café Cubana." James gave me a concerned glance. I kept going. I'd said they *thought* we had mail. "The two men told us it was a coffeehouse chain with Cuban sandwiches and coffee." That part was true. So far I hadn't lied.

"It is. Did you see such mail?"

It was time for someone to tell that first lie.

I looked at James and he hesitated, clearing his throat. Those cigarettes. "We, uh, stored everything in Jackie's — your wife's — storage unit except that mail over there." He pointed toward the narrow table. "And we have no idea what was in your mail."

"Other than my son's finger."

"Hey. We explained that to you. The envelope was" — he paused — "leaking."

Silence.

Finally, I spoke. "We have no information on your son. But because of you and your son we're in this situation a little deeper than we want to be."

James kept shaking his head. I waited to see if he wanted to add anything. He didn't.

"I am truly sorry that you were threatened. I'm not certain that was my fault."

"Actually, it was my fault." James spoke up. "This entire business venture was my idea. However, you're apparently dealing with some dangerous people and a dangerous situation and because of that, Skip and I are in some deep shit."

Fuentes studied James. "Deep shit."

"Deep shit."

I kept going. "Mr. Fuentes, what exactly is your business?"

Fuentes glanced at his wristwatch, a thin gold band and even thinner gold dial. He seemed to be thinking. Finally, he sighed.

"There are some things I can tell you. The two men who threatened you, they are — were — business associates."

"No."

"Yes. But," he hesitated, "not by my choosing. It's a very complicated, difficult story. I'm sorry they threatened you. You see, and this is very difficult to say, they have threatened me as well."

James's eyes lit up. I could see his interest as he leaned closer. "Why are you telling us this?"

"You know Vic. You have a personal relationship with my son and you understand the situation he's in. Am I right?" He looked directly at me, staring intently at my eyes.

I found myself shaking my head up and down. Vic had been there when I needed him and now it was my turn.

"Believe me, I don't know who else to talk to. I would hate to involve you any further, but you need to know that the two men who threatened you tonight may have kidnapped my son."

"And cut off his finger."

"Yes."

"And what does Café Cubana have to do with this?"

"Everything."

His phone rang. I couldn't believe it. We were about to get the story and he gets the perfect out. The little blond, Cynthia, stuck her head around the corner.

"It's the front gate, Rick."

He stood up and left the room.

"Is he going to tell us what's going on or not?" The frustration in James's voice was obvious. "Jesus, this guy is either in a lot of trouble and doesn't know how to get out of it, or he's causing a lot of trouble and we're fucked."

"No middle ground with you?"

"No. But I hope to hell he's *in* a lot of trouble, because I don't want this guy to be on the other side."

"I hear you. We need someone on our side. James, we're looking at accessory to murder." I kept trying not to think about it, but the thought hung out there.

"There's that too."

Fuentes walked back into the living room, a puzzled look on his face.

"The two men who threatened you? Did one of them have his arm in a sling?"

"No." We echoed each other.

"Two men just asked the front gate guard for entrance to the building. They told him they wanted to meet with me. He said they were big men, had Spanish accents, and one of them had his arm in a sling, and did not look well. When he told them he was not to call my number after nine thirty, they left a message."

Neither of us said a word.

"They drove a blue Buick and said they'd be back, and if I didn't turn over my three accomplices, I could expect more body parts in the mail."

CHAPTER THIRTY-TWO

I've always hoped that age brings wisdom. I hope that when I'm thirty-five or forty I'll have a much better grasp on a situation than I do at twenty-four. And then I remember my father left home when he was thirty-seven. Was it wisdom that caused him to leave? Or was it the lack of wisdom?

Did my father realize, at thirty-seven, that he had no more wisdom or maturity than he did at twenty-four when he got married? Do you reach a stage in your life when you find that your emotional maturity has peaked? Would I handle today's situation in a more mature manner in my thirties or forties? If not, what's the point in growing up? Age, just for the sake of age, seems pointless. Loss of hair, muscle, and skin tone, loss of endurance, sexual appetite. If that were all we had to look forward to, what was the point?

"If I had been wise, I would have turned the project down." Rick Fuentes put his glass to his lips as if toasting his wrong decision.

We'd retired to the balcony, sitting on cushioned lounge chairs, sipping Amaretto on the rocks and looking out at the harbor. Amaretto. This for two guys who drank beer almost exclusively unless someone offered wine, usually from screw-top bottles. From fourteen stories up we watched blue and green lights bounce off the still water and cast wavy patterns on the murky surface. A large ship rested on the horizon, its bright lights shining like small pinholes in a black cloth. James had a dream of one day living like this, and at this moment, even with all of our problems, I could understand his passion. It beat the hell out of our cement slab and the dirt-brown ditch.

Fuentes swirled his drink. "I tell you this due to the fact you have put yourself in danger because of my son."

Frank and Joe Hardy would have figured out a way to get the old man to talk. James and Skip had pretty much stumbled into the situation by accident.

"My business is to raise money for business ventures. I'm certain you knew that. And Café Cubana is simply one of those projects. The gentlemen who came to me with the business plan were all successful men. Each, in his own way, had built a small, successful enterprise, and they had pooled their resources to form the new business."

"Why did they need you?" If this group was successful, why would they need more money?

"They were $20 million short."

James drew in a raspy breath. "Twenty million? You could raise that?"

He chuckled. "Of course. I've built an extensive list of investors over the last thirty years. These people have made rather large fortunes investing in my recommendations. The idea was sound. With the popularity of coffeehouses such as Starbucks, and the apparent longevity of the interest in these ventures, I was well on my way to raising the capital."

James was leaning forward, obviously relishing the chance to learn from a master. His father's blood ran through his veins.

"And this was to be a chain of coffee and sandwich shops all up and down the East Coast?"

"Yes. And a chance for each investor to double and triple his money in a very short period of time. Very seldom have I seen such a well-developed concept and potentially successful business. My investors were salivating to participate."

James sat back. "See, it takes money to make money. That's our problem."

"In this case you would have been wise to refuse the offer." Fuentes drained his glass. He stood up and walked to the bar on the balcony, pouring liberally from the bottle. "They had no intention of building the cafés."

It made no sense.

Fuentes drew a deep breath. He studied the two of us for a good sixty seconds, not saying a word. Finally, "Do you know about *Los Historicos*?"

James nodded. "The newscaster mentioned them when she was talking about the fire at the Cuban Social Club."

Fuentes nodded. "These men all came from families that lost property when Castro took control of Cuba. Their families left Cuba vowing to go back one day and reclaim what was rightfully theirs."

"And they attempted to do that during the Bay of Pigs," James said.

"Yes. It was a disaster. Many of my countrymen were killed, and although it has been discussed over and over again, no one has ever mounted a credible attempt since then."

It was way before our time. I'd read about it in eighth grade history class, but my entire image of Cuba was of a rundown country that people tried to escape from — not return to. "People are trying to get out of there. Why would someone want to go back?"

He stared out at the water and I sensed a sadness in his eyes.

"Wet foot, dry foot. If you are stopped at sea, you must go back to be killed or locked up in Castro's jail. If you make it to United States soil, you are allowed to stay. It's very sad. However, these are not people who have anything to go back to. These new refugees, they own nothing. *Los Historicos* have history. History and property."

Cynthia stepped out on the balcony in a loose fitting summer dress and no shoes. Her flowing blond hair hung around her shoulders and I had to admit she was beautiful. She walked over to Fuentes and stood behind him, rubbing his shoulders. As a warm, gentle Florida breeze rustled her dress and hair, I could smell the hint of jasmine in the air. A subtle perfume. I wondered what Em was doing right now.

"*Los Historicos* families owned manufacturing facilities, plantations, large homes, and businesses — hotels, casinos, farms, cigar factories, and so much more. They still believe that if they are able to take over the country once more they will restore Cuba to the way it was."

I also remembered studying the history of Cuba, and how wide open it was in the fifties before Castro took control. Living in South Florida it's hard not to learn something of the history and culture of Cuba. "Cuba was a hotbed of prostitution, gambling, and smuggling before Castro, wasn't it? It seems to me that Meyer Lansky was thrown out of Las Vegas, and ended up running Batista's gambling casinos. A pretty nasty group of people."

"Like the Wild West in the United States in the 1800s? I suppose it was. But these people lost everything. Everything. And they want it back."

"What does a chain of cafés have to do with all of this?" James the entrepreneur, still hanging on to this idea of a multi-million-dollar deal.

Fuentes sighed. "These men were using the money, the

money I was raising, to form an army. They were going back into Cuba to take over the country by force."

We were speechless.

"When I learned of the plan, I threatened to stop raising the money. That's when they kidnapped my son."

"What?" James asked the question; I silently asked at the same time.

"I never should have shared this with you."

"Oh, my God. Vic is being held because of a potential invasion of Cuba?"

Fuentes gave me a stern look. "If you take that story beyond this building, not only will you find the conspirators ready to kill you, but I will also be standing in line. I've said far too much."

I found myself drumming my fingers on the arm of the chair. "Why?"

"Why would you be killed?"

"That should be my first question, but I still want to know why you have told *us* and no one else?"

Fuentes stared into my eyes, maybe trying to find the soul of my being. Maybe trying to scare the hell out of me. I think he accomplished both.

"Because, Mr. Moore. You owe my son. I believe he saved your life many years ago and perhaps I'm telling you the situation to convince you of its severity. I need to convince you to walk away from this and help spare his life. Is that too much to ask?"

My mouth hung open. James was staring at me, frowning. He knew everything about me, yet had no idea what Rick Fuentes was talking about.

"Mr. Moore, I need you and your friends to leave this alone, because if I don't continue to raise the $20 million, they will kill Victor. He will become the first casualty in the new war against Fidel."

CHAPTER THIRTY-THREE

Vic hadn't kept it all to himself. His father knew, so all bets were off. The secret was out. And I suppose, even in my mid-twenties, I wish the story had remained a secret. It's funny how embarrassments suffered at any age stay with you. Weaknesses at twelve remain etched in your memory at twenty or twenty-two and maybe they shape you. Maybe they shape your personality, dictate your personal growth. I don't know for sure, but I still feel the shame.

In junior high, Justin Cramer and Mike Stowe would have been voted most likely to do a life sentence. For any number of reasons. Many of us thought they should go right from seventh grade to jail and stay there at least until we all graduated from high school. Didn't happen. Should have.

The two psychos were rumored to have raped a couple of cheerleaders, beaten a teacher for a bad grade, broken into a dozen homes in our school district, and spent a weekend doing $20 thousand worth of damage to our school. If you're saying to yourself, "These were seventh-grade kids?" the answer is yes. But seventh-grade kids who had flunked at least once and were physically bigger than most high school juniors.

Size and audacity may have been two of the reasons that Vic Maitlin was drawn to Cramer and Stowe. Since he was at the top of the pile, I always suspected he was looking beyond. Two guys with the size and reputation of these two may have intrigued him. Whatever the reason, he hung with them but never was tainted with their reputation.

"Well, the good thing is that Angel didn't kill the guy." James kept his eyes on the road, but his mind was obviously on our situation. "I couldn't think of anything else for a while. We need to find Angel and tell him."

"The bad thing is, Angel didn't kill the guy. At least it would have been one less bad guy to deal with." I rolled down the window and let the warm, humid night air blow through the cab.

"Skip, you don't mean that."

"No."

"First he wants us to find Vic, now he wants us to go away."

"Yeah. Well, things change."

"You gonna tell me about Vic Maitlin saving your life?"

I stared out the window, watching the expensive real estate roll by. Strip malls, concrete, palm trees, and more orange tile roofs. "No."

"What?"

"Maybe it's not as serious as Fuentes made it sound."

"Hey, pard. Tell me."

I said nothing. A buried secret doesn't just come shooting to the surface. I knew James well enough to know the subject wasn't going away.

"What about the rest of it. Do you believe Fuentes?"

"It's a damned good story if he made it up." I tended to take people at face value and Fuentes was believable. He also had a lot to lose.

Three minutes of silence passed. We were both engrossed in our own thoughts.

"And what about Vic? Was he one of the bodies in the fire?"

"God, I hope not." My cell phone went off. "Hello."

"Skip. You could have called. I'm a little frantic right now."

I'd like to think it was the shock of the story and the two Cuban guys showing up at the front gate that caused me to forget to call Em, but some of it is that I'm a self-absorbed asshole. I know my faults. Most of them.

"Em, I am sorry. Really. Listen, Angel didn't kill the Cuban. Big Mouth showed up tonight with his arm in a sling. At least we think it was him."

"Oh, my God. Are you all right?"

"It's a long story. It has to do with—" It was going to be a long explanation. Forty some years of Cuban history, a short course in business and being an entrepreneur, a crash course in Caribbean real estate, and a lesson in modern warfare. I didn't want to do it on the phone. Besides, the minutes cost money. "I'll give you a full accounting tomorrow. Everything is all right for now."

"Skip, we'll talk tomorrow, okay?"

"I've got calls in the morning, but how about we meet for lunch?"

She paused.

"Are you okay?"

"I'm not feeling that good right now."

"Em, what's wrong?" She was strong, never weak. I don't know that I'd ever seen her really sick.

"A little sick to my stomach."

"Are you taking anything?"

"No. Nerves I guess. I'll be all right. Dutch treat tomorrow?"

"No. Fuentes paid us the rest of the money. Actually $3,000. My treat."

She smiled over the phone. I could tell. "Don't forget, partner, a third of that is mine." She hung up.

"I'm going to turn off up ahead and get some oil," James said. "That light is flickering. All we need to do is throw a rod."

"Do you know what that means, throw a rod?"

He looked at me with a sneer. "No."

He pulled off at a gas station and got out of the cab. Hundreds of black bugs swarmed around the yellow glow from the light fixtures above the gas pumps. Catching a glimpse of a car in my peripheral vision, I spun around. No rear window. It must have pulled in behind us. I thought it was blue and big and the brief look I got made me think it might be the Buick.

James sauntered out of the garishly lighted gas station/carryout with a can of oil in his hand, popped the hood, and proceeded to drain the contents into the engine. I got out and looked behind us. No Buick.

We got back in and James pulled back out onto I-95.

"I think that man has problems we can't imagine. He doesn't know where his son is, only that he's been injured. He can't be honest with his investors because if he tells them the truth the people behind Café Cubana will send his son home in a body bag."

I looked out the side mirror and saw lights coming up behind us. Traffic was light, but this guy was hell-bent for leather, pulling alongside of us on the outside line. James glanced over and hit the brakes hard.

My mother harped on wearing a seat belt. Every time I left the house— "Don't forget to wear your seat belt!" I didn't pay a lot of attention to my mother. I bounced from the seat and cracked my chin on the dashboard as James skidded to a stop on the berm.

"What the hell was that all about? What?" I rubbed my chin, gingerly feeling what was going to be a nasty bruise. "Damn it, James."

"Son of a bitch had a gun aimed at my head and I swear he fired it, Skip. It was our big-mouthed buddy in the Buick. That's about as close to death as I think I've come."

Up ahead, a pair of brake lights came on and the car swerved onto the berm. I sat there rubbing my chin as the car ahead shifted into reverse and hit the gas. The big automobile was barreling backward, the rear end swerving back and forth like a fish's tail.

"Jesus! He's going to ram the truck."

"I think it's us he wants to ram, James. The truck just happens to be in the way." I was shouting and not sure why.

James stepped on the gas and we pulled out onto the highway. We passed the blue demon going forty-five miles an hour. The Buick braked again and reversed motion, chasing us at an alarming speed.

"James, we can't outrun that son of a bitch."

"I know."

"Bump him."

"What?" James shrieked.

Now the Buick was three car lengths back, and with my window down I could hear the roar of its engine.

"Bump him!"

"What about the truck."

"Fuck the truck. Think about our lives." Now I knew why I was shouting.

The big blue machine came whining up to the driver's side and when I leaned forward and looked out James's window, I could see Big Mouth taunting us with the gun. With his good hand he waived the pistol as they pulled even.

James jerked the steering wheel hard. He grimaced as he

gave it a vicious twist to the left and for a moment I thought the truck was going to go over. Then I heard the crunch of metal-on-metal.

The crunch, then the shrill scraping sound and sparks flew from the friction. James hung in there, straightening the wheel then spinning it again, pounding the car next to us, again, and again. Finally he spun it to the right and straightened it out one last time, punching the accelerator and heading down the highway.

"What?" I was still screaming and I couldn't see a damn thing. My side mirror showed nothing and with no rear window—which was the reason we were in this situation—I had no idea what had happened.

"Don't talk to me about it, Skip. I don't even want to discuss it until I see how much damage I just did to the truck."

We pulled over two exits later and got out in a deserted shopping center parking lot. Surprisingly, the body damage wasn't terrible. Oh, it was crumpled in spots and the dark blue from the Buick streaked across the white body like war paint, but with my limited knowledge of bodywork, I figured it could be fixed for minimal dollars. I was certain all three of us would have to put money from our profits into the repairs.

James kept pacing, looking at the side and saying, "Damn. Damn. Damn. Damn."

"We'll get it fixed. You saved our lives, man."

"You were right, Skip. Angel should have blown Big Mouth's punk ass away. These guys are bad news."

"Where are they?"

"The last time I hit them, their car rolled. Last thing I saw, it was upside down. It will take a tow truck to get them out of the median."

"Well, we're still in one piece."

"Skip, what the hell do they want with us? Do we know

something? Do they think we still have the mail. Shit, they know we were visiting Fuentes. They must assume we gave him the mail."

"But we didn't give him *all* of the mail, did we?"

He gave me a funny look. "How the hell would they know that?"

I walked back, surveying the truck all the way to the rear. "Hey, pal. Check this out."

He walked back and ran his finger over the hole. "Son of a bitch. They did shoot at us. What the hell do we do now? What do we do now?"

CHAPTER THIRTY-FOUR

We pulled into Gas and Grocery, closed at this late hour. A musty pine scent hung in the air.

"Just because we see him here during the day doesn't mean he—" Angel just kind of appeared, out of the dark, walking up to the truck and resting his elbows on the driver's door with its open window.

"My friends."

"Angel, I've got some good news." James smiled.

"The man wasn't killed."

"How did you know that?"

"Because I shot him in the shoulder. I was fairly certain his friend would take care of him. I may have done some serious damage, but I never believed he was dead."

James sputtered for a few seconds. "Well, then why did you let us believe that he was—"

"People will believe what they want to believe. I have strong feelings for people with belief. But the final proof is in the beholding."

I leaned over. "Who's quote is that?"

"Mine."

"They tried to kill James and me tonight on the highway."

He surveyed the truck in the dim light. "They don't appear to have been successful."

James stared mournfully at the truck. "We just wanted you to know."

Angel nodded. "Leave the truck with me."

"With you?" James stepped back.

"With me. If they come to your apartment and the truck is there, they know you're home. They may try to finish the job. If it's not there, they assume you're somewhere else."

I looked at James and he shrugged his shoulders. "Do you think they'll come after us tonight?"

"I'd like to think they're somewhere licking their wounds," James said.

"But they may be looking for us."

"True. What the hell."

It made sense. At twelve thirty in the morning, it made sense. Angel drove us back to the apartment, past the rows of faded concrete block houses and sparse brown, postage stamp-sized lawns, and we tumbled into bed. I slept a dreamless sleep, but woke with a sense of dread.

CHAPTER THIRTY-FIVE

I SHOOK HIM HARD. Sometimes James could sleep the sleep of the dead and there were times that no alarm could raise his sorry ass.

"Yeah. I'm sick today, boss." He rolled over and pulled his pillow over his head.

"Get up, James. It's safer at work than it is here."

"I don't have to be at work for another" — he glanced at his alarm clock — "hour. For Christ's sake I've got an hour."

"Do you want to walk to work?"

"Walk?"

"Three miles?"

"I'll take the, oh shit, we don't have the truck, do we?"

"Nope."

"I'll walk. Now get the hell out of my room."

I showered, shaved, and put on the cleanest dirty shirt I could find. The tie that had the fewest wrinkles was blue, and it only had the fewest wrinkles because I wore it less than the other three. I didn't like it, but except for the lunch with Em, I didn't care what I looked like. I was lucky to be functioning at all.

* * *

Sammy sat behind his computer, probably checking out a new porn site. He looked up and frowned when I walked in.

"Skipper. I got a call yesterday from an appointment you were supposed to call on."

"Yeah, I missed one late yesterday."

"You never called the lady, Skip." That condescending tone of voice.

"I'll get her today, Sammy." What kind of a name was Sammy? What the hell, what kind of a name was Skip?

"Don't bother. Marie called on her, and it looks like the lady is ready to buy. Call if you can't make the appointment, Skip. If you want to keep this job, call your clients." He dismissed me with a jerk of his head. The jerk focused attention back to the computer.

I called Em, just to make sure lunch was still on. "I'll pick you up?"

"Call me closer to the time, Skip. Right now, I'm sicker than a dog." She hung up and I closed the phone. I still harbor this fear that germs can float through phone lines. It's stupid, I know, but sick people bother me.

I stopped by two appointments, and only one was home. The first call was on a newlywed couple who had lied about owning their home. They rented the little shack, and I couldn't sell them a security system if they'd wanted it. They didn't. They wanted the cheap hot tub.

The second home had a note taped to the door. *We are no longer interested in whatever it was that you are selling. Please don't call again.*

No matter what the placement office at my alma matter had said, a business degree from Sam and Dave will not necessarily open doors for you.

I drove into a mall parking lot, with its pitted, potholed

blacktop and dollar stores and a place called Cheap and Sweet. They aren't stores you usually find in a mainstream mall. I roamed through one of the discount outlets just to kill some time and ended up buying a brown tie that looked better than the blue one. At eleven thirty I called Em and we decided to meet at Esther's. Her dad's construction offices were only a couple of miles away, so it worked for both of us.

I had baked meatloaf and mashed potatoes and Em ordered a cup of soup and salad. The lady in the booth behind us talked loudly with her friend, never slowing down for a minute.

"Oh, my first ex hit me. He did, girl. Mental, verbal, and then physical abuse, and when he grabbed my arm and almost twisted it out of its socket, I knew it was time to leave."

Her friend mumbled some condolences but was drowned out.

"My second ex—you remember Richard? Well, that was even worse. I had to have dental work from that relationship and now he has the kids. They gave him custody. Can you believe what I've been through? The father of my children."

We got up and moved farther to the back of the restaurant.

"So tell me what happened."

When I finished telling her, she smiled. "You think this is funny?"

"My God, Skip. We'd better laugh, because if we start crying we may never stop. You have to admit, this is almost comical. We're just young—almost kids. I mean, we're not involved in any of this. We just happened to be in the wrong place at the wrong time."

"You never read the Hardy Boys when you were a kid?"

She shook her head no.

"Well, if James could have backed up a truck with side mirrors—"

"Told you." She smiled.

"We never would have had the accident, we never would have found the finger, and—"

She folded her hands and was quiet.

"What?"

"Vic. I just keep thinking about this poor guy, kidnapped, his finger being cut off, and his father not having any idea where he is."

"That's the last part of the story, Em. His father warned us to back off. After he begged us to keep looking. He says that if we stay involved, they may kill Vic."

"And there's a good chance Vic is already dead." She buried her head in her hands.

"Yeah. However, I think we should keep looking."

"What?" She pulled her head out of the palms of her hands and gave me a big-eyed stare. "You think what?"

I couldn't tell her. It was just not the right time. I believed there was never going to be the right time. "I just feel I need to do this."

"Give me a break. You guys almost got killed last night. You can't keep getting in deeper."

"Listen, these guys have got it in their heads that we know something. We can't convince them we don't. For some reason they either want to scare us or kill us and we can't just sit around and wait for it to happen. If we can find Vic Maitlin, then Rick Fuentes has his kid back, and he can go to the cops and tell them everything."

She had tears in the corners of her eyes. Once again with the tears.

"It's going to be all right. Really."

She reached across the table and put her hand on mine. "I'm pregnant."

I forgot to breathe. For what seemed like an eternity she looked at me, waiting for my reaction.

Once again she said, "I'm pregnant."

Finally I managed to stammer out a response. "Who's the father?"

She slowly stood up and headed toward the door.

"Em, wait."

She kept walking.

I caught up with her and put my hand on her shoulder. "I'm sorry. Or maybe I'm not. Do you want—" I didn't know what I was saying.

She spun around and gave me a fiery look that even her tears couldn't put out. "You're the father, you ass. Don't you get it? You. Who else did you think it might be?" She turned and walked out the door and I just stood there. I watched her drive away, and I couldn't take one more step to stop her.

CHAPTER THIRTY-SIX

I DID THE MATH YEARS AGO and figured out that my mother was pregnant for three months before she married my father. Maybe that was in his mind when he left home. Maybe he'd been pressured into marriage because of me and never got over that.

I could marry Em. I could do a lot worse, but I still feel that I've got a lot of growing up to do.

I couldn't get a grip on this father thing, and I certainly wasn't going to be able to just accept it in the first minute I found out. I called her cell, but she didn't answer. An hour later I called her at work, but she wasn't in. I called her home, but the machine picked up. I drove to Biscayne Bay, but she wasn't there.

I drove aimlessly, passing the entrance to the causeway where a black guy sat up on a mound of earth, watching the cars go by, his laundry hung out to dry over a guardrail. I ended up a couple of blocks farther at Bayside, a sprawling, colorful outdoor shopping and restaurant community on the bay, with a Hard Rock Café, Hooters, and all the other chain attractions you'd expect. It was almost like a carnival. I had a seven-dollar beer at an outdoor bar and watched a lady with a parrot on her shoulder hustle a mother and her little girl for a ten-dollar picture with the blue and red bird on the girl's shoulder.

I'd blown off two afternoon appointments and figured I may have to find another job. Construction was probably out of the picture. Right now, Em's father might not be in the best frame of mind to hire an unskilled carpenter.

When I pulled into the apartment, the truck was sitting in the lot. Buick-blue streaks and raw-rubbed metal graced the driver's side of our moneymaker. It might take just about all the money we'd made to fix it. Right next to it was a rusted-out Ranchero, one of those old Fords with the front of a car and the back of a pick up. I'd seen it parked there before. It's a junk heap that barely runs and the magnetic sign on the side says *Refinance — let us make your dreams a reality*. As if.

The TV was blaring and James was sprawled on the couch, drinking one of my beers, a box of Cheese Nips sitting on the floor.

"Oh, you've got dinner waiting?"

He grunted.

"Did you get to work this morning?"

"Yeah. There's some cold crab in the fridge. Help yourself."

I'd gotten to hate it almost as much as he did, but when money was tight his perks came in handy.

"The truck?"

"Angel brought it back this morning. He said something a little weird."

"That would be so unlike him."

James smiled. "No, this creeped me out. He said the guys in the Buick never showed up."

"Meaning?"

"I don't know. I took it to mean that he was watching our place to see if they did."

"Our own guardian angel."

James looked up at me. "Honest to Christ, I never thought of that. He really was like an angel."

"Yeah, well you didn't do too bad last night in that role. Thanks for putting the truck on the line."

He grunted again.

"James."

"Dude?"

He could tell it was something important. It's hard to explain that kind of a relationship to someone. I suppose an old married couple could have that relationship, although most of the old married people I know don't really care for each other that much. But James and I understand each other. Most of the time.

"I've spent the last hour thinking about this."

James punched the remote and the television went black.

"Tell me."

I hesitated. I still wasn't sure this was something he should know. But I'd come to the realization that he probably *was* the first person who needed to know. Eventually I wanted to go to my dictionary and look up the word *conflicted*. I felt certain that was an appropriate word for the way I felt about the entire situation. If I'd been high on some hallucinogen I couldn't have been more confused.

"I've got a serious problem."

"Something new going down?"

"No. Nothing to do with what's been happening. This has to do with Em."

James studied me for a moment. I could almost hear the gears turning in his head.

"You've got a serious problem? And it involves your on-again-off-again romance?"

"It does."

"Either she's leaving you or she's pregnant."

"Pregnant."

"Who's the father?"

I knew there was a reason he was my best friend.

CHAPTER THIRTY-SEVEN

THE PHONE RANG at three in the morning. When my cell phone is recharging it will just repeat, "You have an incoming call. You have an incoming call. You have an incoming call."

I grabbed it, still somewhat foggy from what I call half-a-sleep. I hadn't been able to drift off, but I wasn't exactly wide awake. I knew who it was. It wasn't.

"Eugene?"

"Yeah."

"Eugene Moore?"

"Yeah. This is me."

"You have something that we need. If you give it to us, we can call things even."

The Spanish accent gave him away. It was the greasy haired nervous guy from our Cuban duo.

"Mr. Moore?"

"What do I have?"

"You have mail."

Like a computer. "You have mail. You have mail."

"Obviously we've had some confrontations in the last several days that have come to no resolution. I am suggesting that you turn over whatever mail you have and we will stop any aggressive action."

Did they think we still had the finger? And what would happen if they found out we didn't have it? Everything was a blur in my mind.

"Mr. Moore?"

"I'm here. Can I think this through?"

"No. I need an answer."

My head was clearing by the second. I saw movement in the doorway and James stood there, in a T-shirt and boxer shorts, rubbing his eyes.

"What is it, man?"

"What's your name?"

"Carlos."

"Carlos, my partner is here and we need to talk. Call me back in ten minutes." I hung up the phone.

"Whoa!" James had snapped back much quicker than I had. "They want the mail? We don't have the fucking mail."

"Well, James, that's not entirely true."

"One envelope out of two boxes of mail—come on. That could have just fallen out by mistake."

"It's a little too early in the morning for me to figure all this out."

We'd talked until one thirty in the morning, sitting outside on the slab, smoking cigarettes, and getting loose on cheap beer. I kept staring at the building behind us, and the playpen. Two old people praying for a chance to be with their first grandchild, and me, praying that maybe there was a mistake and Em really wasn't pregnant. One thirty in the morning I'd gone to bed, and it was now three thirty. I'm a growing boy. I need a lot more sleep than that.

"I'm having a tough time putting it all together, James."

"Yeah. You've got a full plate, partner. I say we call Rick Fuentes. Tell him that as far as we know he got all the mail we had. Ask him what we should do. Or, we could just tell your pal Carlos to stop by Fuentes's condo and get it for himself." James looked at me, then glanced at my cell phone. Obviously he didn't want to call the man at three thirty in the morning. I sat on the edge of the bed and made the call. The machine picked up.

"Rick Fuentes, this is Skip Moore. We just got a phone call from the two guys who threatened us and, by the way, almost killed us on the way home from your place. They say that if we give them your mail, they'll go away and leave us alone. You've got the mail, Mr. Fuentes. Should we just tell them to deal with you?"

I had this thought that maybe I should have just kept quiet. Once the two Cubans had the mail, all of us were expendable. If they wanted to get rid of everyone who knew about their plans, they'd have to eliminate all of us — including Angel and Emily.

"I need to hear from you in the next ten minutes. It's," I struggled to read the alarm clock, "three thirty-eight in the morning."

I hung up and we waited. James paced and I sat on the bed, thinking for a couple of seconds about actually having a kid, then thinking about how much trouble we were in. Back and forth. Would she even want to discuss marriage? Would these guys actually try to kill all of us because we knew about the plot to overthrow Castro?

Finally, James sat down on an old wooden trunk that I used as a closet and cupboard. "If they get all of that mail, they may kill us."

"Yeah. I was thinking the same thing. And some other things as well."

"My old man, he had fifteen different businesses. That's just fifteen that I knew about."

"And?"

"I never heard of one of them leading to murder. Or even the threat of murder."

"Well, he never had a trucking company. Pretty rough business."

"Yeah."

"James, I think we should just tell Carlos that we don't have the stuff. That's all. We don't have it. What can they do about that?"

"We *don't* have it."

"Yeah. We don't have *most* of it, but they're liable to stop over here and find out for sure." I looked at my watch. "I'll call Fuentes one more time. If he's not there, we'll have to tell this guy that Fuentes has it." I dialed his number and got his answering machine one more time.

"We can't wait any longer." James was pacing again. "If they call back and we don't have an answer—"

"They're liable to come over here."

"Shit. Why won't Fuentes call back?"

Off the charger, "Born in the USA" blared from the little flip phone. "Hello?"

"Skip?"

"Em." I found myself short of breath. " I . . . I am so, so sorry about this afternoon. There was no excuse for that response. I mean, you just shocked me and I—"

"No. I'm sorry. I planned how I wanted to tell you, and, and it just didn't come out right at all. I didn't mean to walk away. I've been an emotional wreck, and—" the receiver beeped. Somebody else was calling in.

"Em, I am so sorry. I've got to take this call."

"At four in the morning? Come on, Skip. Look, if you don't want to talk, fine."

The line went dead. I hit the green button. "Hello?"

"Eugene? This is Carlos. Do we get the mail?"

"Carlos." I let out a slow breath. Em had called and wanted to talk, and here I am dealing with a life and death situation. I guess Em's situation is life and death too. "We don't have it."

"Bullshit."

"No, I'm leveling with you."

"Would you care to tell me where it is?"

I hesitated. I didn't want to put Fuentes in more danger, but this was his battle. And, it was his mail. "Rick Fuentes has it."

There was silence on the other end.

"Carlos?"

"Rick Fuentes has *all* of it?"

"We took it up to him the night you tried to run us off the road."

"Cut the bullshit, Mr. Moore. You have the list of donors for Café Cubana. I want it."

CHAPTER THIRTY-EIGHT

JAMES STARED AT ME, his jaw slack. "He said he knew we had the donor list?"

"Why would I make that up, James?"

"How the fuck does he know?"

There were two ways. "One, they were parked nearby and saw us when we took the envelope out of the box and tossed it back in the truck."

"Possible. We know they tried to get by the gate."

"Number two, they did get by the gate and took the mail from Fuentes. Once they went through everything in those two boxes, they realized the donor list was missing."

"Shit. What do we do, Skip? That donor list was extensive. And potentially damaging."

"They're going to get it somehow."

"They're calling back in—" the phone started it's raucous music.

"Carlos?"

"Yes."

"We've decided to give you the list. Why don't you give me

your number, and we'll set up a time and place where you can pick it up."

He was quiet for a moment, but I could hear him breathing. Then he must have put his hand over the mouthpiece and I could hear his muffled voice talking to someone.

He came back on line. "Do you think I am a stupid fuck, Eugene?"

"No."

"Eugene, you couldn't trace this number if you tried, and I am obviously not going to give you my phone number. I want the list tomorrow night. And I want you to leave it in the trash can that sits outside the Denny's across the street from your apartment. We don't have to meet each other any more, see each other anymore, or threaten each other with guns. Do you understand?"

"Yeah."

"Put the envelope in a plastic garbage bag. Drop it in the trash can around eight tomorrow night. It's that simple. And Eugune?"

"What?"

"Don't make copies. No copies. It had better all bc there. I know what I'm looking for and if it's not there, I'll start cutting toes and ears off your high school classmate. Got it?"

I got it.

CHAPTER THIRTY-NINE

THAT DAMNED FIELD TRIP. Vic was my trip buddy, but there were a lot of things to do, a lot of people to see, and simply being buddies didn't mean that you were chained together. It was just a way for one teacher and one chaperone to leverage a little more supervision. So, we weren't together the whole time. Should have been, but we weren't. And when Vic wasn't around, I figured that he was off with Cramer and Stowe, the goon squad.

It was a park, and we were doing some nature things. God knows, I couldn't remember most of it if I tried, but there was a sinkhole about forty feet deep at the edge of the property. It was surrounded with yellow tape with signs warning us to stay back. For most of the kids, you didn't need the sign. I remember everything about the sinkhole. Everything.

Mrs. Marlow explained how the limestone deposits had built up and eroded and she went through the story about how sinkholes came to be. This particular one had swallowed a garage and two cars. Pretty impressive to a seventh grader. And as long as someone didn't go to the actual edge of the sinkhole, as long as someone stood back maybe a couple of feet behind the yellow tape, what danger could there be?

My trip buddy was nowhere around and I really wanted to see if you could still view the garage or the two cars. The story was that nothing had ever been brought back to the surface. So I worked my way over to the yellow tape, and seeing no one who would stop me, I ducked under the yellow plastic and walked up to the sinkhole, leaning forward and peering into the craggy depths of the pit.

When I felt the pressure on my back, the hard shove, I started to turn, but it was too late. I staggered forward as the ground crumbled under my feet. I can still feel the breathless rush of fear that gripped my midsection. My heart seemed to stop and my stomach rolled in wild turmoil. Feeling my body dropping with the soft earth, I think I screamed and turned in midair, grasping at what remained of the dirt, clawing at it with my skinny fingers. Somehow I hung on. About two feet down. The earth I was clinging to was soft and I could sense it was only a matter of time before it gave way and I would plummet to the bottom of the forty-foot chasm.

I looked up, hoping to see a sign of rescue. Instead, I saw Justin Cramer and Mike Stowe looking down. As I remember, not with glee on their faces. I actually believe I saw raw fear, and it was totally clear to me what had happened. They'd pushed me, for no apparent reason and now were petrified that they'd be found out or possibly they realized they'd finally crossed a line. They had attempted murder.

I screamed again, the cavern soaking up the sound. I watched them turn and run and I felt the fine silt of the earth slowly erode under my fingertips.

And then, there was Vic. When he called my name and I looked up, he was already on his belly, inching forward with his hands outstretched. He reached down, telling me everything was going to be all right. To this day, I can still feel the pain in my knuckles, the cramps in my hands from grasping the dark brown dirt.

Slowly, he reached down as his shoulders and chest cleared the opening. I should have prayed that he didn't fall as well, but all I could do was pray for myself. He wasn't just saving my life, he was putting his life on the line and there's a difference. A big difference. Finally, he reached my wrist and he pulled, breaking my grip and holding my entire weight with one hand. He worked his way back, pulling me with him until he was able to reach down with his second hand and haul me out. How he managed it, I'll never know, but we were both shaking when I reached the surface.

"Vic."

He was breathing deeply, and he looked into my eyes and shook his head. "Don't ever tell anyone about this. Ever. Don't tell them how it happened, and don't ever tell them how you got out. Don't, Skip. Just don't."

I called Emily three times. She didn't answer the first two times. The third time she picked up.

"What?"

"That call was serious. The guys who tried to kill us were on the phone. They want the rest of the mail by tomorrow night or they're going to start chopping off more of Vic's body parts."

"Oh, my God. You still have some of that?"

"And we were trying to call Fuentes and see what his reaction was and you were on the—" the phone beeped.

"Jesus! Em, it's ringing again. I've got to get this, but can we talk tomorrow? Please? We need a serious face-to-face. Em?"

"Take your call. We'll talk tomorrow." She sounded defeated. I'd had one night to consider her earthshaking news. She'd obviously been grappling with the information for a much longer time.

I punched the green button. "Hello?"

"This is Rick Fuentes."

"Rick . . . Mr. Fuentes, since we left your place the other night a lot of things have happened. Let me start at the beginning."

I did. I even told him about the Café Cubana list falling out of the box and accidentally still being in our truck. And by the time I was done, I was exhausted. James sat on the trunk and kept shaking his head as if he was reliving all the highlights.

Fuentes was quiet on the other end of the line. I assumed he was absorbing the information.

Finally, "Mr. Moore, the two men you refer to did stop by here. They have my son, and until I am certain that Victor is alive and well — until I am certain he will return to me, I must do what they tell me. They asked for the list. Apparently you had it when they met you at the storage unit." He was quiet, waiting for my response.

"Yeah, maybe." God I hate getting caught in a lie.

"They picked and sorted through the mail, but the list wasn't there. I convinced them I was not aware of its whereabouts. Apparently they knew where to look."

"Yeah. Well, do you want it back or should we —"

"I asked you to walk away from this situation for Victor's sake. Please, Mr. Moore. Deliver the envelope as they have asked and then just go away. You've done all you need to do." And then he said something I found very strange, but very true. "You know, if Jackie had opened my mail you wouldn't even be involved in this. She was supposed to open the fucking mail."

I thought about that for a moment. He was right. If the wife had opened the mail, she would have found the finger. That probably should have happened, but Jackie never opened any of his mail. She would have seen the list of donors. God, I wish she had. We'd be oblivious to this entire situation.

"Are you surprised she didn't open your mail?"

"Yes. Actually, somewhat disappointed that she didn't," he paused, "and that you did. I asked her to open it. I asked her to please open anything that came to our . . . her house, but that's not the point here. Give them the list and walk away. I can't have your blood on my hands."

I glanced at James, who was chewing on a fingernail. He gave me a look of exasperation.

"We'll make the drop tomorrow at eight o'clock."

"You don't want to go any further with these men, Mr. Moore. Trust me. Please, for Victor's sake, leave it alone. I'll let you know when everything is settled." He hung up the phone.

For Victor's sake. I couldn't put him at risk. I glanced at my two hands, thinking about having a finger amputated. Crudely amputated. A ring finger.

"We're going to drop off the envelope in the trash can at Denny's."

"And that's it?" James seemed relieved.

I thought about it. I thought about the fact that I was still around to think about it. And if it hadn't been for Vic putting his life on the line—

"No. That's not it. We're going to follow these guys and see where Vic is."

"You're out of your fucking mind. You're a madman, Skip."

"You said it yourself, James. Once they get everything they want, they could kill us. I want to know who they are, where they are, and where Vic is.

"Skip! We could get killed. Vic could get killed."

"Yeah, but we're not going to get free of this until we find out where he is."

It wasn't just saving a life, it was putting a life on the line and there's the difference.

There was no other choice. "I'm going to try to get some sleep." Who was I kidding. I lay there for half an hour and finally got up and made a cup of weak coffee. I watched the sun creep over the horizon and cast its bold red rays into the cloudy sky. Red sky. My father had taught me a saying from his Navy days.

Red sky at night, sailor's delight.
Red sky in the morning, sailor take warning.

CHAPTER FORTY

I TURNED ON THE TELEVISION at six and watched the first news of the day. I'd started to doze off when I heard the announcer mention the fire.

"Late last night, fire investigators announced that they had uncovered the identity of one of the bodies found in the explosion and fire in Little Havana."

I held a breath.

"They have positively identified Juan Sistaro, a Miami grocer, through his dental records. The identity of the second victim has not been discovered, but investigators say that the body has some unique physical characteristics."

I sat up on the couch and shook the cobwebs from my head.

"It appears that the ring finger on his left hand is missing. Medical examiners were not certain whether the digit had been severed recently or sometime in the past. Both bodies were burned beyond recognition."

I remember shivering. It was seventy-eight degrees already, and I was shivering like it was below freezing.

"The deaths appear to be the result of a major explosion at the Cuban Social Club, a club that—"

I shut the television off and stood up. The death? Vic was dead? The thought paralyzed me. I stood there staring at the blank screen for at least a minute, then went back to James's bedroom and shook him.

Finally he gained consciousness.

"What the hell?"

I couldn't say it.

"Skip, what the hell did you wake me up for? It's . . . for crying out loud it's six fifteen in the morning. Why do you do this to me?"

"It's Vic."

"What's Vic?"

"The news. One of the bodies they found in the burned-out building. It's Vic."

James threw the covers off and got out of bed. He pulled on a pair of jeans and a stained T-shirt that were thrown on the floor, and walked out of the room. I could hear him banging cups and spoons around as he made himself a cup of instant coffee. In about three minutes he came back in the room. I was still standing where I'd made the announcement.

"You're positive?"

"One of the bodies has a missing ring finger and they don't have a positive ID.

"Vic? Nah. There's no positive ID, Skip. Listen, that guy was tough! Saved your life? He could save his own. It wasn't Vic."

"It's not like we were his best friends, but—"

"Hey, he's someone we knew. Hell, he dated Emily. And now we know his father and stepmother. Are you going to tell me about him saving your life?" He walked to the kitchen table and sat down. I followed him, sat down, and shook my head.

"Is this what it's all about? You owe him?" James went on.

"I don't know. Maybe."

"You won't tell me?"

"James. These guys have tried to kill us. They've killed at least two people that we know of. I don't know if it's Vic. Let's assume he's still alive. We can't go to the cops without putting Vic and his father and everyone else in jeopardy. Isn't that reason enough?"

"I agree we don't go to the cops. But I don't know, pard. It's virgin territory."

"Yeah. I say we follow these assholes and find out if Vic *is* alive. I don't see any other option."

James sipped his coffee, staring out the window at the parking lot. "You agreed to do the college thing so we could start our restaurant. That sort of fizzled. You went along with me on this crazy truck scheme, and God knows where that's taking us. I owe you. I'm with you on *your* crazy scheme. If Vic Maitlin or Fuentes or whatever the fuck his name is . . . if he saved your life, I owe him too. Because of Vic, I've got my best friend by my side. I'm with you, compadre. " He lifted his right hand and we hit palms across the tiny kitchen table.

CHAPTER FORTY-ONE

WE CALLED IN SICK. I'd only done it twice before and once because I'd actually *been* sick. This time I was afraid I might *be* sick. I called Em. She *was* sick, really sick, and asked if I could call later.

I nodded off to sleep about 8 a.m. and woke up at nine. There's a rhythm to my sleep pattern no matter how tired or rested I am. I'm up by seven and even on weekends I can't sleep past nine. I don't care if I've been on a bender, I still am up by 9 a.m.

I called Em again and this time she could talk.

"Are you going to hang up on me again?"

"No." I'd been properly chastised.

"I'm feeling a little better. Can you get away for some coffee?"

"Sure. I'm not going in to work, so let's do it. I'll drive in and meet you in the deli."

The deli is in her condo building. All she's got to do is get on the elevator. A sick person should be able to do that. I had to drive twenty-five minutes.

* * *

She looked great. Cutoffs and a short T, with thin sandals that showed off her sexy legs and feet. For just a moment I forgot she was carrying our kid. Just a very brief moment.

"Em, I'm sorry about last night."

"This morning."

We sat at a table in the large hallway outside the deli, sipping on coffee and chewing on bagels.

"Yeah. Things are happening."

"What things?"

"Do you want to talk about that or about the—" how was I to refer to it?

"The what?"

"The situation?"

"Why don't we just call it what it is, Skip? The pregnancy."

"Okay."

She frowned. "Do you want to say it? Why not try it out."

I didn't like being treated like a kid, however, I knew she was right. If I couldn't even say it, I probably couldn't deal with it.

"Do you want to talk about my phone calls last night or your pregnancy?"

She didn't smile. "First of all, tell me what was so important about last night."

I did. And then I told her about the news this morning.

"Oh, my God." She stared at her coffee. A man next to us opened his *Miami Herald* and I could hear him softly whisper, "Oh, my God." God was a busy guy this morning.

"Em, it might not be Vic."

She said nothing, just continued to look into her coffee. What's the song by Carly Simon about clouds in the coffee?

Finally she looked up. "If it *is* Vic, then we need to call the authorities. This could be murder and we can't let that go unreported." It came to me. "You're So Vain" from some time back in the sixties or seventies.

"What about Fuentes?"

"He's bound to hear the news."

"But do we still drop off the mail? He told me to drop the entire matter, that if we kept getting ourselves involved, it would put Vic's life in danger. But now, if his son is dead—"

"Do you think he'll call you?"

"Fuentes? I don't know. I think he's under a lot of pressure. I may be low priority right now. It's strange, Em. He asked us to find his son, now he wants us to get out of the way."

"Trust me," she said. "Your phone call at four in the morning moved you up to the top of his priority list."

"I'll wait till noon and see if he calls. If he doesn't, I'll call him. Considering we're talking about his kid, I would think he's monitoring the situation."

"It's a plan." She smiled, the first one I'd seen in a couple of days. "Do you want to discuss the *situation*?"

"Sure." But I didn't know what to say.

"You are the father. There's no question about it. I took a home pregnancy test about a week ago, and I would guess I'm five or six weeks."

She looked into my eyes, waiting for some reaction and I had none. It was still a shock to me.

"I've considered my options. I can have the baby and keep it or I can put it up for adoption."

"There's another option."

"Not as far as I'm concerned." She squinted her eyes. "Don't bring that up again, Skip. Ever."

Facing the doors at the end of the hall, I could see Biscayne Bay, the sparkling blue water and several of the big white boats in the marina. A yellow kayak drifted up to the dock. I wondered what it would be like to just sail away with no destination and no master plan. It sounded good until I realized it was kind of like being adrift on the ocean without a rudder. It all depends on your perspective. Right now I was on the ocean and rudderless. Problems seemed to compound themselves.

"Have you been to the doctor?"

"No."

Two chubby Latin babes in too-tight pants and halter tops walked by us, both pushing a stroller with an infant inside.

"I'm going to see my OB-GYN in a couple of days."

I searched for questions. I had a million, but couldn't think of one. Finally, I said, "Does your dad know?"

She sighed. "No. He's going to rave and rant and threaten you—"

"Tell him to stand in line."

"Then he'll settle down and realize it takes two to tango."

There was an uneasy silence. Finally, I had to ask.

"Where do you see me in this scenario?"

"You're the father. Where do you see yourself?"

"Look, Em, I'm in love with you. You know that. I'd have an exclusive relationship if you'd agree to it. That's no secret."

"So what are you proposing?"

I put my hand on hers. "Proposing may be a bad choice of words."

She laughed. Out loud. "God, Skip. I'm scared. I never, we never . . . did you ever—"

"No. I never expected anything like this. Should we get married?"

"Oh, God no. Are you ready for marriage? I don't think so."

"And you are?"

She shook her head with exaggerated swings. "Hell no. I'm not ready to have a kid either. But I'll deal with it."

"Why wouldn't you marry me?"

She took her hand from mine and picked up her coffee cup. Taking a sip she struggled for words. "I wish I smoked cigarettes."

"So you wouldn't have to deal with issues."

"All right," she said, "you want issues? You're immature."

"Well . . ."

"You live like a pig, you and your Neanderthal roommate."

"Not a husbandly trait?"

"You've got a job that doesn't even support you, and you have absolutely no future."

I shook my head in agreement. "Yeah, but I'm cute. And I love you."

She pursed her lips. "All right, let me take those two things into consideration."

CHAPTER FORTY-TWO

I MET JAMES AT THE APARTMENT. He told me he'd slept till noon in between two calls from Cap'n Crab threatening his employment if he didn't get his ass into work. But James has a great sick voice. You'd swear he was going to die. He groans, sputters, wheezes and pretty soon you decide he isn't long for the world. Lindsey at Cap'n Crab told him he'd better be in tomorrow for sure. She didn't fire him, but I think she's sweet on him, so he gets a pass.

"When we have employees, Skip, I hope to hell they're better workers than we are." He lay on the couch sucking on a long-neck beer.

"If they don't show up, we'll have to do all the work."

"Yeah."

I straddled a dining room chair, the screws stripped from the metal legs. It was perilously close to collapsing and we had a bet on how many more days it could support us. The bet was only for five bucks. Probably an immature act on my part.

"James, Fuentes hasn't called. If the man doesn't watch the news, he probably doesn't know about the bodies."

"Call him, pardner. I do not want to get into this mess tonight unless he knows what's going on."

I dialed the number. This time he answered on the first ring.

"Mr. Moore. I assume you're still dropping off the mail tonight?"

"I am, Mr. Fuentes. However, I may have some bad news."

"I don't recall you calling me with good news."

"No. I haven't. However, this may be the worst. They found two bodies in the burned-out building. One of them was missing a ring finger."

He was silent, but I could hear him breathing on the other end.

"Mr. Fuentes?"

"Holy Mary, mother of God. Do they know?"

"No. The last time I heard, they had not identified the body of that person."

"Then there is hope. Continue with your plans, Mr. Moore, and keep your mouth shut. Please. I'll look into this matter. I know some people on the Miami police force and I'll make some immediate inquiries." Abruptly he hung up the phone.

"He was pretty shook up?" James asked.

I thought for a second. "He sounded shook up. Not like I think I would sound if I'd lost a son, but, you know, shaken." It wouldn't be too long before I could relate.

"Do we drop off the mail?"

"He said to go ahead with the plans. Then he told me to shut up. What is that? About the tenth time? Anyway, maybe he's in denial. He said, 'Then there is hope,' so I'm thinking he believes Vic may still be alive."

James drained the bottle of beer and rolled it like a bowling ball into the kitchen area. "You haven't talked much about Em. How did the meeting go?"

How did it go? "It was awkward."

"You'd think, after all the history, that it wouldn't be that tough."

"But it is."

"How did you leave it?"

I shouldn't have told him but I did. "I proposed. Sort of."

His eyes got wide and he slowly sat up. "You really did? This is big, compadre."

"Not as big as her situation."

"Situation? You mean Em being pregnant?"

"Yeah. Pregnant. Anyway, she said no."

"She's not thinking rationally." He stood up and went to the refrigerator, grabbing another beer. "But, then, neither are you."

I bristled. "What would be wrong with that scenerio?"

"Wrong? Jesus, Skip. You're my best friend, okay. I'd trust my life to you, but come on, buddy. You're immature. I mean really. You've got a job with absolutely no future and . . ."

I got off the chair and walked to the door. I needed some fresh air. "And I live with an asshole roommate who not only is an asshole but a complete idiot. Fuck you." I walked out and slammed the door, almost taking it off the hinges. The door, like everything else in our apartment, was dirt-cheap.

CHAPTER FORTY-THREE

I DROVE AROUND FOR A WHILE. Down to the stadium, then onto I-95, and I lost track of time. When I finally got back to Carol City, I drove over to Gas and Grocery. I parked, walked in, and pulled a bottle of Pepsi out of the cooler. I paid and asked if Angel had been around. The girl simply shrugged her shoulders and turned around, stocking cigarette packs behind the counter.

He was sitting on the hood of the Prism when I walked out. Knowing how cheap the car was, I was concerned he might leave a dent. Hell, the car had so many dents already one more wouldn't be noticed.

"Angel!"

"Man, how does it go?"

"It goes. Listen, tonight we're dropping off a piece of mail from our truck into a trash can at Denny's."

I'm sure he thought I was crazy. He cocked his bald head and looked at me as if I'd lost my mind.

"You can give it to me. I'll throw it away right here."

"No. The Cuban guys asked us to drop it off. They're going

to pick it up and we're going to try to follow them. We can see where they go and, hopefully, find our friend Vic."

He shook his head. "You guys are crazy."

"Yeah, well . . ." I knew he was right. Angel was much smarter than we were. "Do you want to come along?"

"Yeah. I do."

The guy was as crazy as we were. Somehow that made me feel better.

"Do you want the complete package?"

"We do."

Angel smiled, his white teeth contrasting with his dark skin. "Okay, man. I'll bring everything. We'll find those sons of bitches."

The three caballeros. For justice, for a way of life. It was a stupid move on our part, but we were young and there's an age when you understand death, you watch it happen around you, but you, you are invincible. Soldiers going into war must feel like that. Fear, trepidation, awe, but no doubt that you'll come away alive and victorious.

"I want to show you something." Angel motioned to me and we walked behind the Gas and Grocery.

I was invincible. Then, I thought about Em and my kid. I shook. This probably wasn't a good time to be putting my life on the line.

CHAPTER FORTY-FOUR

"A JEEP?" James looked shocked.

"A Wrangler. Midnight black. He parks it behind Gas and Grocery. Honest to God, James, it looks like he polishes it every day. Showroom new."

"What about the Prism?"

"Angel is right. These guys have seen my car parked here. If they see that eyesore behind them they'll know right away we're following them. They've never seen the Jeep and it's a perfect car for tailing them. If they go off road, we can go off road. It's dark, not that iridescent shit-green color of my Prism."

"What the hell. Let's take the Jeep. In half an hour I'll walk across the street and put the envelope in the trash can. I'll walk back here, and you guys pick me up in the next complex."

"As long as they don't grab it in the first five minutes we should be able to get the Jeep in position and see them when they take it."

"It's gonna be a strange night, pardner." James was wired. Six cups of coffee and ten cigarettes will do that to you.

"No stranger than it's been, James. And it's been pretty strange."

Half an hour goes very slow when you want it to go fast. James dropped the envelope and the list into a garbage bag, tied the straps on the top of the bag, threw it over his shoulder like a South Florida Santa Claus in cutoffs and a Mötley Crüe T-shirt and walked out of the apartment. I stood on the porch and watched him as he walked it across the street, through the field, and into Denny's parking lot. It was still light enough to see and I watched him take the top off the plastic container. He stuffed the bag in, replaced the top, and started back. Nothing to it.

I went out the back door just in case they were watching the front. The old black man was sitting in a cheap aluminum chair on his slab reading a magazine. He nodded as I walked by, never looking up. The empty playpen had a new powder blue blanket draped over the side.

Angel was in the next lot, sitting in the Jeep Wrangler.

"Hey, man. Nice clear evening. We should be able to see everything."

"Anybody watching me? Do you see anybody?"

"Nah. My feeling? They think you want to be done with all this. You pass on the mail, you're done. The last thing in the world they gonna think is that you follow them."

I slid in the passenger side. James could ride in the back. "My feeling? I should tell you this, Angel. I think that once they get the mail, they could kill us."

"Why they gonna kill you? Huh? What did you do?"

"They think we know what's going on."

"Do you?"

"Yeah."

"Then maybe you're right."

"You still want to go?" I looked him straight in the eye.

"Seems to me I'm the one who shot one of those boys. I'm in pretty deep already."

James came around the corner, watching behind him as he sprinted for the Jeep.

"Hey, guys. I didn't see anyone. Where do we go from here?"

Angel started the engine. "Spot up by the ditch has a gravel bed like a pullover. When they were digging it out I suppose they put the heavy equipment and dump trucks there. We can see Denny's pretty well from there." He pulled out of the parking lot and down the narrow road pulling into the gravel. He turned the Jeep around and we faced the back parking lot of the eatery.

"It's going to be dark soon." James leaned forward, staring intently ahead.

"Those lot lights stay on pretty late," I said.

We sat there, at least one of us feeling pretty stupid. We were way out of our league, playing James Bond and not having a clue what we'd do if we did stumble on a hiding place. My gut reaction was that Vic was dead. The last time they found us stalking them, they warned us. This time they could do much worse.

"If we don't do this, they may kill us." James sounded like a continuation of my thoughts. "I mean, we all agree, right? The object is to find out if Vic Maitlin is alive or dead. Once we know, we'll have to report this whole thing." Pretty serious comment from a guy who hated the authorities.

"If we report it now, and Vic is alive, they may kill him. We know they've threatened to send more body parts to Fuentes." I was embarrassed at how we were trying to justify this escapade. We were nervous and scared, but I believe all three of us were raring to go. We finally had some adventure in our lives, something a little out of the norm.

"Hell, we should have just walked away from the whole thing." James lit up a cigarette.

"Five thousand dollars for a little stakeout, James.

Remember? A simple little job. Sure, Mr. Fuentes, we can do that."

He blew a stream of smoke at my head. "And Vic, Mr. Fuentes's son, saved your life, pardner. Correct me if I'm wrong."

Angel didn't react, but reached across me and opened the glove compartment. He pulled out a black leather case and opened it. "Binoculars."

The man had thought of everything.

"You said you wanted the complete package."

James tapped an ash out the window. "It's almost like you've done this before, amigo."

Angel put the glasses to his eyes and surveyed the area. Windows down, there was no breeze.

A hot, sticky, humid Miami night. My T-shirt was already sticking to my skin and I hoped we'd be moving soon. Anything to get the air circulating.

A white Cadillac swung around the back and pulled up to the trash can.

"Here we go, boys. He's getting out." Angel kept his gaze fixed on the car. "He's going up to it, standing there, looking both ways . . ." he paused.

We could see the guy on the far side of the car, but we couldn't make out what he was doing.

Angel kept the glasses steady, the long seconds stretching out.

" . . . and he's dumping an ashtray or something into it, and," he paused, "now he's pulling away."

I let out a long breath.

We were quiet for a minute or more.

"Do you ever think about death, Angel?" James spoke softly, as if afraid the insects buzzing outside might hear.

"Death?"

"Yeah. Do you ever wonder when you'll go. Or how? Skip

and I have talked about it, and it never has really registered. My dad died at a relatively young age, and it took me a while to get over it, but my own demise just never computed. I always assumed I'd live forever, or damned close to it." He let it hang out there.

Finally, Angel said, "And?"

"All of a sudden we're in a situation where our lives are being threatened. I'm starting to wonder when it's going to happen."

"You miss your father?"

"I do. There is so much I wish I'd asked him."

Angel stroked the steering wheel. "I never knew my father. And my mother walked out on my sister and me when I was fifteen. I've seen a lot of bad things. I've seen people die in a number of strange ways, and I've contemplated my own death. I have."

I picked up a strange feeling. "Angel, have you ever killed anyone?"

He was quiet and I felt I'd gone too far.

"Not unless they needed to be killed."

"I'm sorry I asked."

James jumped on it. "Does it bother you?"

"No. Old and young, we are all on our last cruise."

I finally had something to live for. Hell of a time to start contemplating death. I tried to avoid thinking about Angel killing people or my last cruise.

What looked like a black Ford Focus crept through the parking lot and Angel picked up his binoculars once again. The car slowed down and one of the kitchen help opened a rear door and walked out, her silhouette outlined by the light from the doorway. She appeared to lean down to the window of the car and converse with the driver for about thirty seconds. Finally she went back in and the car pulled out with a burst of speed and a squeal of tires. You could hear it from where we sat.

I could sense the tension in the Wrangler drop.

"Emily, the girl I met earlier, she's your girlfriend?" Angel watched my face, maybe for confirmation.

"Yeah. Sort of. It's a strange relationship."

"I believe they all are."

James tossed his cigarette out onto the gravel in a bright burst of spark and ash. "When this is over, I'm going to call Jackie again."

"Oh, really? I thought she said she wasn't interested."

"She never said that, pardner. She said her lawyer told her not to get interested. She thought I was cute."

"Yeah, well—oh, by the way, did you get the drift of the phone conversation I had with Fuentes?"

"I heard your half of it. Why?"

"He said something strange. He said that if Jackie had opened his mail, she would have found the finger, and we would have been off the hook."

"What's so strange about that. It's true."

"For a brief moment he sounded like he was pissed off she didn't open his mail. He actually asked her to open it and call him if there was something important. She didn't."

"I'm pissed off she didn't," James said. "We'd be back at the apartment, drinking a beer and eating Fritos, blissfully ignorant of this entire mess."

"This guy, Fuentes, he's been caught cheating on his wife. He moves into this condo with his little girlfriend and then asks his wife, Jackie, to open any mail that might mistakenly come her way? Why would he do that?"

"Mail never stops, Skip. I mean, my family moved one time and for two years people mailed stuff to the old address."

"Yeah, yeah. But Fuentes was begging his pissed-off ex-wife to open his personal mail. And he made a point to tell me that."

James pointed his finger at me. "You're making this into a big deal, pard. It's not."

The night was quiet. The faint smell of greasy fried food mixed with the brackish odor coming from the ditch wafted in the air.

A cream-colored Lexus swung around the corner of the restaurant and pulled up to the trash container. Angel watched through the glasses.

"A white guy, he's just stepped out. Polo shirt and khaki slacks, he's headed toward the container."

I couldn't make him out. It was getting dark and the lights from the lot at that distance were dim.

"He's talking to someone in the passenger side. Now the passenger is getting out. Can you see him?"

"I can see the passenger. Looks like he's stretching." Just a dim shadow. The binoculars would have made the picture much more clear.

James leaned forward staring through the windshield. "Are they waiting for someone? Looks like they're surveying the surroundings."

Angel kept the glasses trained on one spot. "Don't think so. He's struggling with something on the far side, I can't quite make out — there it is. He's got the garbage bag, he's looking into it. Now he's pulling the envelope out and —" I wished to hell I'd had better eyesight or else I had the glasses.

"The trunk is opening and he's laid the envelope inside. He's back in the car —" Angel lay the binoculars on my lap and started the engine. "Gentlemen, we're about to take a ride. Hang on tight. Let's see if we can stay with these guys."

CHAPTER FORTY-FIVE

I HAVE TO ADMIT I WAS SURPRISED. I thought we'd be pitting ourselves against the two Cubans in a blue Buick. Instead, we were following what appeared to be two new guys in an expensive luxury sedan. Everything was black and white, except the bad guys were in white and we were in black. And maybe that was good, because black makes a great disguise at night.

"I was a caddy at a country club when I was young." Angel kept both hands on the wheel, staying well behind the Lexus as it cruised at a safe speed toward the highway.

"You?" James seemed surprised.

"Yes. I was quite good."

"So you know the game." I'd played golf before but I didn't have the patience for it.

"I don't play. But there are two basic rules when you caddy. Understand the lay of the land and keep your eye on the ball."

"And your point is?" James leaned forward.

Angel looked over his shoulder. "Watch where we are going and keep your eye on the Lexus."

"Ah."

It wasn't difficult. The Lexus rode the entrance ramp and thirty seconds later we followed.

"They're heading toward Miami." James was getting with the program.

I wondered how much Angel knew. "You agreed to get involved with this without knowing much about the situation, Angel."

"It's about Cuba."

"Yeah. I don't know how much you want to know, but it's about arming soldiers to take Castro out."

"My friend, it's been tried many times before." Angel looked pensive. "Do you know what Castro wants most of all," Angel asked.

I knew. "He wants his brand of Communism to succeed. It's been the entire focus of his revolution."

Angel was quiet, watching the car ahead, but staying a respectable distance behind. "Castro gave up on his Communism long ago. When the Soviet Union folded, Castro understood that Communism would not work in his country. Fidel is building a new economy based on tourism. People from Europe, Canada, other Caribbean countries are all flocking to his country. They spend dollars, Cuba invests in new resorts, but the United States won't allow its citizens to participate."

"Wait a minute." I couldn't let him go unchallenged. "Are you suggesting that Castro is a capitalist?"

"No. I'm stating that fact. Granted, he makes it work for the party rather than for the people, but little by little the people are understanding how to make capitalism work for them."

James chimed in. "So why get rid of him? His life is on the decline. Why not let nature take it's course? He's going to kick off soon. He's in his late seventies, isn't he?"

Angel nodded. "He'll die soon. Old and young, we're all on our last cruise."

The Lexus did about seventy and Angel was about five car lengths behind. Occasionally he'd let a car get in front, then pass it a mile or so up the road. Just a normal guy trying to get to the city without attracting attention.

"Castro wants a legacy. Right now his revolution has failed. That is not the way he wants to be remembered. To be a hero, he must get the United States to repeal their embargo. Not to mention the billions of American dollars he will reap."

It made sense. If Castro was able to open tourism to the United States, then he could also open trade. It would be his final victory and the Cuban people could point to his leadership as the beginning of a new Cuba.

"But Miami is a stumbling block. *Los Historicos* want two things. They want Castro to fail so that he will have no positive legacy. His history will be littered with failure. And they want their property back. They want their farms and factories and homes. As long as Fidel Castro is in power, neither of those things can happen. So, the good Cubans of Miami and South Florida keep the pressure on. They threaten elections here in the United States, they fund revolutionary groups who promise to take Cuba back, and for a small band of patriots, they cause a great deal of international turmoil. They will not let Castro be victorious."

James asked from the backseat, "Do you know what's happening with the mail that we're chasing?"

"Maybe. Maybe the less I know, the better. But it would appear that you've gotten yourselves into a Cuban jam. If you are involved with radicals who want to take back the island, you may have bitten off more than you can chew."

I stared straight ahead. I knew the lay of the land and watched the white Lexus as it signaled for an exit.

"Should we be for or against an invasion?"

"I think the United States should stay out of it. That's what I think."

"You're in this almost as deep as we are, Angel. Do you want to get out?"

He smiled. "I live for this adventure."

"We could all be putting our lives on the line."

"I know. They threatened us with guns. I haven't forgotten. Emerson wrote, 'A good indignation brings out all one's powers.' I would think that all three of us should be indignant and, with our combined powers, we should be invincible."

CHAPTER FORTY-SIX

So I KNEW NOTHING about world affairs. We all knew that Cubans living in South Florida had a strong lobby. And we all knew that when Castro finally abdicated the throne it could be a boon to all of us who were within a stone's throw of the island. James and I had even discussed a restaurant in Havana. We were stoned or drunk at the time, but I remember talking about it. But now I'd been briefed by a genuine Caribbean, a Bahamian, someone who understood the politics of the region and I realized I didn't know what I thought I knew. It had never affected my life before. Now, I wondered if it could affect my death.

The Lexus veered to the right and took an exit into downtown Miami. Angel smoothly followed, winding past palms and brush, and turning under the highway. There was no reason for the two men in the Lexus to be concerned. Three other vehicles pulled off at the same time.

"Do you know the area?" James obviously didn't.

Angel's face was grim. "Industrial. About twelve blocks up is the Miami River. Shipping, warehousing."

We could see the car leading us in the next block. Now there was just the Jeep and the Lexus. We drove by boarded-up buildings and a commercial dry cleaning establishment. At this hour of the night there wasn't much happening. Angel turned right and the Lexus went straight.

"Whoa!" James shouted from the backseat. "Angel, man, he's going the other way."

"I'm going to go up one block, then cut back in. Just in case he noticed us following him."

I looked at the black guy with admiration. "You *have* done this before, haven't you?"

He gave me a little smile. One block up he cut left to the main road, then right. Now the white car was two blocks up, but well in sight.

James clapped his hands. "Bravo, Mario Andretti. Your driving skills are to be admired."

The buildings were now all concrete block or vinyl and metal siding. I could make out cranes and heavy construction equipment for almost an entire block, and I could smell the water. An iodine, rotting seaweed, and decaying fish odor mixed with an oily smell, the kind you associate with diesel engines.

We drove three more blocks and I could see the end of the street. The Lexus's headlights bounced off a metal guardrail with diagonal red-striped tape and Angel pulled over and killed the lights.

"Too close. We'll see if he goes right or left, then we'll pick him up."

He turned right.

The taillights had just cleared the corner when Angel pulled out from the curb. He flipped on the lights and raced to the dead end. As he eased out, we all three peered down the side street that ran along the water to the right. There was absolutely no sign of the Lexus.

CHAPTER FORTY-SEVEN

Angel inched down the street as we stared into the gloom, watching for driveways, entrances, or side streets. There was no Lexus in sight. Glancing to the left I saw the river, lights from the highway that ran above casting shimmering yellow and white snakes on the inky black surface. We could make out crumbling concrete curbs and a one-story stucco building with piles of weathered wooden lobster traps stacked next to it. On a warped piece of plywood someone had painted *Miami River Lobster and Stone Crab*. Dark clouds covered the moon and stars, and the entire atmosphere was claustrophobic.

"Maybe he noticed us and pulled off up ahead." James was concerned.

"And maybe going down this street, we're driving into an ambush." Now there was something I never thought I'd say.

"Gentlemen, be patient. I feel certain the two men had no idea they were being followed. And I feel confident that if they're here, we'll find them."

We were quiet, creeping through the deserted neighborhood, watching for some sign of activity. The moon broke through for a moment and I could see an old rusted fishing trawler rolling with the current. *The Peggy Anne.* Ghostly, gutted buildings on sagging frames threatened to collapse into the river at any moment, and dark shadows played along the bank.

Five minutes at ten miles an hour and we were beyond the warehouse district. It was obvious we'd lost them.

"Man, it would have been a great break."

"James, think about it. The last time we staked out a building we were warned. Now we know these guys play rough."

"I know, amigo, but remember, Angel brought the complete package."

"Jesus, let's not get into shooting people again. All we want to do is find Vic, report the story, and go home."

Angel pulled into a drive, turned around, and we headed back the opposite way. "This Vic? He was a childhood friend?"

"Sort of. We didn't know him that well. He was the kind of kid everybody looked up to. President of student council, big shot football player, good student, and looks to kill. His dad is Rick Fuentes."

James chimed in. "You left out the part about his girlfriend. And the fact that he apparently is responsible for you being alive today."

I ignored part of the sentence. "Vic dated Emily when we were in school. For a very short time, I might add."

"And," James continued, "we're hoping he wasn't killed in that fire."

We drove slowly down the street, still not believing that we'd lost them. Their car was going to pull out onto the street at any second.

It didn't happen. Angel kept it slow. The occasional halogen lamp spilled light into a deserted parking lot outside a small factory or warehouse, and then we were back to the street we had driven in on.

"We can go back to Carol City and admit defeat. We can go back and hope that the Cubans will leave us alone, and maybe they will." Angel took a deep breath. "Or we can try one more time."

"What are we going to see that we haven't seen?"

"Probably nothing. But we can try."

"Nah. We lost them, Angel." James figured we'd given it a shot.

Angel spun the Jeep around and headed back down the street one more time. No Lexus.

"Give it up, man." I was tired, and it wasn't going to be a good idea to take tomorrow off from work. I'd already blown off several appointments and an entire day. The only good thing about my job was that losing it wasn't the end of the world. And I was afraid it would come to that.

Angel picked up the speed and we headed back the other way. Forty minutes later or less we'd be back at the apartment. I wondered if Em could sleep. She had to be thinking about the baby, and when things bothered her, they really bothered her.

"Angel," James called from the backseat. "Stop. Back up. About three properties."

Angel put it in reverse and eased it back.

"Slow down. Right here."

Absolutely no Lexus.

"Look down between the two buildings."

The two low-roofed buildings were blue corrugated metal, and a dim floodlight mounted on a pole highlighted a small parking area. Between the two buildings I could barely make out a forklift. "James, there's no Lexus."

"Angel, do me a favor. Stop right here and kill the lights."

Angel pulled into a gravel parking lot and shut the engine off.

"Let's walk up there. Just humor me."

We walked slowly, no traffic or people in sight, just dim shadows.

"What the hell did you see?" I couldn't see anything.

"Up ahead."

Angel looked back over his shoulder. The Jeep almost disappeared in the dark.

"I thought I saw movement. Honest to God. Like someone going between buildings. I figured if there are people here at this hour of the night, maybe the car is here."

"Quite an imagination, James."

He shot me a look. "You got a better idea?"

We walked down between the two buildings, about fifteen feet apart. The yellow forklift was parked close to the outside wall. It was old and beat up, the yellow paint chipped and faded, and the fork tines themselves looked worn and shiny.

"There." James walked up to the building. "A door, right here." He was whispering. "And right over here, a door on the other building. I knew I saw something. Someone went from one building to the other."

We looked at each other. It meant nothing.

"Ah, fuck it. I thought maybe—" He drifted off. I started back to the Jeep.

"Skip!" A loud, course whisper. James was pointing wildly, beyond the forklift.

I walked back and followed him. Seven car lengths from the forklift the dark sedan sat against the wall, passenger side out. The dark blue paint was scratched to the bare metal, and swatches of white streaked across the surface. The top of the car was severely dented and the windshield had a crack from top to bottom. It appeared that in the battle of the box truck versus the Buick, the truck had won.

CHAPTER FORTY-EIGHT

The Cubans' Buick sat there in plain sight and a line from *The Pit and the Pendulum* came to mind.

> *A fearful idea now suddenly drove the blood in torrents upon my heart, and for a brief period, I once more relapsed into insensibility.*

There. I'd like to see James, Angel, or Em identify that line. But it was true. I lost all sensibility and felt my heart beating about triple speed.

James rubbed his fingers over the white scratches. "Sons of bitches."

Angel smiled and in a hoarse whisper said, "I recognize the car. The Cubans with the gun. So," he looked around, "the white car must be in one of these buildings."

"And what are we supposed to do? Just open the doors and see for ourselves?" This Hardy Boy fantasy was getting the best of me. Actually, the idea of looking inside didn't sound bad.

No one answered.

"All right, we came to find Victor. If it wasn't his body in the burned-out building, my guess is he's inside one of these. I suggest we sit in the Jeep and wait. For maybe an hour. Let's see if there's any activity. It's almost midnight. Let's give it till one o'clock."

We walked back to the Jeep and Angel parked it in the next lot. From there we could see the two metal buildings and just get a glimpse of the space between them. If the Buick or the Lexus left, it had to drive out the front.

We waited. Three amateur sleuths not knowing what we'd do if we found our evidence. The biggest fear was thinking we might not find it. We were silent for ten minutes. Across the street on the river was a beat-up ocean trawler, probably loaded with bicycles and used automobiles, ready to head down to South America, while up ahead was the gleaming tower that is the Four Seasons Hotel. Construction cranes sprouted up everywhere around the skyline, rising into the black sky like shadowy robots. Em called Miami "Crane Town."

"I may be sick again tomorrow, pal."

I laughed. "James, you pull it off better than I do. I try to sound sick and I come off like a bad actor in a high school play."

"You were *in* the senior play, pardner. And if I remember, you weren't convincing at all. Lieutenant Cable in *South Pacific*, right?"

"How about you, Angel?" I decided to probe.

"What? Was I in a high school play?"

"No. Do you work? Have a job?"

He didn't answer.

We spent three or four minutes in embarrassing silence, the stifling heat and lack of a breeze closing in on us.

"Maybe we should call Fuentes," James said. "We could ask him for some overtime."

I thought about calling Emily. I needed to tell her that she didn't need to go through this alone. So I was immature, I didn't have a future, and hung around with questionable characters, but it didn't make me a bad person. Deep inside you know who you are, you know what kind of a person you are or what you expect to become. I was going to be successful. Wildly successful. It just wasn't something that I'd figured out yet. I don't know if it's age or experience that eventually gets you to that point in your life, but I knew, and I know now, that I will be successful. And in the back of my mind I believed I could be a good father. I would be a good father. No question.

"Self-employed."

"What?" I'd been lost in thought.

"You asked what I did." Angel reached for the binoculars, took them from their case, and trained them on the buildings.

Another ten minutes went by and I wiped the perspiration from my eyes.

"I wasn't that bad an actor. Hell, I got an award for outstanding senior in the school play."

"Yeah. However, if I remember, Heidi Moose was the only other senior who had a lead and her rendition of Bloody Mary was abysmal at best."

"Abysmal?"

"She sucked."

I checked my watch. If we left at one, were in bed by two, I could get about five hours of sleep.

I could deal with that. I had to hang on to the security sales job. At least till the next best thing came along or until I was wildly successful.

"James, if you call in sick—you'll still have a job?"

"Shit. Lindsey isn't going to fire me. The last time I was with her she told me I was the best thing that ever happened to her."

"You and Lindsey?'

He shrugged his shoulders. "Something to pass the time, Skip."

"Someone just stepped outside."

Angel handed me the glasses. I strained to see in the dim light. I could make out a man carrying a briefcase. He stood by the forklift, looking around. Instinctively, I slid lower in my seat.

"What?" James leaned forward. I handed him the binoculars.

"Probably one of the men who picked up the mail."

"I say we call Fuentes and let him come down here and check it out." James didn't sound as confident as he should have. "Really, Skip. Tell him we found the place and let's get out of here."

"You forget one thing, James. Fuentes told us to drop off the envelope and leave the entire thing alone. He was adamant about that."

"Shit."

A heavy cloudbank broke and for just a moment the moon lit up the area like daylight. I could see the guy with the briefcase motioning to someone inside the doorway and a second later the ribbed steel door in front of the building groaned and started rolling up. I reached back and retrieved the binoculars.

"That is one huge overhead door." It was sliding up, exposing a massive opening. Now the clouds covered the moon, but lights burned inside and the glow spilled into the parking lot. I could see the white Lexus on the concrete floor, headlights on, ready to leave the building.

"What's stacked up in there?" James pointed toward the opening.

I concentrated but could only tell they looked like wooden crates. "Boxes."

Angel took the glasses and looked at the scene for a minute.

Three men were standing around the car having an animated conversation. With our windows down we could hear voices but nothing specific.

Angel handed the glasses back to me. "Do you recognize anyone," he said softly.

I concentrated. "The guy on the far left looks like one of our Cuban friends."

"That's what I thought. The one I didn't shoot." Angel chuckled.

I handed the glasses back to James.

"That's him. Jesus, I wouldn't forget that guy. He drove the car when they banged up the truck."

He handed them back to me. I put them to my eyes and continued to watch.

"I don't know that we're going to figure anything out from back here." James was ready to leave. I wasn't going to argue. Other than finding the warehouse, I wasn't sure what this trip was going to prove. The three men shook hands and stepped back.

"Shit. Wait a minute. The big guy was the driver. The tall guy on the right, sitting in the chair—" I handed the glasses back to James. "Look hard, James. Very hard."

He took his time. "Yeah. Some tall—oh, fuck. That can't be. Nah, we haven't seen him in—"

"About five years? Hair's a little longer, he looks a little heavier—I'm not sure, but I think that's him, James. If it's not him, the guy could be his brother."

"Jesus. Vic Maitlin. We've found him."

CHAPTER FORTY-NINE

Of course I saw him for five more years — all during high school — but right after the sinkhole incident, he avoided me. If I was walking in the hall, Vic would stop and talk to someone else, making it obvious he didn't want to have to converse with me. He seemed almost embarrassed about what had happened. I built scenarios in my head. I thought maybe the goon squad, Cramer and Stowe, had threatened him, telling him not to ever talk about it, and to make sure I didn't. Or maybe he didn't want to be known as the guy who saved Skip Moore's life. But later, midway through the eighth grade, he made a point of stopping me after a class just to see how things were going. And from that point on we were okay. Not good friends, not social in any way, but okay. The last time I'd seen Vic was a couple of weeks after graduation. I ran into him at one of Jordan Trump's parties. He walked up and nodded.

"Everything came out all right."

I remember giving him a questioning glance.

He smiled. "Hey, we made it. We graduated. Everything

came out all right." He paused. "You know. Everything is good. I'm glad you're around."

I mumbled some response and he reached for my hand, the second time in his life. I offered it, and he squeezed it tight, shook, and walked away. I hadn't seen him since.

"Can you tell if anything is missing?"

James handed the glases back to me. "Nah. Too far away. Now I'm not sure it's him. It looks like he's either sitting on his hands or they're behind him. Could be tied up."

"Your friend doesn't seem to be missing a finger?"

I shook my head, having second thoughts. "We can't tell. And maybe it's not our friend."

"Damn, Skip, it sure looks like him."

The white car pulled away and the overhead door on the building rolled down. Clouds filtered across the moon and the parking lot was filled with eerie shadows and dim light. The three of us stayed low as the Lexus drove by us and made a turn down at the main street.

"If Fuentes's kid is alive, I think he'd like to know."

"It's gonna be tough, James. We weren't supposed to follow these guys."

"Well, shit. We did. Trouble is we don't know for sure if the kid we saw was Vic Maitlin. If it was, he's not the burned up body. If you had a kid, wouldn't you—ah, I'm sorry, Skip, you're about to have a kid. Shouldn't we tell Fuentes there's a chance his kid is alive?"

Angel shook his head from side to side. "You know nothing. You both admitted you weren't sure who it was. You're not sure of anything. What are you going to tell his father? Something that calms him? Maybe something that upsets him?" Angel sounded disgusted. "You know nothing."

I felt chastised. He was right, we couldn't call and tell him what we didn't know.

James tapped me on the shoulder. "I say we head back, pardner. It's late and I think the party is over."

I hesitated. "I want to know."

James shook his head. "No, compadre. Let's get away from this right now."

As long as this hung over our heads, we didn't know what kind of trouble we might be in. I wanted an answer, and the worst part was I didn't even know the question. I opened the door and stepped out. I started walking toward the building.

There's safety in numbers. However, no one followed me, and with the moon behind the clouds and the dim light as my only guide, I felt very much alone. If the guy in the warehouse was Vic, I wanted to know. I can't explain what drove me to make that walk. It wasn't a macho thing. It was a chance to make up for something that had haunted me for eleven years. And at the very least there was a father who thought his son might be dead. I was possibly in a position to prove that theory wrong.

The walk took forever. Finally, I stood between the buildings, staring at the door from which James had seen someone walk between the two structures. I turned the knob, knowing full well that it was a futile gesture. It most certainly was locked. Instead, the door handle rotated a half turn and the door opened on well-oiled hinges. So much for futile gestures.

It was time to put up or shut up. I eased it open and stuck my head around the door jamb, peering inside. The bright interior lights had been switched off and just a dim glow from some mounted wall fixtures covered the room. Thank God no one was in sight. Wooden crates lined the far wall and another forklift was parked in the center of the cavernous space. The floor was smooth gray cement, and I could make out a small glass-windowed office to my right at the far end. What the hell was I doing?

Here I was, playing the Lone Ranger and boldly taking on

my mission with no support from the troops. I couldn't just abandon the task and admit failure. I should have. But I didn't. I pushed farther and walked in, casting furtive glances in all directions. Everyone seemed to have vanished. To my immediate right stood five metal cylinders about four feet around and five feet tall. They looked like they contained some sort of gas, with escape valves and a faucet handle to turn them on or shut them off.

The room echoed with silence, and I stood still for a good minute, afraid that any motion would immediately alert the Cubans to my presence. Assuring myself that blue jeans and a black T-shirt would help me blend into the surroundings, I stepped behind the first cylinder, staying close to the wall and keeping track of how close I was to the door. For the first time, I glanced toward the ceiling, noticing a balcony that hung out over the back of the room. The protrusion extended maybe four feet into space and was surrounded by a railing. There was no one on the upper level, thank God.

It was eerily quiet, and when I heard the first voice it startled me. I jerked like I'd been shocked with electricity. To make matters worse, I didn't understand a word. Whoever was speaking was speaking in Spanish, and having taken two years of German in high school, I didn't have a clue what was being said.

Obviously they weren't speaking to me. I couldn't see anyone, but the voice was to my right. A second speaker answered and a conversation ensued. Instinctively I flattened myself against the wall.

I looked up again as someone turned on a bank of fluorescent lights, and at the far end of the balcony two men appeared, one smoking a cigar. They leaned against the railing and the older of the two was flicking ashes to the cement floor below. If they had looked toward the door, they would have seen me in an instant. A third man walked out of the office at the end of the room and motioned up to the two men. They disappeared and a moment later came walking out of the office. I assumed there were stairs in the back that I couldn't see.

Silently I cursed James, the truck, and whatever had gotten us into this confusing mess. The three conversationalists were lost in their dialogue and I was the last person who wanted to disturb them. They started walking toward my end of the building and I felt my heart jump. Crouching, I made every attempt to become one with the metal cylinder.

They stopped at the first set of wooden crates, almost directly across from me, and I recognized our Cuban friend as he pointed to the closest box. The man with the cigar picked up a crow bar from the floor and pried the top from the crate, puffing on his stogie the entire time. He tossed the lid onto the floor and reached inside. I realized I was holding my breath.

He pulled out a long metal object, partially hidden by their three bodies. I had a good idea of what it was before he turned and held it to the light, admiring its sleek lines and form. I knew nothing about firearms, but this appeared to be some sort of a high-tech rifle, not the kind you'd go hunting with in the woods. I let out my breath. Boxes and boxes of rifles. Enough for a small army.

They turned to the boxes, their backs to me.

It was time to get the hell out of Dodge. Practically dragging my feet, I measured my distance to the door. I slid silently, afraid that actual footsteps would resonate throughout the hollow building. I could sense rather than see the door, and I was sure that with two more steps I would be within reaching distance. It was at that moment my phone blared "Born in the USA" at full volume.

CHAPTER FIFTY

I GRABBED FOR IT, yanking it out of my pocket as I reached the door. I was tempted to throw it on the ground and run, but I took one extra second just to see who the hell was calling me at the most critical time in my life. I couldn't explain then, and I can't explain now, why I would have checked the caller's number, but I did. And as I twisted the door handle, pulled it open, and ran, I could hear the angry shouts from inside. I fully expected to be tackled from behind or have someone firing bullets at my back, but what surprised me more than anything was the gunshot from in front of me. One shot, a cracking sound like someone with a whip, then two more shots and I hit the pavement, just as the floodlight went dark.

Glass shattered and rained down around me onto the parking lot surface, and looking ahead I could see headlights flashing a rapid off and on pattern. I stumbled to my feet and ran again, my legs pumping like pistons, my chest heaving, gasping for air. How far was the damned Jeep. The passenger door was wide open and I leaped in as Angel tromped on the gas. We shot out of the parking lot and hit the road doing at least forty.

"I put a little extra in the engine." Angel smiled in the dim light.

My breathing was ragged and I couldn't get enough air into my lungs. Feeling like I might throw up, I leaned out the window, looking behind us. There was no sign of anyone following.

I gulped humid night air into my oxygen-starved chest and said nothing.

"Great shooting, Angel." James reached out and patted the driver on the shoulder. "Hey, amigo, Angel shot out the floodlight. Trying to give you a little cover while you made your escape."

I wanted to thank him, but all I could do was inhale.

"So what the hell did you see? And who saw you?"

I waved James off. If I talked in the next minute I knew I'd go into a coughing fit.

We were all quiet for that minute; the only sound was me trying to suck up all the air in the car. God, I was out of shape. This was the wake-up call. It was time to exercise, eat right, and lay off the beer.

Angel hit the main road back to the highway and I stared straight ahead as he blew through the first stop sign, and the second, and then a red light that I didn't remember from before. I glanced at the sideview mirror about eighty times and never saw the first sign of another vehicle. We finally got to the entrance ramp to I-95 and I could breathe a little slower. Maybe I'd just cut back a *little* on the beer and just exercise occasionally. No reason to make a radical change.

"Guns."

"What?" James didn't understand.

"That's what was in the boxes. Guns. Rifles. Sleek-looking rifles. If I knew anything about rifles, I'd say they looked like they were automatic with long clips. But I don't have a clue. All I know is, there are boxes and boxes of the black things and they had one out when I ran. I don't know why they didn't shoot me."

"They weren't loaded." Angel, with the complete package, probably knew a whole lot more than I ever will about guns. "Some of those boxes probably contained ammunition."

"I'm telling you, Angel, they could start their own army with all those weapons."

James leaned forward. "They probably have."

I glanced over at the speedometer and saw Angel was doing about eighty miles an hour. Given the hour, he probably figured the cops had better places to be.

"Okay, pardner, what happened while you were in there?"

I took a deep breath, feeling weak and somewhat disoriented. "How long was I in there?"

"Five minutes. Damn, it seemed like an hour, but Angel timed you."

I told them about the cylinders, the boxes of guns, the balcony, and the three men.

"So it was the second Cuban?" Angel asked.

"No doubt. But I didn't recognize the other two men and I didn't see Vic. Maybe we were wrong."

"Maybe." James was cautious. "If it was Vic, my guess is they took him away in the Lexus."

"Well, I didn't see him. The three guys opened one of the crates and pulled out this black rifle and my phone went off."

"What?"

"My phone. I swear it's going on vibrate tonight and I will never program another song for a ringtone. Bruce Springsteen almost cost me my life."

"It went off while you were in there?"

"Are you listening? It went off. Loud."

"And what did they do?"

I shook my head. "Jesus, James. I didn't stick around to find out. You saw the result. I think I ran the hundred in ten flat."

"Who was it?"

"I looked. Habit. Look down and see who's calling. All the time I'm thinking, 'This is going to slow me down. They're going to catch me because I'm checking the number on my cell phone.' "

"Em. Had to be."

I thought of her for a moment. I was convinced that the kid almost lost a father tonight, and the thought made me sad. I at least wanted to meet the baby when he came into the world. All the work his father had done so far was pure pleasure and I needed some of the angst, pain, and agony to make it a real experience. I should probably quit putting myself in such dangerous situations.

"No. It wasn't Em. It was Rick Fuentes."

"Fuentes almost got you killed?"

"Caller ID said Rick Fuentes." I pulled the phone from my pocket, punched in my code and listened.

"You have one unheard message. First message."

"Eugene Moore? This is Rick Fuentes. I hadn't heard anything, and I'm hoping you took the mail to the designated spot. Once again, I'm sorry you are involved and it will be much better for everyone concerned if you now just walk away."

"Fuentes wants to know if we dropped off the mail, and he wants us to wash our hands of the entire affair. What else is new?"

James piped up from the backseat. "I think that suits me just fine. We can bill him for the overtime and finish with this whole mess."

I looked back over my shoulder. "You got us into this, James. And now we stumble on Vic or someone who looks like him. I want to know if he's still alive. And, we've just staked out the headquarters of this organization and we—*I* was found out. That doesn't let us just 'finish with this whole mess.' "

Angel kept both hands clamped to the wheel. "You're right.

You are now a prime target, and you have to finish what you set out to do."

"Christ, I've lost sight of what we set out to do."

"Find your school friend. You were hired to find out where he is. This Vic."

Headlights filled the side mirror as a lone vehicle rapidly approached. Angel hit the gas, approaching a hundred miles per hour and the vehicle kept coming, gaining by the second.

I watched our speedometer hit one hundred and five. What was it Angel said? " I put a little extra in the engine." One ten and climbing.

The car behind us spurted around Angel's Jeep like we were standing still and continued down the highway, it's taillights winking in the dark black night.

I caught my breath for the third or fourth time that night. If someone didn't shoot me, beat me to death, or kill me in some other way, I knew I'd die from a heart attack or nervous exhaustion.

"I think tonight you should stay with me." Angel was calm and straightforward. "They don't know where I live."

"Neither do we." James put his hands on the back of my seat. "Friend, I thank you, but I think we've gotten you in enough trouble. Besides, I've got a job. And I assume that Skip needs to get to work tomorrow too. I don't think we're going to hear from these people again."

"Where do you live?" I was intrigued.

"If you're not going to visit tonight, you have no need for that information." Angel kept his eyes on the road and his foot on the gas. I couldn't wait to get home and hit the pillow.

CHAPTER FIFTY-ONE

"YOU HAVE AN INCOMING MESSAGE. You have an incoming message. You have an incoming message."

I blindly reached for the phone, interested more in shutting off the obnoxious alarm-clock voice than in hearing from a caller at the ungodly hour of five in the morning. The phone read "unknown caller."

"It's five o'clock in the morning. This had better be good."

"Skip Moore?"

"Yeah."

"Skip, this is Jackie Fuentes."

The lady who started this whole mess. Well, actually Em started it by suggesting we help clean out Jackie's house. No, James started it because he bought the cursed truck, but Jackie was high on my list of people to blame.

I didn't say anything. It was her call.

"Skip?"

"Mrs. Fuentes, I'm very tired. I had a rough night last night —" I wanted to say something about the mail and looking for her kidnapped stepson but I didn't.

"I know."

"You what?"

"We need to talk. You, Emily, and your friend."

"James?"

"Yes."

"Listen, Mrs. Fuentes, if you want any of that stuff back, we don't have it."

"When can we talk? This morning?"

Apparently people with money have no concept of working for a living.

"I've got to be at work in three hours, Mrs. Fuentes. That leaves another two hours of sleep, if I can get back to sleep, and one hour to get ready."

"Skip, this is very important."

Now she was pissing me off. "So is my income."

She was quiet for a moment. "What time do you get off work?"

"I'll be home by six."

"And James?"

"Usually works from ten to seven."

"Can you please meet me at my house tonight? Around eight?"

I looked at my watch. Fifteen hours. I had trouble figuring out the next three hours.

"Sure."

"I'll have Emily here and we can discuss this situation. Thank you."

I lay on the bed, my hands behind my head, staring at the ceiling. There was no way in hell I was going back to sleep. And if I couldn't sleep, the son of a bitch that got me into this mess shouldn't be blissfully sleeping. I got up and walked into his room.

"James."

He rolled over and looked at me through squinting eyes.

"One of your girlfriends just called."

"Called you?"

"Yeah. Apparently you're unlisted."

"Who?"

"Some girl named Jackie Fuentes."

His eyes widened, and he sat up. "What the hell did she want?"

"To apologize for not going to dinner with a stud like you. She wants to make up for it by seeing you tonight at eight."

He got this shit-eating smile on his face. "No kidding?"

"Well, she would like Emily and me to be there too. It seems there's some sort of a situation she'd like to discuss."

His face fell. "Wouldn't you like to go back to that first day, Skip? And just turn down the Fuentes job?"

"Come on, James. Think Penske, U-Haul, Ryder."

"Fuck you." He rolled over and pulled the pillow over his head.

I walked out into the tiny kitchen and thought about coffee. Instead, I pulled out a beer. Budweiser, breakfast of champions. I could feel tightness in my thighs and calves and remembered running for my life last night. I also remembered swearing off beer.

I sat on the back porch, sipping my beer, and watching the first pink fingers of color stretch over the sky. Red sky in the morning, sailors take warning.

The old man behind us stepped out the back door, looked at me suspiciously, and nodded. He picked up the blanket on the empty playpen and replaced it with a new one, then walked back inside.

I took a long swallow and leaned back, watching the sky turn colors. I closed my eyes and opened them forty-five minutes later.

CHAPTER FIFTY-TWO

I MADE A SALE. Not only did they sign on the bottom line, but the young couple put down two hundred bucks. I was surprised anyone in Carol City had two hundred dollars in cash. And this *was* cash.

I called the order in and Sammy actually put the phone down on his desk and applauded so I could hear him. I was embarrassed for him.

"Skipper," he was bubbling over, "I knew you could do it. See? And these aren't the only people out there. You watch. Your sales are going to start soaring."

I made two more calls and decided to blow off the rest of the afternoon. I'd tried Em's number but got her voicemail three times. Then she called me.

"Skip, you called."

"How are you feeling?"

"Sick. I'm seeing a doctor tomorrow."

"Good." I didn't know what else to say.

"Jackie called this morning."

"Yeah. Does she always get up at five in the morning?"

"She sounded frantic. I have the impression someone called her and she was shook up."

"Em, are you going to her place tonight?"

"Sure."

"Assuming this meeting breaks up at a decent hour, do you want to go out and—"

"And what? Mess around? I'm not up to it Skip."

"Em, we need to talk some more. I've had some time to get used to this."

"Get used to this? Oh, good. I'm glad you're used to it, Skip because I'm not used to it. How do you ever get used to it?"

"Well, I mean I'm not used to it but—"

"Skip, I don't feel like talking to you or anyone about this. I'll see you at Jackie's tonight." She hung up the phone.

Obviously she was going through some emotional thing that I didn't understand, and I was being shut out, which bothered me. Besides, she was sick every day and that couldn't be too pleasant. I don't know why God had women take all the crap that goes with childbearing, but I'm glad He did. I don't think men would be strong enough to handle it.

James came home dragging ass. "Long day, bro." He threw himself down on the stained sofa and closed his eyes.

"It's going to be longer, James. I have a feeling that this meeting with Jackie Fuentes isn't going to be pleasant."

"What do you suppose she wants?"

I walked to the refrigerator and grabbed two beers, handing one to him. "Obviously it's something to do with her husband. And probably the mail. And I feel certain the Cubans will come into the conversation."

"And let's not forget Vic. Our classmate will probably figure predominantly in this meeting." Swallowing about half his beer, James belched. "Shit, we gotta leave here in ten minutes if we're going to make the powwow. I'll splash some water on my face and we'll get out of here.

"We'll take my car?"

"Good idea. I think the truck needs oil, and every once in a while there's some sort of rattling sound."

"Our future."

"Yeah. Once we get this behind us, we'll just be a little more selective in what we haul." He went into the bathroom and came out a minute later, looking as ragged as he had when he went in.

The drive took longer than I expected due to a tractor trailer accident on I-95, but when I finally got through the gatehouse and pulled into Jackie's drive, Emily was just getting out of her T-Bird.

"Do you know how good you look?" She wore khaki cargo pants and a halter top that showed a lot of skin.

"As a matter of fact, I do," she frowned. "God knows enough guys tell me on a daily basis. It gets a little old." She nodded to James. "Asshole."

"Em."

She walked ahead of us, past a Lexus SUV and a BMW 325i, to the back door of the house. She rang the bell and Jackie Fuentes answered, wearing a pair of faded jeans and an orange blouse, her hair pulled back and tied with a matching piece of orange cloth. The housemaid look did nothing to detract from her beauty.

Jackie escorted us down the hall that James and I had walked back and forth about forty times, and into a small library, complete with built-in bookshelves, a stone fireplace, and what looked like a custom-designed desk. It occurred to me that for two guys who made next to nothing and were up to their eyeballs in debt, we were seeing a lot of how the other half lived.

"I needed to talk to all three of you together." We sat in leather chairs, sipping brandy from small glasses. No shit.

Brandy. She poured the drinks from this fancy glass decanter, and even though I'd never tasted it before, I think I sipped it like a pro. James, on the other hand, downed his in two gulps and kept eyeing the decanter. Emily drank Evian. One of the reasons she might be upset with me was that she couldn't drink liquor for the next nine months. There was probably more to it than that.

"This was going to be a simple job. I wanted you to haul my husband's possessions out of this house and deposit them in a storage unit. In retrospect, I probably should have hired a professional moving company." She paused and leveled her gaze at James. "Hell, there's no *probably*. I should have hired someone who could drive a truck. Obviously you can't do that."

My roommate cringed.

"You couldn't back up a truck, and you have gotten us all into more trouble than even I can imagine." She took another sip, poured herself another glassful, and ignored James's pleading look.

Em spoke up. "What brought all this on, Jackie? We told you what happened. The guys are just starting out and—"

"First of all, I guess I mentioned to you," she pointed to Em, "that I thought Rick might be mixed up with a terrorist organization."

"You said something to that effect."

"Well, I'll stick by that story. Only now we know what kind of terrorist organization."

"Cubans," James said.

"Cubans who don't care how they get what they want. They dismember people, kill people, blow up buildings, and threaten those of us who just want to be left alone."

It didn't make sense. "Why are they threatening you?"

"Because my husband—soon to be my ex-husband—heard that I was going to call the authorities."

"Huh?"

"I had mentioned to another friend that I suspected Rick was involved in some terrorist organization. This was after my husband and I pretty much abandoned any hope of reconciling our differences. I told this person that I was considering calling the CIA."

"Wow."

"I've been getting phone calls in the last couple of days threatening me. Telling me that if I report any suspicions to the authorities not only will Vic be killed, but I'll be on a hit list as well."

Em sat her bottled water down on the side table by her chair and stood up, tugging her top to make sure it didn't slip. "That's some serious shit, Jackie. But we had nothing to do with any of it. If anything, we've been threatened as well, and we never suggested reporting what we know."

A bell rang somewhere in the house and Jackie stood up, holding up a hand as if to quiet us. She walked out of the room and we looked at each other, not knowing exactly what to say. Inside of thirty seconds she reappeared, a man in his thirties trailing her.

"This is William Krueger, CIA."

He nodded. Krueger looked official enough. He had a buzz cut, open-collar blue shirt, and a tan sport coat and slacks. His shoes were layered with a coating of shiny wax, and when he grabbed my hand I winced, certain that he'd broken a finger.

"Mr. Krueger is with the CIA in Miami. He contacted me about a week ago, and—"

I broke in. "You never contacted the CIA yourself? After your threat?"

"As I was saying, Skip, he contacted me. Right, William?"

"Yeah." Slow. Something about the delivery of the one word.

"He told me that there was some concern about my husband's business." She nodded to Krueger.

"Yeah. I told her we were investigating some of the dollars he was raising and some of the people he was hanging out with. She shared quite a bit with me."

"So you think Rick Fuentes is involved in this attempt to unseat Castro?"

"No. Not anymore. We feel that with the kidnapping of his son, he's only going through the motions to protect his kid."

"So what do you suggest we do?"

"Drop everything. Don't involve yourself anymore."

"Last night—"

"We know. You visited a warehouse down by the water. Forget whatever you saw."

James stammered, "B-But we think we may have seen Vic, Rick's son. And we saw—Skip saw guns."

Krueger nodded. "Drop it. Don't tell anyone what you've seen and don't try to see anymore. We'll take it from here. Mrs. Fuentes here has her life on the line, and so do you. Don't push it any further, got it?"

James shook his head up and down vigorously.

"Do you have identification?" I wasn't comfortable with the guy.

"I'm not getting through to you, am I?" He reached into his back pocket and pulled out a wallet. He flashed a badge and stared at me, slipping the wallet back into his rear pocket. "This is serious stuff, kid. Don't fuck with me."

"How do you know where we were last night?"

"We know. That's what we do, we get information. We're the Central Intelligence Agency. Intelligence. Understand?" He stood up and walked toward the door, turning to us for a final word. Or two. "Pretend you never heard of Rick Fuentes. Pretend you don't know his son Vic. If you continue to involve yourselves, you're not only putting Vic in danger, you're putting yourselves in danger."

"Mr. Krueger," James finally got some backbone, "Vic is already in danger. If it wasn't him we saw last night, there's a good chance he's dead."

"Then forget about Vic." Krueger smiled a disingenuous smile. "Worry about yourselves, because you're in danger right now. You could walk out the door of this house and never even make it to your cars. Understand?" He turned the corner and we could hear him walking down the hallway. We understood. To some of us, it didn't make any difference, but all four of us understood.

CHAPTER FIFTY-THREE

"YOU HAVE THE RIGHT TO REMAIN SILENT, so shut the fuck up. If you can't afford an attorney we'll find the dumbest son of a bitch on earth to represent you." James flicked his ashes on the cement and drained his second beer. I could have told him it was from *Lethal Weapon 4*, but I wasn't in the mood.

"It's not funny, James. The CIA is involved and apparently we could get in even deeper than we are."

"Deeper?" James was close to shouting. "Christ, Skip, they were already trying to kill us. How much deeper can we get?"

"Yeah. And are we running for our lives?"

"We should be scared shitless."

"And we're not."

"We're invincible, amigo. We think about death but we don't seriously believe it's going to happen to us."

"Is that it?"

"I don't know. I'd like to know what happened to Vic." He popped number three, and handed me my second.

"Me, too. I'm tired of getting the runaround from everybody." Especially from Em, although I didn't want to admit that to James.

"Speaking of runarounds, was Emily giving you the run-around tonight?"

"What?"

"I noticed she wouldn't talk to you when you spoke, and she pretty much ignored you the rest of the time."

"Yeah. She thinks I'm immature, have no future, and I've got a jerk for a roommate. I'm not husband material. Apparently not father material either."

"Jesus. I wasn't serious last night when I said that."

He was. "*She* was. I think she wants to distance herself."

"From you?"

"Seems to be the plan."

"Sorry, pard."

"So do we call Fuentes? Forget about what the CIA guy said?"

James stared into the darkness, waving his cigarette, making a bright orange arc in the air. We were both quiet for a moment.

"We've got another party involved here." He sipped his beer.

"Emily? Jackie?"

"No."

"Who?"

He smiled. "Angel."

"And your point is?"

"He's had pretty good instincts so far, Skip. I say we tell him about our meeting and see what he thinks."

"I agree." Angel had probably saved my life twice. Once when he stopped the Cubans at the storage unit, and just last night when he shot out the floodlight at the warehouse. It wasn't a bad idea to see what his opinion was.

"How about I swing by Gas and Grocery tomorrow on my

way to work, and I'll see if he's around. I'll take a break about three. Any chance you can swing by Esther's?

"I'll do it. I may not have to worry about a job."

"Oh, come on, pard. I have a feeling your sales are going to soar."

CHAPTER FIFTY-FOUR

I PULLED INTO WORK about half an hour late, thinking about Em and thinking about what Krueger had said last night. *You might not even make it to your cars tonight.* Something like that. I thought about all the movies and stories I'd read where somebody puts a bomb in your car, and the minute you turn the key, BOOM! I thought especially of that movie, *Casino*, starring Joe Pesci where De Niro's car blows up. I would have checked the engine on my Prism, but I had no idea what to look for. Then I thought about a fatherless kid. And maybe she was right. I was pretty much useless, nothing more than the sperm donor to fertilize the egg.

But when I walked into the office I got a nice surprise. Maybe the job was getting better or I was getting better at the job because another client bought a system. Not only did this guy and his wife buy one, but he wanted a system for his office. I think he was an accountant or something. Sammy was ecstatic.

"Contract was on the fax machine this morning, Skipper. Two more sales. I think someone took our little conversation to heart."

I cringed. I kept my mouth shut, but I cringed. I didn't take him seriously, much less to heart. The guy was a flaming asshole and whatever had happened must be pure, dumb luck.

I called Em from the office phone. It saves minutes. She answered like it was a business call, very formal. Then when she heard my voice she got even more cold and distant.

"Em. What do you think?"

"About what?"

I knew the kid issue wasn't her favorite subject at the moment. "About last night."

"What about last night?"

I was getting slightly irritated by the attitude. "Were you there? I thought I saw you. I know you didn't talk to me, but I would swear you were there. Jesus, Em. About the CIA guy and Jackie."

"What's there to talk about? If you keep meddling in this thing, Vic is going to be in even more trouble, Jackie could be in trouble, and you and James could be in trouble. You heard him. I thought he was very clear." Her smug voice came through the receiver loud and clear.

"Listen, I don't know what I did to piss you off, but I wish you'd lose the attitude." I started to build up a head of steam. "It seems to me that we've got a couple of things on our plate that need to be dealt with, and your shitty attitude isn't going to help us get through them."

She was quiet for a moment. "Maybe I should look at that other option."

"What other—" and it hit me. "Really?"

"I don't need a kid in my life right now, Skip."

"I can't ever imagine a time when I will." I should have kept my mouth shut. "I don't mean that. I mean, I'm like you. It's going to take a while to adjust. I think it's a wonderful thing and if you decide to have this baby, I'll be the best father that—" It suddenly occurred to me. "Em. I've had three sales in the past two days. Three. I'm not sure this is a dead end job." I was sure. More than ever. This job was totally dead end, but to be stuck with this loser image in the mind of the woman I love—well, you know.

"Congratulations."

That was it.

"Well, I could buy a playpen with the commission."

"I told you, I'm considering other options."

"Would you tell me before you do anything? After all, I did have something to do with this."

"Yeah." She sighed. "I remember what you had to do with this." There was a long silent pause. "I'm busy, Skip." She hung up. Just like that.

My first two morning calls weren't home, and my third took almost two hours. They asked me dozens of questions, and gave me an extensive tour of their four-room house. After an hour and a half I found out neither one of them had a job and they were about to be evicted. Then they had the nerve to ask if they had won the hot tub. I told them yes. They were the grand-prize winners. I gave them Sammy's cell phone number, told them he'd arrange delivery, and I drove down to Chili's for lunch. Sammy was going to be so pissed.

The cute little waitress, Nancy, who had come on to James, waited on me.

"You're James's roomate."

"Yep."

"He hasn't called."

"He's been a little busy."

"The second job?"

"It's become more than that." I ordered a boneless rib sandwich and a beer.

She brought the draft to the table and tucked a strand of hair behind her ear. “What kind of a car do you drive?”

“Car?”

“A Cadillac?”

“Hardly. A Geo Prism. Ugly green. Why?”

“James told me that the next time we went out he was going to pick me up in a brand new Cadillac. I figured he could hardly afford one, working at Cap’n Crab.”

CHAPTER FIFTY-FIVE

ESTHER'S PARKING LOT was half full at three, with James's truck right out front and a fire engine parked on the side. Five uniformed firefighters crowded into one booth in the front, and they were discussing a morning rescue as I walked by.

"Hey, pard." James nodded to me as I approached his booth. "Angel's on his way."

"I had lunch at Chili's. Nancy says hi."

"Oh, yeah. Nancy. I should probably call her."

"She says you promised to pick her up in a new Cadillac?"

He tilted his head. "I probably had too much to drink."

"That would be so unlike you."

"Someday, Skip. Once we get this Fuentes thing settled." He sipped a Coke and pushed around a spoonful of potato salad on his plate. "You having anything?"

"Nah. I'll wait and see what sumptuous dinner plans we come up with tonight."

"I'll have it someday, Skip. A Cadillac. They got that new convertible out. What? You don't believe me?"

"For you or for your dad?"

"Angel's here." He pointed toward the door.

Angel sat down and I noticed his Jeep outside the window.

"I filled our Bahamian friend in on the meeting last night. He says he wants in on the project. Right, Angel?"

Angel nodded.

"Let's lay out the entire scenario."

James was in his business-planning mode. The thought crossed my mind that the last time he did this, we got into our current mess. That thought crossed my mind. How deep do you dig your hole before you realize the shovel is the problem? If you toss out the shovel, you don't have to dig anymore.

"Rick Fuentes is helping fund a terrorist group that wants to overthrow Castro."

There it was. Plain and simple. The enormity of that statement made me shiver. I knew everything that James knew, but for some reason the far-reaching implications of what we were involved with had never been that clear. If my child *was* born, he would read about this in eighth-grade history class. Our entire country's economy could be affected. Lives would be lost, fortunes would be lost—and won. And even though the three of us —four, counting Emily, were major players, I saw absolutely no way this situation could benefit *us*. If the Cuban element thought we were a threat to their plan, they'd kill us. Not a benefit. If we ignored them, they could be successful or not and whatever fortunes were won or lost, James, Em, Angel, and I would never see a penny. If anything, we could lose. Our jobs, our relationships—again, not a benefit.

"Vic Maitlen may or may not be in jeopardy," James continued. "Up to this point, we've avoided going to any law enforcement agency because Rick Fuentes has asked us not to. He was afraid that his son might be killed if we pursued this any further."

"But now—" I knew what he knew.

"But now, the law enforcement agency has come to us." He

swallowed a gulp of his Coke. "So the question is, do we continue to try and find Vic Maitlin?"

"And," I interjected, "don't forget that Jackie Fuentes's life has been threatened."

"Hell," James said. "Seems to me our lives were threatened too."

I nodded. "So, do we tell Rick Fuentes what we've learned so far?"

"You know nothing." Angel scowled. We'd been through this with him before and he'd made his point. Apparently, not strongly enough. "You saw someone who might have been Victor Maitlin. If you tell the father that his son is alive and you are wrong, he'll be devastated. If you tell him that you followed the Cubans, he'll be furious. Whatever you tell this man, it will do you no good and could do irreparable damage."

Nothing stood between James and his food. He shoveled down a forkful of beans and nodded, apparently agreeing with Angel.

"Let's assume Vic is still a victim. And that he's alive." I believed he was alive. I hoped that was him in the warehouse. "If he is, and we can witness it, we can still go to the authorities." I wanted to identify the goal.

"But," Angel crossed his arms, "you claim the authorities have already come to *you*. If you identify anything, it's simply for your edification. We need to do two things."

James chewed furiously, swallowing and choking on his food. "Wha . . . wha . . . .what things? All we need to do," he cleared his throat with a rumble, "is to identify Vic. This time for sure."

"No. What you need to do is to prove that he is a victim. Prove it. Prove that your high school friend has one finger missing. Prove that he is being held so that Rick Fuentes is forced to sell shares in Café Cubana to save his son. Then, and only then, can you go to a higher authority. I don't believe that the CIA, FBI, or the local police department will argue with any of us if we can prove that Vic is a victim."

I pondered the statement. He'd said *us* at the end of his rant. *Us*. Everything else had been *you*.

Angel was on the team. And he was right. We needed another trip to the warehouse and a more positive report on Vic Maitlin. Why? Because our lives were in jeopardy. Because until we settled this situation once and for all, we would be involved. Because I owed Vic Maitlin my life.

And because I wanted my child to read his eighth-grade history lesson and not find that his old man screwed up.

"Angel, you still missed the most important part of this scenario." James polished off the potato salad with one final bite. He chewed thoughtfully, washed it down with a swallow of Coke and in dramatic fashion laid his hands flat on the table and gazed at the two of us. "The CIA has told us to stay away from this. The CIA, gentlemen."

Angel, in an equally dramatic presentation, lay his large, black hands on the table. "You may never have met with the CIA."

"Did you not hear the story I told you earlier today?"

"I listened very carefully."

"And what?" James turned his hands palms up. "You don't believe me?"

Angel looked at me. "You believed you saw a police officer the night of the fire. Now, you believe that same man was one of the two Cubans who tried to kill you."

"And your point is?"

"Our beliefs change. Depending on new information."

"And do we have new information? I hadn't heard of any."

"You now have *my* information. The CIA, under current guidelines, does not get involved in the investigation of American citizens."

"But—" James and I had both talked to the man.

"They don't."

James shook his head. "So you think the guy was phony?"

"The Bureau of Alcohol, Tobacco and Firearms may get involved."

That made sense. These guys had massive amounts of what I assumed were illegal firearms.

"The FBI may get involved. But not the CIA. The second thing you must do is start asking for more positive identification when you meet these imposters."

We sat there for a minute, James and I looking at each other, both wondering the same thing. Did Jackie know the guy was a phony? Finally, I said, "Angel, how the hell do you know this?"

"It's not important how I know. I know. I also know this. If there is a plot to overthrow Castro, the CIA would not try to stop it. They'd probably applaud the effort."

CHAPTER FIFTY-SIX

I HAD SOMETHING TO RUN FROM. Something I could leave. A woman who wasn't sure she even wanted my child, and an international plot to overthrow a dictator. I'd gone from wondering if I could pay my bills, to the possibility of fatherhood and war with Cuba. My God. Life and death. Freedom and Communism. Had my father been faced with such problems, maybe he would have stayed. Nah, my father would have left even earlier. The heaviness, the weight of the world in one decision, all rested on me. And on James. And on Angel and probably on Jackie and Emily.

I couldn't comprehend all the consequences. And when you are unable to fathom the depth of a problem—when you are incapable of sorting out the logic in a situation, then I guess the best thing to do is to cover your ass. And in a brief moment of sobriety, that's what I decided to do, although protecting my ass meant protecting *my* ass, Em's ass, and the unborn baby's ass. Still a weighty problem.

"I stopped by Gas and Grocery and got a case of oil. You

owe half. I'll get you the bill." James walked in, and before any polite greeting, he hit me with the fact that I owed him.

"If I'm going to get socked for the bill, where's the oil?"

"I put it behind the false wall in the truck."

He walked to the refrigerator and took out a beer, frowning at me on the couch. I'd been home for two hours and he was just getting off work. He twisted off the top and took a long, slow pull on the bottle. Cans this week were cheaper at several outlets, but our one guilty pleasure was glass bottles. Somehow, the beer tastes better. It just does.

"So what do you think?"

He didn't ask about dinner. He didn't ask how Em was or if I'd sold any more systems. He just went right to the heart of the matter.

"Well, everything Angel said made sense."

"And what about that Angel? Jesus, he seems in tune with exactly what we're doing and what's going on around us. It scared the hell out of me."

"James, if he's right, he could be the best thing that ever happened to us. And if he's wrong—" I hadn't thought that through. He seemed so logical, I didn't doubt him. Two weeks ago I thought he was a crackhead. Today, I was willing to bet my life on him. Literally.

"Let's assume he's one hundred percent, pard. If he is, if the CIA guy was phony, then there's a strong possibility that Jackie is involved."

"Oh, come on. She was duped too." I believed in her, if only because she was Em's friend. "That's assuming that he was phony."

"Why are they coming to her?"

"James, she told us. She spread it around that she thought Rick was involved in illegal activities. Jackie found out that her husband is involved with the plot to overthrow Cuba. The two of them have already decided to break up, but now she thinks she has something on him. So, she threatens to go to the CIA or another authority. Maybe she wants a bigger settlement."

"Got proof that it happened that way?"

"I told you from the beginning what Jackie told Emily. She told her that Rick Fuentes was involved in a terrorist plot."

"Yeah. But Jackie didn't know that Rick was being blackmailed. If you're right, and she considered going to the CIA, she thought he was a willing participant. And, she probably was hoping he was guilty. I have a feeling she'd like to see him squirm a little bit."

"But now she's getting threatening calls."

"If this Krueger is really from the CIA, they'll help her."

I shook my head. "Oh, yeah. What are the three things people have learned not to believe? The check is in the mail, I won't come in your mouth, and I'm from the government and I'm here to help you."

"Angel seemed pretty sure Krueger wasn't for real."

"Angel also said if the CIA knew of a plot against Castro—"

James finished the sentence. "They'd applaud the effort. Jesus, you don't think that Krueger and the CIA are —?"

"Let's find out."

"What, now we're going to stalk the CIA?"

"Nah." For a buck fifty I dialed 411.

"Information. What city and state?"

"Miami, Florida."

"What listing?"

"Central Intelligence Agency."

There was as short pause. "I have no listing for that agency."

"Can you just try the initials, CIA?"

"Oh. Like the *CIA*?"

I wasn't sure how to answer that one.

"There is no listing."

"James, you've got Internet at the Cap'n?"

"Yeah."

"Let's Google the CIA."

James smiled. "All right, amigo. And Lindsey is working late. Maybe I'll get lucky and she'll invite me to spend the night."

Lindsey was glad to see him. Cap'n Crab was busy, but the petite brunette found time to hang around the back room and chitchat. She seemed to be good at that. She told him what had happened between the time he'd left and right now, then she told him how she anticipated the night would go, then she asked if he had any plans later on, and I figured that both of them already knew what the night would bring. And so it went. James kept her busy while I Googled.

There's a home page for the CIA in Langely, Virginia, and they list an information number. When Lindsey and James walked out front, I called the number. The girl who answered was very officious. She asked if I was with the press, and since I wanted her to answer some questions, I told her I was. When she asked me what publication, I should have said I was a freelance journalist, but she'd taken me by surprise and I really didn't know what to say. Directly in front of me lay the latest copy of *Food Industry*, so that's what I told her.

"*Food Industry*."

"And what can I help you with?"

"If a group of American citizens were to be involved in a coup on a foreign government, would the CIA investigate?"

I heard her take a breath, then pause. "And again, who are you with?"

"*Food Industry*. We're doing a story on, uh, food and the CIA."

"Uh-uh." She wasn't buying it. "Regardless, the CIA does not investigate American citizens."

“You wouldn’t do surveillance on a couple of guys who may have seen something or know something they shouldn’t?”

“I have no idea what you’re talking about. However, you can tell *Food Industry* that the Central Intelligence Agency does not investigate, follow, or worry about American citizens on American soil. Okay?”

“One more question. Can you tell me if there’s any roster of CIA employees?”

“No. We couldn’t give out that information.”

“Okay. Thank you.”

I hung up and picked up a copy of the Miami phone book. I thumbed through the Ks and found one William Krueger. What the hell. I dialed the number, wondering where I’d found this new courage. When you’ve been threatened, shot at, almost burned alive, pissed off the CIA, and knocked up the most beautiful girl in town, there’s not much left to be afraid of.

A lady answered.

“Um, is Mr. Krueger in?”

“He’s not home at the moment. I do expect him within the hour. Can I take a message or would you care to call back?”

“I want to be sure I’ve got the right William Krueger. Does he work for the CIA?”

“Yes. You’ve got the right one.”

I hung up. If they traced the call, Lindsey could take the heat.

CHAPTER FIFTY-SEVEN

JAMES DROVE ME HOME in the truck, grabbed his toothbrush and a change of clothes, and went back to see Lindsey. I grabbed a beer and walked out back, sprawling on the plastic lounge chair and listening to the night birds harmonize. There were no lights on in the apartment behind us, just the ever-present playpen.

I sat there for maybe half an hour, working things through my feeble mind. Maybe the lady on the phone was part of the scheme. Maybe she played along, telling everyone that Krueger was CIA, when in fact he was something else. "Born in the USA" blared from my pocket, and I remembered I hadn't set the phone to vibrate yet. You'd think it would be the first thing I would have done.

"Hello."

"Hi, Skip."

"We're talking again?"

"We're talking. I'm not happy with the way I've been. Usually I can control my emotions a little better."

"Hormones and all that."

"I suppose."

"And you're seeing the doctor when?"

"Tomorrow. I can't put it off any longer. I keep thinking if I don't get medical confirmation, then it isn't real."

"But, of course, it is."

"Of course."

"And your other option?"

"I can't do that. You know me better than that."

"I thought I did. I guess I do."

"You do."

"Here's a stupid question. Really stupid. With all that's going on, this is going to sound really dumb."

"Shoot."

"Have you thought of a name?"

She laughed. And it sounded so good. "As a matter of fact, I have. If it's a boy, Eugene is not on the list."

"Thank God."

"I like Troy and Aaron. For a girl I always thought I'd pick Alison."

"One L?"

"One L."

I took a long swallow of cheap beer and smiled. In spite of everything, Em was talking to me and, better yet, we were talking about the baby. Our baby. It meant that not everything in the world was fucked up.

"Tell me what you and your crazy roommate are cooking up."

I told her about our conversation with Angel and my call to Krueger.

"You could always just assume that everything is going to be all right."

"But it's not. Vic may be in trouble, these Cubans have threatened our lives, and now we've been warned by the CIA. And it appears the CIA shouldn't even *be* involved. Your friend

Jackie is getting threatening phone calls, and we know something we're not supposed to know. We know there's a plot to invade Cuba. If we can prove any of this, we can go to the authorities."

"And if we can't prove any of it?"

"They may try to make sure we never do. Look, Em, there's a much bigger risk now."

"You mean because of me."

"Yeah. I never had anything that I really cared about. Ever. I never took us—you and me—that seriously. I just never thought we'd end up together. I mean, I wanted to, I think, but now it's different."

"I'm not sure we're going to end up together. Obviously the connection is a lot stronger, but, Skip, I'm not making any promises."

"I'm not asking for any promises. But I do believe it's worth fighting for. If I let this Cuban thing take over I'm putting everyone at risk."

I could hear her breathing softly on the other end. "Don't be a hero on my account, Skip. You have no idea what you're getting into."

"No. I don't. I also have no idea where we are right now. I've got to take some initiative here. I've got to get some control of my life and quit letting other people make decisions that affect my life. Your life."

"So, what do you propose?"

"I think we have to check out the warehouse one more time. We've got to find Victor. It's the only thing that makes sense."

"And you could get killed looking for him. Really. You could be killed."

"And I could get killed if I don't."

"Skip? There's more to this, isn't there? "

I wasn't sure what to say.

"Skip?"

"There is."

"Want to tell me what it is?"

"Not everything. Just this. Vic Maitlin saved my life eleven years ago."

Now it was her turn not to know what to say. Finally, "He saved your life? Vic? My God, Skip, how?"

"That's it for now."

"Pretty heavy stuff."

"Yeah. And he risked his life to save mine. It's just something I have to do, Em."

"So there's something else you care about."

"Yeah, I guess. All of a sudden I have some things in my life that really matter."

There was nothing left to say.

Justin Cramer and Mike Stowe got busted our sophomore year in high school. They got caught selling drugs to an undercover cop and were expelled a week later. The cop posed as a student and she not only caught the goon squad but two other students, a student's parent, and a wrestling coach.

It seemed like the perfect time to tell my story, but I didn't. After Vic pulled me out, the sinkhole incident was on my mind every day and I saw the players every day, but in my sophomore year, three years after it happened, I often thought maybe I'd dreamed the entire occurrence. Now, after Rick Fuentes threatened me with my obligation to his son, I felt I could finally let it out. But it wouldn't come out. It had been buried too deep and too long.

CHAPTER FIFTY-EIGHT

I MADE A HANDFUL OF CALLS the next morning, stopped at the Cap'n for lunch, and told James that Em and I were back to normal.

"There's no normal with you guys."

"Well, as close to normal as possible. Listen, I want to go back to the warehouse one more time."

"I'm not that stupid, pard."

"Well, I am."

"You're on your own this time, Skip." He headed back into the kitchen to make someone a crab sandwich and I finished my po'boy and left.

He pulled up in the truck about seven fifteen, stepped into the apartment, and immediately walked to the refrigerator, pulling a beer from the inside of the door. "What time do you want to go?"

"Go?"

"Oh, fuck. You know I can't let you drive down there by yourself. You'll do something stupid like the last time and get yourself shot. I'd have to call your mom and try to find that worthless asshole father of yours and tell them you've been killed, and I'm not going to go through all that shit. What time are we leaving?"

"Nine?"

"Just the two of us?"

"I thought about that. If we need a gun, we need Angel."

"Shit." He pulled the keys to the truck from his pocket, took a long swallow of beer, and motioned to me. We walked out, got into the truck, and drove to Gas and Grocery. The tiny carryout was open, but Angel wasn't there.

"What do we do now?"

I shook my head. Angel had always been there. "Stick around a couple of minutes."

Half an hour later I went inside and asked the old lady behind the counter to leave a message for Angel.

"What the hell I look like? Voicemail?"

"No, I just thought if he happened to stop by—"

"We close at nine. You want him to get a message, you go find him."

I walked back to the truck and shrugged my shoulders. "We're on our own, James."

"Been that way most of our adult lives, Skip. I think we can manage."

We drove back to the apartment, pulled in beside the rusted-out Ranchero, and went inside. James finished the warm beer.

"This is about paying a debt, right?" He wiped his mouth with the back of his hand.

"Some of it is."

"You and me, Skip, we'd do that for each other."

"Sure."

"But you'd do it for someone you don't really know. You'd try to save someone because they saved you."

"There's other reasons."

"You want to protect your lady and the new kid."

I remember glaring at him. His psychoanalysis was getting a little overbearing.

"I'm right."

"James, maybe I'm doing this because I'm afraid for my own life. If I don't get them, they'll get me."

He smiled that cocksure smile of his. "Nah. You care about people, amigo. You've got people and situations that you really care about. It's what makes you a strong person. It's what I like about you, pard."

"And you? What are you really in this for?"

He didn't pause a second. "Because you're in it. It's you and me, Skip. Hell, I guess if you and what's-her-name ever do get married, you'll have to have a guest room for me to live in." He grinned.

"Fuck you, James."

"I said you're my best friend, buddy. But I won't go that far."

CHAPTER FIFTY-NINE

We left at eight thirty. I had James swing by the carryout, but there was no sign of our black friend or his black Jeep. James hopped on I-95 and he opened it up to fifty-five miles an hour. We should have taken the Prism, but James had insisted.

"Need to open up the truck a little bit. Guy told me if you want to keep it tuned up, open it up once in a while."

I listened to his bullshit for another couple of minutes. Finally I'd had enough. "You know, James, you couldn't even *open up* that sorry rust trap pickup you had in high school! Christ, I think top speed was thirty *if* the damned thing started. You always sound like you know so much about cars and trucks—"

He was silent for a while. I probably should have just shut up, but I was riled. Vic Maitlin, Emily, James—they each had special meaning in my life and I could do something to help them. Protect them. But I had no idea what that something was. As it stood, I was playing David to Goliath and the only person in my corner tonight was James. Probably not the person to be pissing on.

"You're in a tough spot, Skip. There's a lot going on in your life. Just don't take it out on the people who are here to help you." Son of a bitch knew what I'd been thinking.

We were quiet the rest of the ride.

James pulled off the highway and we headed down to the river on North River Drive, past Garcia's, downtown's freshest seafood. The sign says so. Past the sewage plant next door to Garcia's, and past the rust-bucket container ships with their loads of housewares, food, autos, and whatever bound for Honduras, Columbia, Belize, Puerto Rico, and other ports south. He slowed down, concentrating on something.

"You hear something?"

"What am I listening for?"

"Just listen." He jazzed the engine and we scooted ahead for a moment.

"Hear that?"

"What?" I hate it when people do that. Tell me what the hell I'm supposed to be listening for.

"That. Right there."

I heard it. A clunk.

"Yeah, a clunk. Why couldn't you say, 'Listen for a clunk'?"

James ignored me. "Shit. I'll bet we're low on oil."

"Just like that, you know?"

"Had a friend who was driving home with some girl and clunk. Car threw a rod because of low oil. Had to catch a bus home."

"We're back to a rod again?"

"Just shut the fuck up, Skip."

I could see our warehouse just up the street, lit up by a new floodlight in the parking lot.

He pulled over, three lots from the one with the forklift next to the building. Three lots from the parking lot where I'd run my ass off. Three lots from the warehouse where I thought I'd seen Vic Maitlin.

"What are you pulling over for?"

"Check the engine."

"Shit, we should have driven the Prism."

"Makes no difference. They know every vehicle we own. Besides, we can park the truck here around back of this building and walk over to their warehouse."

"What I meant was, the Prism doesn't drink like it's dollar beer night."

"Yeah, and the Prism hasn't made us one fucking penny by hauling anything either."

"And, James," I was ready to bow out after my last shot, "the Prism hasn't almost got us killed!"

He stepped out and walked around to the front. I sat in the passenger seat watching him. He reached under the hood, flipped a lever, and raised it. I could hear him tinkering, probably pulling out the dipstick and trying to figure out if we needed oil.

"Shit. It's dryer than a witch's womb."

"And what do we do about that at nine o'clock at night?" I yelled through the windshield.

"Put oil in it, asshole."

I put my head out the window. "And, Mr. Lessor, where the hell do you think we're going to find oil at this time of night?" I could just see us stranded by the water. Tomorrow morning we'd both miss work again, and I'd have to beg a ride home from Em.

"If you will be so kind as to fold down the passenger seat, open the door behind the seat, you will find that closet with the false wall. Inside you'll find a case of oil. You see, I do know what I'm doing."

I'd forgotten. James, for once in his life, was prepared. I got out of the seat and gently folded it down. In the dim light it was hard to find the door. If you don't know it's there, it's hard to see.

Finally I found the small metal pull, opened the door, and stepped into the dark closet. James had set the case of oil to the right. I fumbled for a can, lost my balance, and ended up on my knees as the door swung shut and I was lost in the pitch black.

And then I heard the second noise that night that frightened me. The sound of a car pulling up beside the truck and a voice asking, "Having engine trouble?"

I knew the voice. There was no question whose voice it was.

"I asked if you're having engine trouble."

I could hear James's trembling voice. "Yeah. I just—look, I don't want any trouble."

"Ah, Mr. Lessor. I'd help you. I really would. But it seems my arm is in a cast and a sling right now. A little hunting accident from the last time we saw each other. I don't know why you're here, but it could be the biggest mistake you've made in your whole life."

CHAPTER SIXTY

I HELD MY BREATH longer than I've ever held it. I used to practice in the public swimming pool when I was just a kid. Other kids would say they'd heard of guys who could hold their breath for two, three minutes. I may have made it for about fifty seconds but that was it. I swear that night I made three minutes easily.

"Where's your partner?"

It was Big Mouth, the guy who'd rolled the Buick.

"He had some late calls to make. He's in sales and—"

I heard a thud, then James grunted.

"He's not here."

Another thud.

"Don't mess him up too bad. We may need to get some serious information from him."

There was some rustling around, then the voice that I assumed belonged to Carlos. "You look like a fucking trussed-up pig. I'd put you on a spit and watch you twist in the fire."

There was no sound. I pictured James, tied with rope and gagged, thrown in the backseat of their car, or worse, in the trunk. I thought about coming out. For about half a second. There was no earthly good I could do.

"I'll drive the Buick. Carlos, you follow in the truck. We'll park inside the warehouse in case he was meeting someone. Post someone outside to see who drives by. We can't take the chance on any company tonight. Especially tonight."

The car started and pulled off. The driver's door opened on the truck and I took another deep breath, praying the door to my closet had latched. All I needed was for that door to spring open. It didn't.

Carlos started the engine, let it idle for about fifteen seconds then said to himself, "What the fuck is that noise? Thing goes clunk. Clunk."

The truck started moving and I started counting the seconds. Less than forty-five and I heard other voices as Carlos pulled into the warehouse then the sound of the big overhead door as it rolled over the top of the truck and slammed to the concrete floor. I was blind, but my ears were picking up everything.

"Where is the partner, Juan?"

"He doesn't want to say. I suggest we play pass the pig."

A voice I didn't recognize said, "Push him over here."

There was a soft thud and a grunt. James was getting the shit beat out of him and there was nothing I could do.

"Where is Eugene Moore?"

"Take the gag out of his mouth."

"Where?"

James spit. I could hear it even through the thin door. I thought he was spitting to clear his mouth after losing the gag.

"You motherfucker. You spit on me—" Whack. Whack.

If my boy lived through this I would have to give him all the credit in the world for taking this beating on my account. But as long as one of us was still undetected, there was a chance I could get out and get help. I just didn't see any opportunity at this point.

"Want to tell us? Where is your partner? The other night, he was running like a scared rabbit. Maybe he is in his briar patch?"

"Yeah. Maybe." James croaked. "Maybe if he was here he'd run again. Seeing as you guys don't have any weapons on you, maybe he'd take off running and bust out the side door like he did the last time and—" Whack. Thud.

"Fucker just wants to mouth off."

I ached for him. Maybe they were doing some irreparable damage. He'd given me a clear signal that with the element of surprise I might get out the door. No guns? No guns that he could see. And how far could I run? Far enough to get my cell phone out and call 911? What if I called now? Shit, I knew I'd have to say something and they'd pick up even the faintest whisper.

"So what do we do with him?"

"If it was me?"

"Carlos, it's not you. If we made decisions based on what you thought we should do, we'd be nowhere right now."

"Both of you shut up. We don't need a hassle right now. The truck is coming in an hour to take the boxes to Key West to be put on the boat. It has to be tonight and we don't need any screw ups. If he's got a partner who's going to be looking for him or coming by later, I want to know about it." Still another voice. By my count there was Carlos, Juan, and at least two other men.

Thud. "Anybody else coming by, pig?"

I couldn't let this continue. I don't know what I thought, maybe he had broken ribs, a concussion, but I had to do something.

"I can't hear you, smart-ass."

I reached into the case and picked up two cans of oil. Not

exactly weapons of choice, but ones of necessity. If they were effective, Pep Boys and Gas and Grocery would have a whole new advertising campaign.

"Mr. Lessor. We can keep beating you, but we seriously don't want to do that. What we simply want to know is who else is coming. Surely you didn't come by yourself. You've always got company. Let's see, you were with your friend and his female companion the night of the fire—you were with the black man at the storage unit, you were with your two friends the other night when you spied on us."

I eased the door open, just an inch, clutching those two oil cans like they were hand grenades.

The door was hinged on the right so I peered out to the left. I could see through the driver's window, but I'd have to open the closet door a lot farther to be able to see through the windshield.

The back of a small man blocked my vision. His hair was thick and coal black and he wore a green shirt, about the same puke green color as my Prism. Should have brought the Prism. I would bet that they wouldn't have recognized that car.

"Come on, James. You protect someone else, but then you can't protect yourself. You see what I'm saying?" Thud.

Someone else was kicking or hitting him. My green-shirted guy stood motionless.

I pushed the door open farther, becoming increasingly bolder. Now I had a clear view through the windshield. James was on the hard cement floor, his hands behind his back. The first thing I noticed was blood running from his face. Juan, Carlos, and someone else stood around him, Carlos bouncing on the balls of his feet like a prizefighter waiting for his opponent to get up off the canvas. James wasn't getting up.

Juan, his arm in a cast, kept taunting James. "Come on, Mr. Lessor. You're not so tough without your friends. Tell us who else is coming. If they come before we load our truck, we'll have to show them how we treat our visitors."

I pushed the door even farther and no one noticed. They were concentrating on my roommate, face down on the cement, blood flowing freely, staining the concrete floor.

Putting the oil can I had in my right hand on the floor, I reached for the passenger-side door handle. It opened quietly. With the seat folded down, I could reach the door with my leg. I picked up the can and pulled my leg back. I kicked the door wide open, leaped from my dark closet, jumped to the cement floor and fired a can at Big Mouth's head. I hit him on the back of his neck and Carlos went down.

Running for my life I turned and fired the second can, catching the small guy with the green shirt in the middle of his back. He stumbled and fell. I reached for the door handle on the side door of the warehouse and the door popped open. Head down I ran one, two, three steps and hit a stone wall.

"Hey!" Arms wrapped around me, binding me up. I struggled, kicking and fighting to get free, as my assailant turned me and put his arm around my neck. He was squeezing, applying serious pressure, and I could feel myself choking, gasping for air. Lights popped off inside my head, brilliant flashes exploding behind my eyes, and I fought for consciousness.

"Don't kill him. Tie him up and put him in the office and we'll decide what to do with him later."

I was passing out, but I recognized the voice. It was the second time Vic Maitlin had saved my life.

CHAPTER SIXTY-ONE

My head was splitting open. Someone had taken an axe and cleaved it. I can't even describe the incredible pain. And then I opened my eyes and concentrated on consciousness. And there was James, propped up against the wall next to me. He was tied with thick rope, and maybe because the light was dim, he appeared to have a gray hue to his skin.

My hands were numb, tied too tightly behind my back, and my head really did ache. Part of me hoped that James was passed out so the pain of his beating wouldn't be so hard to bear. The other part of me wanted him to wake up fast so we could try to make some plans. Hardy Boys novels didn't seem so glamorous this time.

Someone had been stationed outside that door. Knowing I'd snuck in before, they must have decided to secure the entrances. And someone who sounded like Vic Maitlin had stopped the guard from strangling me. I couldn't be wrong about that voice. He wasn't dead. But it didn't appear he was being held captive, either.

My head throbbed, and my neck was raw and bruised. And

that was minor compared to what James must be going through. His nose appeared to be left of center, and he had a large swelling over his right eye. Someone had wiped the blood from his face, but fresh blood was dripping from his nose and a cut on his lower lip. His breathing was shallow and raspy, and I was afraid if we didn't get medical attention soon, he might go into shock. I didn't want to speculate on how much worse he might get.

Sweat beaded on my forehead and I could feel my T-shirt, moist and sticky on my skin. It must have been over one hundred degrees in the small office. Gently I twisted my head and surveyed the surroundings. Four walls and a window that seemed to look out into the warehouse. A gunmetal gray desk, swivel chair, and two filing cabinets were shoved up against the far wall. A faded calendar with a dark-skinned girl in a bikini smiling seductively hung on the far wall. It just seemed out of place. I figured we were in the office that I'd seen at the far end of the warehouse. The balcony would be above us.

The faint aroma of a cigar wafted through the small room and low voices murmured outside. They were talking about a truck arriving, picking up the guns, and driving down to Key West. Then there was something about a boat. So the guns were being taken to Cuba tonight. The invasion must be soon.

What the hell was the deal with Vic Maitlin? I tried to picture a scenario where he would be in a position to order someone not to kill me. This from a guy who's finger had been severed and was being held for ransom. A ransom of twenty million dollars in shares of Café Cubana. It made no sense, but my head hurt, I was dizzy, and my best friend was next to me, unconscious and barely breathing. I wasn't thinking clearly.

I wondered if the truck had arrived yet. I don't know how long I was out, but if people were still in the warehouse it would appear that they were still waiting to load the guns on a truck. I glanced at James and there was no change. Sweat and blood soaked his shirt where his head hung down on his chest and his rough breathing didn't sound good.

Footsteps and Spanish-speaking voices approached the office and I closed my eyes. Let them think both of us were unconscious until I knew what they wanted.

The door opened and several people walked in.

"You guys have got to stop with the Spanish." A different voice. "It's been too long, man. I can't follow you."

I didn't recognize the voice.

"They have been nothing but a thorn in our side. This entire part of the operation would have been trouble free without these two."

"Not altogether true, Israel. What about the grocer and his gay friend?"

"Castro's spies. There is no doubt."

"They caused problems."

"And they were dealt with. But these two—"

"These two are here, under our control, and we can now get rid of them."

Only two voices speaking and one of them was Carlos.

"Maybe there is another alternative."

It was Vic.

"Maybe we can keep them tied up here in the office. Jesús is staying here and he could keep an eye on them until our operation begins."

Everyone was quiet for a moment. Finally, Carlos spoke. "Keep an eye on them? What the fuck are they, children to be watched? Listen, Victor, we talked about collateral damage. People will die. Some innocent, some not. It will happen. It's a necessary part of war. Are you losing your courage?"

"I was born with more courage than you'll have in a lifetime!" There was venom in Victor's voice.

"Then show some. Here is my pistol. Shoot them both, and

we'll throw their bodies in the water. Casualties of war, Victor. Here, take it."

It was time to open my eyes. I wanted to have some say in the matter.

"Vic."

He looked down at me. The same good looks, dark skin and eyes, and big hands, one of them wrapped around a pistol. There seemed to be five healthy fingers on each one. "Hey, Skip."

Carlos stood in the doorway, smirking. A third man watched with wide eyes and an unhealthy grin plastered on his face. He seemed to be eagerly awaiting my demise.

"Vic, I'm really glad to see you have all your fingers." Vic's fingers. One of the main reasons I was in this predicament.

He gave me a vague smile. "Yeah. That was never for your benefit."

"Jackie?"

"Jackie. She was supposed to open the envelope, realize my father was being blackmailed, and stay out of the way for a while."

"But she never opened the envelope. I did."

"I'm truly sorry you got involved. Ironic isn't it?"

I ignored the comment. "But, whose finger was it?"

He glanced at Carlos, who was leaning against the door frame, amused at the story Vic was telling.

"There was a Cuban grocer and his significant other who stumbled onto our little plan. We took them to the Cuban Social Club and—"

"We talked to them." Carlos laughed. "And then we cut off the finger of one of the men when they refused to tell us what we wanted to know. He squealed like a baby."

The third man spoke. "But they told us everything. They were reporting back to Cuba about our plans for invasion. It's very simple really. You just remove body parts to get a full confession."

I was trying to put it all together. "You decided to send the finger—"

"And Victor's class ring."

"The finger and the ring to Jackie?"

Vic nodded. "It seemed like a good idea at the time."

James was wheezing, his chest almost jerking with every breath he took.

"Vic, James doesn't sound good. He could use a doctor."

I saw the indecision in his eyes. He glanced at Carlos, then to James, and back to me, and sighed.

"Saving someone's life once in a lifetime should be enough. It should be more than enough."

I didn't mention that he'd saved my life again by stopping the guard from strangling me.

Vic pointed the pistol at James, held the pose for a moment, then swung the barrel so it was aimed directly at my head. He cocked the hammer and a chill went down my back and I shivered in the stifling heat of the office.

Then he turned and handed the pistol back to Carlos. "I am responsible for this man's life. While I may not save it again, I cannot take it. It has nothing to do with courage, but everything to do with the laws of life."

Carlos stared at the pistol in his hand, then shrugged, released the hammer and stuck the handgun in his belt. I breathed a sigh of relief and said a silent prayer. I'm not a religious person, but sometimes you just feel that someone upstairs is watching out for you.

Carlos put a hand on Victor's shoulder. "You think what you did was admirable. You would like to think everything you do is noble and well thought out. You are no better than the rest of us. You do this not just for *Los Historicos*. You do it for your own greed."

Vic shoved his hand away and glowered at him. "I do this for the people of Cuba who beg for freedom."

"And people will die. Innocent people will suffer. It's like your explosives expert who made one small mistake on the bomb that was meant for Castro. It brought down the Cuban Social Club—killed the two spies *and* your bomb maker. You have already been responsible for lives, Victor, and the war has yet to begin." Carlos spun around and walked out into the warehouse.

The third man, I guessed his name to be Israel, just stood there, giggling. Vic looked down at me, a scowl on his face. "Maybe there's a lesson here. The life you save may come back to haunt you. Don't haunt me, Skip. The greater good is that I am successful in this mission. Don't stand in my way."

I remembered the last person who had asked me to get the hell out of the way. Ricardo Fuentes, Vic's father. Only he was asking me to step aside so his son could live. I wondered what Rick Fuentes would think now.

CHAPTER SIXTY-TWO

"TRUCK'S HERE," someone shouted from out in the main room. Truthfully, I'd had about enough of trucks. I could hear the overhead door rattle as it raised up, and the sound of a diesel engine as the truck pulled inside. The door closed and the choking smell of diesel exhaust filled the area.

James coughed.

I tried stretching my arms to see if there was any play with the rope. There was no feeling at all in my hands. I stretched again and thought maybe there was a slight easing of the tightness. Not enough to make a difference.

"Skip."

I jumped.

"Skip?" James' eyes were *almost* closed, droopy at best.

"James. Man, I'm glad you're back."

"Man, what's happening?" His head still hung low, his chin resting on his chest.

"You took a pretty good beating."

"You think I don't know?"

"James, I tried to get out. Took two of them out with

my pitching arm and a couple of oil cans, but they stopped me."

He was quiet for a moment, still drawing short, raspy breaths. "You're gonna have to pay for that oil, pard."

"Vic is here. Alive."

"No shit. They've got him too?"

"No. He's got us. He's one of them, Vic and all of his ten fingers." I filled him in on the rest of the story. Half way through my CliffsNotes version his eyes closed and I thought I'd lost him. "James?"

"Yeah. I'm listening. Trying to block out the pain."

When I finished, he lifted his head, looking at me with one eye open. "They were going to kill us?"

"Oh, I think they intend to kill us even now. But they're loading the truck at the moment, and we're not high priority."

We could hear the sound of the forklift sliding under the boxes, then loading them into the truck.

"So if everyone is busy with the truck, now would be a good time to escape." James even managed a weak smile.

"I agree. Let's get out while we can."

No plans, no chance of any escape.

"I think they may have cracked some ribs. My right side aches and when I breath it feels like something's sticking me."

"Man, I wish there was something I could have done."

"You tried, amigo."

I hadn't heard them approach, but someone was turning the door handle. They shoved open the door and stepped inside and I got a glimpse of a shoe before I raised my head to see the rest. Heavy wax coating on a black shoe. I looked up. Buzz cut and open-collar shirt. Krueger from the CIA.

"Jesus, am I glad to see you."

He smiled. "Told you boys to mind your own business. Remember I said it might come to this?"

I smiled back. "I should have listened. Mr. Krueger, I can't tell you how glad I am. I believe James and I are on a list to be shot in the not too distant future."

He laughed out loud. "Yes, I believe you are." Someone walked in behind him wearing a shoulder holster with a wooden handled revolver inside. "Mr. Moore, Mr. Lessor, let me introduce you to Mark Spense. Mark's with the Agency as well."

"Thank God. Listen. James is in pretty bad shape. They beat him up and he thinks he may have some internal injuries. Can we get these ropes off and get some medical attention?"

Krueger laughed again. A jovial guy. "Mr. Moore, I'm afraid you're mistaken about my reason for being here. Actually, there are several reasons, but right now my primary business is to attend to your death. And you can't say I didn't warn you."

CHAPTER SIXTY-THREE

I WONDERED IF MY OLD MAN would ever find out that I'd been killed. Collateral damage. My mom and sister would be busted up, but my dad? He might shrug his shoulders, but you can't miss something you don't claim as yours. And James's dad? Now, like his father, James was never going to amount to much in the world of business, and he certainly wasn't going to be driving that new Cadillac.

"Mark, get 'em on their feet, and bring in their friend."

My heart jumped into my mouth. Jesus, they couldn't have Em. Oh, Jesus Christ, please, not Em.

Jackie Fuentes walked into the sweltering office, a quirky smile on her face. "Hi, boys."

James raised his head gingerly. I watched Jackie flinch when she saw the damage done to his face. James wasn't so cute anymore.

"So you're in on this too?"

"Not so you'd notice." Mark Spense followed, the gun out of his holster and pointed at Jackie's back. He pulled me up with his free hand, then eyed James. There was no way James could stand on his own. "You two," he motioned to Jackie and me, "pick him up. We're taking a little stroll across the street to the water." Agent Spense untied my hands and I worked the circulation back into them. Then he untied James's hands.

For the first time I saw panic register on Jackie's pretty face. "They're really going to kill us, aren't they?"

"We are, little lady. We are."

I gently took James under one arm and Jackie lifted the other.

"I don't care if you have to drag him, we're going outside."

I stared hard at Krueger. "Before we go, tell me one thing."

"Oh, Jesus. This is just like the fucking movies. 'Please, tell me how all this happened before you kill me.' "

"This isn't the movies. It's my last request. I just want to know. Is Victor in charge of this little band of malcontents?"

"No. Now shut the fuck up and move."

"One more question?"

"Move."

"Are you and your partner really with the CIA?"

Krueger had pulled out his gun and was waving it at me.

"Yes? No?"

"Yes. Get moving."

James grunted as we helped him stand, but he was able to put one foot in front of the other.

We entered the main area and I could see the large box truck being loaded with the crates of guns and ammunition. The yellow forklift was working off one of the pallets about half way down the wall. Carlos was driving the lift and Vic and Israel were inside the truck helping load the boxes. Juan, his arm in a cast, stood off to the side. All things considered, I figured he would rather be helping. A handful of workers were busy with other projects, two of them carrying the metal canisters that I'd hid behind the other night.

We were herded to the side door and into the parking lot.

"Chains and blocks are across the street. May as well put them on over there." Mark Spense nodded to Krueger.

"Keep moving."

"James, if it comes down to it, know that I loved you like a brother. There's nothing I wouldn't do for you."

James grunted. We were pretty much dragging him now. He couldn't move on his own.

"Skip, James, I'm sorry about all of this. I never meant to get anyone else involved. Really." Jackie's voice quivered.

Krueger pushed the barrel of his gun into my back. We crossed the street and stood by a crumbling three-foot high cement barrier that ran along the water as far as I could see in the murky shadows.

"Sit him down." Krueger motioned to James, and I eased him down against the wall.

Jackie stood stock still, looking like a frozen Barbie doll in tight jeans and a simple white T-shirt.

"Put that chain around his ankle."

I glanced down and saw a chain wrapped through and around a cement block. They were going to toss us into the water and either let us drown or shoot us first. There wasn't a damned thing I could do to stop it.

"Wrap the chain around his ankle." Krueger raised his voice. "Mark, do it for her. We've got to get this show on the road."

Mark Spense put his pistol in the shoulder holster, bent down to take the loose end of the chain, and fell flat on his face.

"What the fuck?" Krueger took a step closer, leaned down, and gasped. "Christ, he's been shot."

He grabbed Jackie by the shoulder, pulling her in front of

him. He gave James and me a hard look, then furtively glanced in all directions.

"Please, don't hold me so tight, it really hurts." Jackie was squirming, trying to loosen Krueger's grip.

"You should be dead by now, so this really isn't so bad, is it?" His arm reached around her chest, mashing her breasts with a death grip. "Whoever is out there, I'll shoot this little girl. Swear to God."

Silence. I could hear the water lapping at the cement wall and across the street I could hear the commotion as the workers loaded the truck behind the overhead door.

"Show yourself or I'll shoot her, so help me."

No response. James and I huddled by the seawall. I could smell the rotting seaweed and oil that floated on the surface of the flat black river water. His eyes were closed, but I had the feeling he was not missing any of this.

"One more chance, and I'm going to put a bullet in her head." Krueger yelled. His voice echoed off the steel building across the street.

I closed my eyes. I had to do something. Jump up, shout, throw myself at him. I flexed my legs, ready to leap.

"Time's up."

Krueger's head swiveled back and forth, trying to find out where the shooter might be. He put his gun to Jackie's head and I heard the sound. As if someone spit, loudly. The shooter's bullet hit the cement seawall inches from where I sat, and particles of concrete showered the area. Again, the spitting noise and this time the bullet hit gravel in front of Jackie Fuentes.

"Please, please let me go."

Krueger took aim somewhere in the darkness and fired. The loud explosion surprised me. He pointed in the same general direction, firing again, and holding Jackie tight to his chest.

"Move!" He shoved Jackie in front of him and moved

double time across the street toward the warehouse. I watched him as he reached the building, pushing her inside.

"James?"

There was no answer. I grabbed my cell phone from my pocket and dialed 911.

"911 operator. Do you have an emergency?"

"Man, do I only. There's a guy trying to kill me and two of my friends. And they're loading guns and ammunition to take to Key West, and sail over to Cuba for an invasion."

"Sir, this is an emergency number. It's against the law to use it for anything else."

"Lady, this is a fucking emergency. I know you record these calls. Give this to someone. I'm in a warehouse district off North River Road, down by Garcias. You tell somebody things are going to get pretty hairy in a matter of minutes." I closed the flip phone.

"They're already pretty hairy, Skip. I just killed a government agent." Angel stepped out of a shadow and kneeled down next to James. "You're going to be all right, James. This whole thing is about ovcr."

CHAPTER SIXTY-FOUR

We carried James to the Jeep parked in a small grove of pine trees a block from the warehouse. Krueger was protecting his own ass and it was time to protect ours. James was breathing steadier as we stretched him on the backseat.

"We need to get Jackie Fuentes out of there."

"We need to get James to a hospital."

We looked at each other, then back at James, breathing regularly.

"Okay, all right. But if 911 gets busy, they'll have someone here soon. We should just stay out of it."

"Skip, James will be all right. He was awake and making sense. I doubt if there is a concussion and he's breathing well right now."

"How the hell do you know all this stuff?"

He motioned to me and we left the Jeep.

"What do you plan to do? My God, these people have hundreds of guns, ammunition, the CIA—"

"I was wrong." Angel stayed close to the buildings we passed and I stayed right behind him.

"Wrong? About what?" The moon stayed behind clouds and we were probably hard to spot.

"Your CIA friend. I believe he *was* from the CIA."

"So the CIA is involved in this invasion?"

We approached the warehouse. There were no guards outside the side door.

"I don't know. Maybe three rogue agents, maybe the entire agency."

"Three? There was a third?"

He motioned to me and we headed toward the back of the corrugated steel building. We walked past the outside forklift and the Buick was still parked. He walked me behind the building and put his finger to his lips. Whispering, he pointed to an outside metal fire escape. "There's a door up there. I believe it opens onto a balcony that surveys the entire warehouse."

I whispered back. "How the hell do you know?"

"I was up there earlier this evening."

I shook my head. The guy was a regular James Bond.

He motioned to me and we quietly climbed the steps.

You'd think that international terrorists would lock their doors. But they don't. These guys didn't. The door opened easily and Angel stuck his head inside.

"They're busy down there. Come here."

He eased in, kneeling, and watching under the railing that ran along the four-foot wide balcony. I followed.

The truck was about loaded. There were four more pallets of boxes and one more canister left to lift onto the truck.

"Down there." Angel pointed.

Jackie was standing against the wall, midway down the floor. Someone I didn't recognize held a gun on her, and Krueger was nowhere in sight.

"You can see everything from up here, can't you? The entire operation." The voice behind me surprised the crap out of me. I'd been shocked so many times tonight this shouldn't have fazed me, but it did.

"Stand up, put your hands behind your backs and walk down the stairs. It's time we get rid of you assholes once and for all." Rick Fuentes shoved his pistol deep into my ribs and pushed me toward the stairs. He grabbed Angel by the collar and brought him along. "I swear to Christ, Moore, I'm going to kill you myself."

CHAPTER SIXTY-FIVE

He shoved me and I stumbled down the steps, landing on my tailbone at the bottom. He kicked my ass and told me to get up.

"I suppose now isn't the time to tell you that your son is still alive."

Fuentes slashed at me with the barrel of his pistol, and I felt the skin rip on my cheek. I touched it and felt hot blood running down my face.

"You keep fucking things up. Where's your partner?"

"He took off. I have no idea where he went."

Fuentes hit me again with the gun. I moved my head with the blow and it wasn't as severe.

"Do that again, and I'll take the gun away from you."

He looked at me with wide-open eyes. Angel spun around and looked at me. Fuentes raised the gun and I grabbed it. I don't know where I got the strength or the courage, but the adrenaline was flowing and I twisted hard, kicking him in the crotch at the same time. Fuentes went into a crouch and let go of the gun. I've never shot a pistol before, but I figured there was a first time for everything. I pointed the barrel at him, closed my eyes, and pulled the trigger. The explosion was ten times more powerful than I'd imagined and the recoil jarred my shoulder. When I opened my eyes Fuentes was lying on the ground, grabbing his thigh.

"They heard that for sure, Skip." Angel had pulled out his gun. It was like the Wild West. "Quick, both of us go in with guns and we'll get Jackie to safety."

"One minute, Angel."

"Skip—"

"Mr. Fuentes. You're spearheading this revolution?"

He glowered up at me, holding his thigh, and stemming the flow of blood. Even in the dark I could see the fluid staining his gray slacks.

"You and your son? There's got to be a family connection over there. What, your father owned property, a factory?"

No answer.

"The finger was to throw Jackie off your trail. Right? Then why did you hire us to see if Vic was at the Cuban Social Club?" I waved the gun menacingly. I tried to appear like they do in the movies, but he didn't scare easily. He already knew I was a lousy shot.

"Go fuck yourself."

"Just tell me if I'm right. Once *we* knew about the finger, you had to do your little act for us too—so we'd go back to Jackie and tell her how sad it was that you were being blackmailed with the kidnapping of your son. It really would have been a lot easier if we hadn't gotten involved."

"Skip, let's go."

"One more question, Angel, then we'll go." I kneeled down on the ground and in the dim light I could see the grimace of pain on Fuentes's face. I was just thankful I hadn't killed him. "What about the list of donors? Come on, tell me what that was all about."

He gave me a hateful look. "That was a huge mistake. You were never to have seen that list."

"But these people were investing in what they thought was a business venture. They didn't know about the invasion."

Fire leaped from his eyes. "Some of them. And some of them donated to the cause. Some of them knew exactly what they were investing in. And you're fucking with a very powerful group of people. There will be repercussions. That list was never to have been seen."

I thought about some of those names. Huge power players. Politicians, entertainment moguls. Did they know? Did they "donate to the cause"?

"These people will smash you like a bug. Like the bug that you are. They will hurt all that you love, and take away everything you believe in."

Angel grabbed my shoulder. "Don't listen to the madman." We ran around the side of the building, past the Buick, past the outside forklift to the side door.

"Walk fast, as if you know what you're doing. We hold our guns at our sides, walk to the far wall, tell the guard that she belongs to us, and we take her."

If my face didn't hurt so much I would have laughed. "Angel, they're killers. It just doesn't work like that."

He put his hand on mine. "Friend, if you believe it will happen, almost always it will happen. Do as I say and you will see the success."

Angel pushed the door open and strode in. I followed as closely as possible. Christ, I'd been free and clear three times now, but I kept going back. What the hell was wrong with me? James had said I cared about people and maybe that was it. Or maybe I was just born stupid.

We were halfway across the floor and no one had said a word. The workers were busy pushing everything into the back of the truck so they could close the door. Big strides, guns by our sides, my face streaked with blood, and it was as if we belonged.

"We're here to take the girl." Angel grabbed her by her shoulder and pushed her toward me.

"Huh?"

The guy wasn't the brightest bulb on the circuit.

"We'll take it from here." Angel walked away.

"Hey, wait a minute." The guard shouted.

I looked over my shoulder, Jackie by my side. The guy had his gun up and was pointing at us. Angel spun and fired. The guard collapsed in a heap on the floor.

"Run!"

We did. I grabbed Jackie's hand and we ran faster than any of us had ever run before. Out the door, through the parking lot, and down the block. The sirens were screaming as we screeched to a halt at the pine grove. Police car after police car, horns honking, sirens wailing, came racing to the warehouse.

"I called in the address before I shot the CIA agent," Angel said.

"So you had all of this in hand?"

"Not everything. Obviously you played a big part."

He opened the Jeep and James was lying where we'd positioned him, breathing deeply. I heaved a sigh of relief.

Jackie stepped in and sat by his head, stroked the matted hair, and talked softly to him.

"We're going to the closest hospital." Angel started the Jeep. "I think our friend needs a checkup."

CHAPTER SIXTY-SIX

THEY DIDN'T SAY HOW LONG he'd be in, so I left at one thirty. As I walked into the apartment, "Born in the USA" blared from my pocket. Two in the morning.

"Em. Boy do I have a story for you."

"Skip, I've got one for you too."

I went into the bathroom and examined the dressing they'd put on my face. A long strip of gauze covered the hideous gash from Fuentes's gun.

"Skip, I saw the doctor today, well, yesterday."

"Oh. I thought it was —"

"I went. You need to know."

"What? I need to know what?"

"I lost the baby. Or, the baby was never totally there. It's called a blighted ovum. It makes no difference. We're not having a baby."

I had nothing to say. Neither did she. We spent a minute not talking to each other.

"Em, I'm sorry. I'd gotten used to the idea."

"Me too. Lots of ups and downs." She sounded like she was ready to choke.

"God, I hope you're okay with this."

"I made a decision."

"What?"

"I'm taking some time off."

Time off? "A couple of days?"

"Months."

I lost my breath. "How many?"

"Two, six, I don't know. I told Dad—"

"About—"

"No. He doesn't have a clue. I told him I needed some time. If you want to stay at the condo once in a while you could keep an eye on it for me and—" she was crying.

"Em, where are you going? God, I don't want you to leave for months. Do you know how much I love you?"

"Yeah. I do."

"And still you're leaving for months."

"I am, Skip. I have to. I'll call." And she was gone.

I lay awake most of the night, getting up at eight and calling Sammy.

"Sam, I had a rough night. I won't be in today."

He cleared his throat and I could tell he was pissed. "Skip, did you tell somebody they won the hot tub? What the hell are you doing giving out my private cell phone number. You know better than to—" I hung up the phone, grabbed a beer, and lay down on the couch, flipping on the television. My face was itching like crazy under the gauze.

Maybe it was too early and they didn't have the entire story or maybe the entire story was never going to be told, but the only news mention of the warehouse incident was that police had been called and found some illegal firearms. I guess that's accurate. There could have been some murders committed and thank God that didn't happen. There was no mention of a dead CIA agent.

I thought about going to the authorities. But what authorities? I wasn't sure whom to trust and, unless our names came up in the investigation, I figured we were better off sitting on the sideline.

Em was leaving, James was going to be out of it for a while, and it seemed to me that maybe I had some serious growing up to do. Somehow I should be taking a life lesson from this entire experience, but for the life of me I couldn't figure out what it was.

About nine I wandered out to the cement slab, sipping on my second beer of the morning.

I glanced at the playpen behind the apartment and did a double take. A little black boy was sitting on the mat, grabbing at a plastic yellow duck. The patio door opened and the old man stepped out. He nodded.

"This is my grandson, Jason." Very matter of fact. Like the little kid had been there for months.

I nodded back. He picked the boy up, grabbed the blue blanket, and walked back into the apartment. I took a deep swallow for myself, then one for James.

I called the police and reported the truck stolen. They called back and informed me they'd found it and were holding it for evidence. I could pick it up in a week or two. And, I visited the hospital for three days straight, but James was never awake. I'd sit for an hour then leave. They'd seriously medicated him for the pain.

I thought about going back to work but hadn't made the effort. It seemed easier to sleep late, drink beer, and feel sorry for myself. I drove by Gas and Grocery a couple of times, but the old lady said Angel had disappeared. All I know is he was more than just a casual bystander. By the third day, the story had also disappeared from TV, radio, and the newspaper.

I called Jackie. Maybe twenty times. She never answered, and after three days her number was disconnected. And then our apartment phone started ringing two or three times a day, but no one was ever there when I answered, and when I tried to get the number, it was blocked. I kept hoping it was Em, but with my luck it was one of the big money guys trying to scare me for ruining their invasion. It worked. I was a little frightened.

But, I've got my backup. I copied the list of donors and put it in a spot that no one will ever find. Then I sent a letter—you know how that works, a letter to an attorney that says, "In the event of my untimely demise, please find the following information, etc." I felt stupid when I did it. I don't feel so stupid now. I'm not going to say a thing to you or anyone else, but trust me, there were some huge names on that list.

The fourth day, three o'clock in the morning, my cell phone went off and I grabbed it during the first two notes. "James?"

His voice was gravely, like he'd been coughing. "I'm s'posed to be resting, pard. But I needed to thank you for savin' my life. Remember?"

"Yeah. I remember. I found out that saving someone's life doesn't necessarily mean much."

"It does to me." He was quiet, like he'd drifted off to sleep.

I smiled. He was still on medication. Slurring his words, sort of drifting in and out.

"Skip?"

"Yeah, James."

"We're gonna make it big. You wait 'n' see."

"Yeah, James."

"Skip?"

"James?"

" 'Member that Cadillac my dad never drove?"

"I remember."

"I'm gonna get one, and I'm gonna drive it for the old man. We're gonna make enough money to get a big Cadillac and drive it downtown Miami."

"I'll be by your side, James."

"Gonna happen, pardner. You have my word on that."

"Your word. Got it."

He was quiet for a moment. Then, "All I got is my word and my balls, and I don't break them for nobody."

"Al Pacino, *Scarface*."

"Hold down the fort, amigo. I'll be home soon."

EPILOGUE

THE BODY OF AGENT SALVIDOR SANTORI, a Cuban-American CIA operative, was found on the roof of the Colony Hotel in South Beach six days after our bizarre incident at the warehouse on the Miami River. He'd been shot in the face, but the bullet stayed in his skull.

Several weeks later I caught a blurb in the *Miami Herald.* It mentioned that a government employee named Mark Spense had been found shot to death. The story went on to say that the bullet seemed to be of the same caliber and from the same gun that killed Salvidor Santori. That's all I ever saw. There's been no more news about the killings.

I know who killed Agent Mark Spense, just before he was about to throw three of us in the Miami River. I can only assume that the same person killed Santori.

It's been over a month and no word from Em. I keep hoping I'll hear from her, but she has a lot to work through.